Mother of Dreams

BreAnn Hanks

Hanks Publishing
Publishing Co.

Follow us, Hanks Publishing, on Instagram!

Edition 2

Book Art and Design by BreAnn Hanks

Dedicated to my readers and fans.
Thank you so much for your support.

Trigger Warning:

If you have been a victim of rape, please reconsider before continuing this book.

Prologue

Amari walks into the bedroom, getting greeted by a man that she was hoping not to see tonight.

His silver-gray eyes glow in the light of the setting sun, his clothes tight on his massive frame. The two top buttons on his black button up are open, showing off his chest hair. The sleeves are rolled up and showing off the muscles in his forearms. His jeans cling nicely to his hips and thighs.

Amari growls, unsettled by this intrusion. First, he mind links with her, telling her to wait. Then she comes in here to find him waiting for her?! This is uncalled for! What is he doing here?! He didn't come to the coronation or to congratulate the happy couple!

What gives *him* the right to show up unannounced and in the bedroom?! Amari doesn't want Allah here! She him out, far away from here!

"Get out," she threatens in a growl, her fists clenched tightly at her sides. She's not having it. Not on her wedding day!

"No," Allah replies coldly. He holds Amari's cold stare and lifts his chin, not moving another muscle. His eyes somehow shine in the moonlight, the gold rings missing.

"What?" Amari snaps. "Do you have a death wish?"

"I have a wish and it's not for death!" Allah snaps, glaring at her with broken eyes. "My wish is to have you!"

Amari dug her nails into her palms. "You're too late! And you can't change my mind!"

"Amari, don't do this," Allah threatens with a slight growl, trying to convince his second chance mate to rethink what she's doing. He has no right! He had his chance and he blew it!

"You had your chance to sway me and look what happened!" Amari snaps as she walks over to Allah, her finger pointed at him. "I have your mark when we *both* agreed not to mark each other!"

"Yeah, well, I'm not the one that broke that promise first!" Allah snaps angrily.

Amari winces, dropping her hand. "Fine," she scoffs in disbelief. "I'll sever the mate bond if that's what you so wish!"

"No. Amari. Wait." Allah reaches for her, panicked, but she slaps his hand away.

"Don't touch me," Amari threatens with a growl. She shakes her head. "You don't get to touch me! Not ever, again!"

"Look. I made a mistake."

"The fuck, you did!" Amari looks Allah over from toe to head, noticing nothing's changed.

He's still the same. So, why is he fighting for her so suddenly? Did his wolf come back? If so, she's in trouble.

Tears form in Amari's eyes as she thinks about what could've been with Allah if his wolf wasn't so one-minded and bullheaded. He shakes his head at her.

"Blame me all you want. But it's Ragnar that messed it all up. He got jealous when he saw you riding Raja in the forest. He's the one that wanted to mark you. I wanted a different release for his pain."

Amari scoffs in disbelief. "And you think sex is any better," she asks dryly, unimpressed and still furious. She can't believe Allah would do this! Here and now!

What is he thinking?! He can't just do this! Not after the wedding *and* the coronation! This is bad timing on his part! "It's better than leaving a mark for the whole world to see!" He's not happy. It seems like he was prepared for a fight. He came expecting it.

"You're lucky I have Sirena to fix that!" Amari snaps, not wanting to continue this conversation. "She was able to cover up my mark for my wedding and Viggo's coronation," she yells, pointing at the location where her mate mark is. "He never has to look at it ever, again!"

Allah winces. "Amari."

"Don't '*Amari*' me, Allah. We're done." Amari turns her back to Allah and starts for the bathroom, done with this infuriating conversation. "Get out of here!"

"Amari, wait." Allah grabs Amari's hand and she thrusts it out of his hold.

She turns to face him. Her hand stings as it slaps across his face, her glare deepened. "You may be my mentor. But you'll *never* be my lover. Not ever, again," Amari growls.

Allah searches her eyes, looking for a way in to her heart. She shakes her head at him, giving him the impression he won't get a way into her head.

"Not in this life. Nor the next. You messed it all up when you marked me. And to *think*." Amari gets in Allah's face. "I just about considered you after Garrett's passing." She shakes her head before turning her back to her fated mate. She walks out of the bedroom, into the hall, leaving him there and hoping he'll be gone by the time she comes back with her newlywed husband.

She starts down the hall, leaving her frustrations behind.

∞

Viggo trails his hand down Amari's arm, standing right behind her.

He wants to be gentle with her. He knows what she just had to go through. She let it show in front of him but put on an act with everyone else. She's so strong, making him admire her for that.

Viggo puts his nose in Amari's hair and breathes in her scent, letting lavender and vanilla fill his nostrils. The night of their wedding and his coronation… And *he* came to ruin it. At least tried to. Viggo is going to help Amari forget about it. He loves her and doesn't want her stressing. She deserves to be happy.

Viggo kisses Amari's hair as he wraps his arms around her, comforting and reassuring her. He knows how she must feel. All her life she was mentored by a man old enough to be her dad. She never once had feelings for him, but he toyed with her emotions, made her believe that there was something there. He used her emotions to his advantage, getting her in bed a few times.

Viggo unzips Amari's dress from the side. She lets it fall to the floor. Not wanting to push her into anything, he just helps her undress. He undoes her corset from the back. As it loosens so does she.

Amari takes a sharp inhale and Viggo feels his member arouse. She shouldn't have this effect on him. But when he's falling in love with her more and more every day, he hates to admit that she's starting to have *every* effect on him.

Viggo's lips land on Amari's naked shoulder. He trails soft kisses along it and up her neck. When he comes back down his lips meet where her mate mark should be. Thanks to Sirena it's not there as long as she wishes it not to be.

Amari turns around. She undoes Viggo's new tribal belt, her lips brushing against his. She doesn't fidget or falter. Her hands move swiftly, removing his clothes with his consent. Viggo takes his shirt and tunic off, helping his beloved wife. He steps out of his pants after they fall to the floor.

Fully naked in front of each other Amari and Viggo take it in, looking each other over. The soft glow of her skin looks brighter in the moonlight, her lightly fair skin nicely tanned by the sun. Her round breasts have perfect little nipples that are pointing out, ready to be taken by Viggo's mouth and marked.

Amari's scar on her neck is a reminder of the war that took her life as a regular Goddess. Now, she's immortal thanks to Viggo. He's grateful to have her back.

Amari gets on her tiptoes, pressing her lips against Viggo's in a gentle kiss. She cups his neck as he opens up to her, his arms wrapping around her. Their tongues spar. Soon, Viggo loses himself in Amari's embrace. He devours her and doesn't care to take a breath, wanting to keep her close.

She comes up for a quick breath, letting him take in the crisp air from outside. It penetrates his lungs that are screaming for air. Viggo picks Amari up by her thighs as he makes eye contact with her. He gets between them, pressing them into his hips.

Amari clings onto him, wrapping her arms around his neck and her legs around his waist. Viggo's member pulses and screams for a release. But he's not ready to go there just yet. He wants a moment to pleasure his wife with just his touch.

He lays her down on her side of the bed, staying above her. His lips instantly go to her neck. He trails soft and gentle kisses down it to where the mark should be. He decides to do it, moved by the love he has for her. His territorial side comes out.

Erasing Allah's mark, Viggo sinks his canines into Amari's skin, giving her a new mate mark. One that will stick forever no matter what. Amari gasps at the sensation, holding Viggo's head in place. Her free hand trails down his torso and her fingers feather against the tip of his cock. She strokes it as Viggo finishes up his work.

He groans into her neck as she opens up her thighs for him. Viggo looks Amari and their brown eyes meet. She nods her head and presses her hips into him, inviting him in. Viggo guides himself into her wetness to the hilt and she gasps, awakening the beast inside of him.

Amari moans in pleasure, relaxing underneath Viggo as he watches her. He holds himself up with just his hands, wanting to watch her orgasm. He moves inside of her slowly at first, her tightness clamping all around him. The moment she wraps her arms around him and slides her hands down his back he can't hold it in. He's got to have that honeymoon baby.

Viggo thrusts into Amari hard and fast, making her go quiet. Her eyes roll to the back of her head as she chokes on a gasp of pleasure. He picks up the speed. The headboard bangs against the wall with every thrust. A small sound manages out of Amari's lips.

At the top of her ecstasy, it's going to be a while before she comes back down. Viggo groans, watching the love of his life as she orgasms. His cullions tense up and he knows he's close. Gods, yes! He knows it's quick. He should draw it out. But he's so close he can't hold it back.

Viggo thrusts into Amari harder as his cullions jerk from the stroking of her tight core around his pulsing cock. He spills his seed inside of her as they pant in unison. She clings onto him, shaking from her intense orgasms she just had.

Viggo pulls Amari into his arms and he holds her tight. He's never letting her go. He's never going to stop loving her. He has so much to promise her and he intends to keep each promise.

He's going to be the man that she needs and wants in every way.

1

6 Years Later

Amari picks up her son as he cries. She holds him close in her arms, looking at him lovingly.

She starts to sing a song that worked on her two older children. A song that's also a memory from her life before this one. A life in Homba. When she was just a child herself.

The song is from a movie she enjoyed at a young age and still does. A classic to her and everyone else like her, she can't help but smile at the words. Memories of her childhood fill her mind while she sings.

Amari takes Clay's hand and his fingers wrap around her thumb. Oh, her heart. As Amari continues to sing the song and calm Clay down, she can't help but smile at all the memories she's made with Viggo and their two older children, having flashbacks.

In one flashback, she's on Viggo's ship with him, the wind whipping her hair back with their daughters in front of them, their blond and brown hair whipped back. In another flashback, Amari and Viggo are making hot, intimate love as they consummated their marriage. All the flashbacks that follow, Clay starts to calm down and watch Amari with his bright blue eyes as she continues to sing to him.

Going out to sea and seeing the world in the eyes of a Viking, their two girls with them. Helping set the sails and replace a yard whenever they started to notice rust eating it away. Memories and flashbacks fill Amari's mind and she can't help but smile sweetly, knowing she will make new ones with Clay now born.

"'You'll be in my heart. Always." Amari sings sweetly.

Viggo wraps his arms around her, making his presence known and making her jump. He moans as he puts his lips to her temple. "I love it when you sing," he says lowly, sounding love stricken.

Amari huffs and smiles. "Thanks, babe," she says softly. She lays her head on his shoulder, looking at their first son.

Viggo sets his massive hand gently on the top of Clay's head and kisses it. "Good job," he whispers. He looks at Amari and his chocolate brown eyes pierce her hazel brown ones. "He's beautiful."

"He looks like you," Amari says softly.

Viggo leans in and his lips caress Amari's in a sweet and soft kiss. "With my dad's eyes."

Amari sighs and relaxes in Viggo's arm as he pulls her into him. She's so grateful to have him so close. Their adventures out on the ocean have brought them closer to each other. No matter where they are, though, the memories they make bring them closer as a family.

Amari can't imagine an even better life. She doesn't think there is one! She wouldn't trade this best life she has for the world. She's got everything she wants right here.

Amari dreads meeting up with Madi, her cousin, in a while, but she knows she's got to go. Viggo kisses her forehead.

"Emma is outside playing with the cats," he says, feeling like he has to give his wife a report every day. "Raja is keeping an eye on her."

"Of course, she is," Amari replies. She looks up at the man that she calls the love of her life. Her best friend. "Raja blessed Emma. They have a connection."

Viggo nods, chuckling. "That's true."

"Did you put the devil down for a nap?"

Viggo suppresses a laugh and nods. "Ramein is asleep in her room," he says lowly.

Amari grunts in disgust. "Terrible twos are more like terrible threes."

"She gets it from me."

"Yeah, she does," Amari drawls out. "I remember that stories your brother told me."

Viggo laughs quietly as Clay starts to fall back to sleep without a sound. "Let's not go there."

Amari snorts. "Only because Ramus tells them in an embarrassing way."

"And I prefer we don't ask him for anymore."

Amari moans a laugh, burying her face in Viggo's chest. Standing a foot shorter than him, it's easy for her to get away with an easy slip of the teeth on his peck. She likes to nip him there whenever he thinks about getting into trouble with her.

Viggo tenses up and Amari knows it's for that typical reason. He did something… She sighs and sags.

"Alright," she says nonchalantly. She looks up at him. "Out with it."

"I may have created something new," Viggo puts in.

"What?" Amari drawls out, getting suspicious.

Ever since Viggo's coronation as God of Hallam he's been able to create life like Amari. He tends to create some that isn't needed, whatsoever, and Amari's creatures wind up getting overrun by Viggo's.

Luckily, they find a balance and some of Viggo's creations become prey to some of his and Amari's. Her life gets the same treatment, but everything comes out evenly and everybody wins.

"Don't get mad," Viggo drawls out.

"Viggo, it's you. You always make the stupidest creatures."

"You can't call Medusa stupid."

Amari sighs and sags in disgust. "She's part of Greek mythology. I should *never* have taught you some of it."

"Well, too late."

Amari looks at her husband in disbelief. "What did you make?"

Viggo holds up a baby Pegasus the size of his forearm. Amari drops her jaw in awe and blinks, gaping. That is the cutest thing she has ever seen! "We now have mini-Pegasus."

She wants to keep it as a pet. And it's so fluffy! The baby Pegasus is white with a gray muzzle, its short fur fluffed out with a winter coat already. Amari just wants to love on it. Why does it have to be so damn cute?!

Amari looks up at Viggo, her lips slightly parted in awe while cuteness overload takes over her and gives her a boost of serotonin. "Babe, have I told you how much I love you?"

Viggo gives Amari a lopsided grin, slightly showing his pearly white teeth. "I knew you'd like it," he says softly.

"This is the cutest thing ever! I wanna keep it as a pet."

"Good. Cause there's nine more of them."

"You're just trying to find more ways to knock me up, aren't you?"

Viggo leans in and lets his lips brush over Amari's lips, teasing her and sending sparks through her. "More or less," he seduces lovingly.

"Clayton is only four months old and you wanna get me pregnant, again, already?"

Viggo makes an uncertain sound. "No."

"You hesitated."

Viggo pulls his head back and looks at Amari. "As much as I would love another right now, I just don't think a year between our third and fourth is a wise choice. Plus, your body needs more time to heal. Clay's birth was brutal on you," Viggo says as he points at Clay with his eyes on Amari.

"Good." She gets in his face. "Cause, I think we should wait until he's at least nine months away from turning two years old."

Viggo smiles at Amari genuinely. "Just like Emma and Ramein."

"We waited a little too long to have Clayton, by the way. We should've done it sooner."

"We did. You had a miscarriage. Remember?" Viggo sounds a little nervous talking about the incident.

Amari sighs and sags. "Don't remind me," she says lowly.

"And then it took us almost a whole year when we started to try, again."

"Again," Amari warns softly. "Not helping."

"Sorry, Mare." Guilt shows on Viggo's face and he pulls Amari into his arms, leaving room for Clay so he doesn't squash him. Viggo kisses Amari's temple. "I love you," he says lowly.

"I love you more." Amari leans her temple into Viggo's lips, closing her eyes and enjoying the touch. Oh, she loves this man so much! She can't believe her luck! She's so glad she chose him!

He groans into her temple. "Do you wanna know what else I love," he asks in a low, husky tone.

"Hmm. What?" Amari whispers.

"Our red room," Viggo seduces.

"Oh," Amari drawls out as she looks up at her beloved husband, getting seductive. "Are you trying to turn me on?"

"No," Viggo drawls out innocently. He and Amari both know he's not no matter how hard he tries, though.

Amari smirks and presses her lips together. "We haven't been in our red room since Clay was born six months ago."

Viggo leans in and brushes his lips over Amari's seductively. "I'd like to change that," he whispers.

Amari gasps as she thinks about the new toy that she and Viggo have yet to try. It gets her going.

∞

Madi paces as she breastfeeds her second child. Just a newborn, her little boy is easy to take care of. But her two-year-old boy is getting into mischief, keeping Ryker busy.

After five months he came around and they got married. It's been almost six years, now, and Madi and Ryker are happy together with their little family. They took a while before they decided to start having kids.

Madi moans, dreading what's about to come. She's constantly seeing Amari at one of their estates to take care of business. Madi's got to leave soon for their next meeting. It's a good excuse for their kids to get well acquainted and the give the parents a break. They see each other almost every day, at the moment. But that will change after a while, making the meetings happen only once a year.

Hell's Fire is almost its own world, now. Madi is hoping it can be given a different name in this next meeting. It'll be better that way. Hell's Fire sounds too cruel.

Madi spots a hellhound trying to sneak out and two hellcats chase him back to where he belongs, right on his tail. Madi shakes her head. Lucifer is always trying to get out and cause havoc in Hallam. Madi won't put up with it. He needs to learn manners!

The dog yelps and whines with his tail between his legs, running back to guard the dead with the cats hard on his heels. Madi hangs her head and moans in disapproval. She swears that dog is only trouble. He's so lazy, too!

A male hand lifts Madi's chin and Ryker kisses her, distracting her. Oh, he's good at that.

"Where's Miles," Madi asks softly, her eyes closed with Ryker's forehead on hers.

"Playing with the hellhounds," Ryker replies softly. "I asked them to keep him company."

Madi grunts in disgust. "The terrible twos."

"He'll grow out of it." Ryker kisses Madi. "You got somewhere to be."

"Yeah, I know. Amari will have her kids there, so I'll take him with."

Ryker nods. "I'd come with, but it's only you ladies that go."

"Well, there's also Viggo there."

It's Ryker's turn to grunt in disgust. "I hate that man," he says lowly. He shakes his head. "I don't like his way of living. And he snaps your head off with the simplest mistake." Ryker shakes his head, again, looking at Madi. "No. You go." He kisses her and their lips mend together in perfection.

Madi loves this man. She didn't want to get married right away or just in five months. She wasn't ready. But when Ryker started to come around, she felt as though it was right. He's the one that makes her feel like herself and he encourages her to be herself.

Madi enjoys the love Ryker has for her. She can't help but reciprocate it back to him. She's fallen irrevocably in love with him and there's nothing that she would change about him. He's the best thing that has happened to her. Madi won't be letting him go. He's stuck with her for as long as they live.

∞

Viggo stands in the doorway as he watches Ramein sleep.

Amari is in her meeting with Madison and Emma is outside playing. Clay is in Amari's office with her while he plays. Although Viggo can watch him. Viggo and Amari left early, not wanting to wake Ramein up when it was time to go. She and Viggo know first-hand what happens if they wake the beast from her slumber. They don't want to deal with her wrath.

Ramein sleeps peacefully. Her light-brown bangs fall in front of her face while the rest of her hair is tied back in a Dutch braid. She's a beautiful girl with her one green eye and one brown eye. She's almost a mini version of Amari. The only difference is her chin. She gets it from Viggo.

He's grateful that all of his kids with Amari are hers. Not a single one is Ada's. After having Emma, Amari promised Viggo she would get rid of Ada's eggs. She did. Amari spilt every single one back into Ada a year after Emma was born.

Viggo finds the rare gene odd… But at least he doesn't have to worry about it anymore. While Ada is still Amari's mistress, they strictly stick to dildos when they want penetration. Viggo prefers it that way but he didn't ask Amari to do that. He just caught her with one when she came home from shopping. Her eyes met with his and only on thing came out of her mouth.

"I'm not risking taking her eggs, again," Amari said when the green rings around her brown eyes lit up.

She walked away after that and left Viggo dumbstruck but happy all day. He pleasured her all night that night and they were sore all day the next day. But he doesn't regret it.

Viggo watches Ramein sleep for another ten minutes before slipping away quietly and headed for the kitchen. He passes Manny, who is holding a little one while he has a picnic basket in his free hand.

"Manny," Viggo says. He follows the young takal, lycan hybrid to the back door and opens it for him. "Who's this little one? I don't think we've met."

"Mine," Manny replies. He looks at Viggo. "Maylee and I finally decided to try for kids. This is our first."

"Congratulations, brother!" Prouder than he's ever been, Viggo watches the man he wishes could've spent more time with. But someone got in the way.

"Thank you." Manny walks out the door Viggo is holding for him. "And thank you." He stops and turns to look at Viggo. "You and Amari have treated us so well. I can never thank you enough."

Viggo nods, love filling his heart. "Just because the wolves and takals don't you, it doesn't mean you're worthless."

Manny shrugs. "My battle form is different from the rest of our kind. It intimidates them."

"As it should. Your wolf knows what he's doing with you. He gave you the form as a sign of respect."

Manny shrugs, again. "Maybe. I just know that if I ever get a pack of my own, I'll be that alpha Mars promised me to be."

Viggo nods, looking at his son proudly. "Oh, I have a feeling you will," he says in a low tone. "I'm proud of you. Son. My wife was right to take you in."

Manny smiles at Viggo, showing his pearly white teeth. "I'm grateful for her. And to have you as my father."

Viggo nods, again. "Tell your siblings I miss them."

It's Manny's turn to nod his head. He turns around and joins his wife for a picnic under the white dogwood tree that separates some hedging. He was raised right, Viggo being there whenever he was welcome. He just couldn't take his kids he has with the Asgard Lycan Princess with him and spend time with them alone. It was forbidden.

Viggo is grateful that he gets chance to do that, now, with Manny. He plans to do it right the first time. He closes the door behind him as he gets back inside the estate and someone walks out of Amari's office quietly.

Amari and Madi are heard talking about the issue that they both have with some of the werewolves. It goes quiet, the door quietly closing. Viggo passes May as he goes back up the stairs, but May stops him.

"My God," May starts quietly, addressing Viggo.

He stops halfway up the stairs and looks at May, his chocolate brown eyes meeting her green eyes. She's holding Clay on her hip.

"Amari would like to visit the were-cats kingdom once she is done with Madi and she would like for you to join her. Would you like me to pack a lunch?"

"Has my wife eaten?"

May shakes her head. "No, she has not."

Viggo nods briefly. "I will talk to her about it once she is finished up in her office."

May nods. "Of course."

"Thank you, May."

"You're so very welcome."

Viggo walks up the stairs and heads for the bedroom that he shares with Amari while they are here. They spend most of their time in Heaven's Light, taking care of all the creatures that have passed on. They don't need much, but it keeps the god and goddess busy most of the time.

Viggo gets in the bedroom in the west wing and he walks over to the end table with his paperwork. He has a few to sign and look over. His office isn't quite finished here yet.

Viggo shares Amari's office most of the time and they enjoy it. They get some alone time together and it's where they've created baby number two and three. The renovations on the estate didn't sstart until earlier this year. Viggo and Amari have had no desire to put in an office for him, mainly working back home in Heaven's Light. But since they decided to revisit the conversation, they decided it would be for the better so Viggo can work in his own space while Amari had her meetings in hers.

Viggo tends to come with her a lot so they can have a little vacation with her family. He works for a few minutes when Amari mind links with him.

I'm done, handsome, Amari seduces, sounding like she wants to continue where they left off earlier.

Oh, Viggo drawls out in the mind link. *And you're horny?*

Well, when you got me going right before my meeting you have a price to pay.

Viggo chuckles, letting Amari hear him. His member grows at the thought of her punishment for him. She knows just how to torture him. It gets him every single time. *Then get up here and punish me, beautiful.* He seduces.

Oh, no. You're meeting me in my office. Amari seduces. Oh, she's quite the tease!

I'm on my way. Viggo forgets about the paperwork and he hurries out of the bedroom, down the hall and stairs, and right into Amari's office to find her still talking to Madi.

Her brown eyes meet his in a sly grin. Oh, she's good. But how long is Amari going to torture Viggo before he gets his way with her? Amari looks at Madi.

"Well, let's plan on the were-cats' help. And the feline Guardians. Dogs may be their natural predator, but most big cats are the natural predator of a lone wolf. We'll have the upper hand in certain situations." Amari has always been able to come up with a solution on certain problems.

Madi nods. "Of course. I think that will work well."

"Thank you, Madi." Amari stands up and she throws her bangs back, her eyes piercing Viggo's. She's challenging him. "I will talk to my husband about our plans."

Madi stands up and starts for the door. "I appreciate being able to bring Miles here. He's got quite the attitude at the age of two."

"Ramein didn't have the terrible twos. She has the terrible threes."

Madi sighs in disgust. "I'm hoping Miles won't be like that at three." She stops at the door and Viggo keeps his eyes on Amari, seducing his wife with just a look.

Amari keeps her eyes on Madi, ignoring him. "Well, good luck. You're gonna need it."

"Thank you." Madi walks out of the office and closes the door behind her, leaving Viggo and Amari alone.

Viggo raises an eyebrow at Amari. "You lied to me."

"I played you," Amari replies seductively. "There's a difference."

Viggo starts for Amari and she starts around her desk, their eyes peeled to each other. "You know I don't like being played."

Amari sits on the front of her desk and Viggo meets her there.

"It's a dangerous game."

"And here I am still standing," Amari says in a breath as she wraps her arms around Viggo's neck.

He thrusts her hips into him, getting in between her thighs and making her eyes fill with lust. "More like sitting." His eyes go to her lips. "You're about to be on your knees," he growls seductively.

"Make me," Amari seduces in a whisper.

Viggo's lips crash on Amari's lips and she holds onto him as their tongues clash and spar.

2

Amari unbuckles Viggo's belt as his hands ravish her skin, caressing over her with a purpose. They tear her shirt in two at the seam on her left shoulder and she barely has time to grab her remote and press the button to turn her office into the red room that she built with Viggo. It's something they worked on together, wanting to pleasure and punish each other whenever they wanted.

Viggo groans into Amari's mouth, his hands caressing her breasts. She rips his perfectly good shirt and tunic with muscle she got throughout the years as his Viking wife and Chiefess. He growls into her mouth in warning. Oh, she gets to torture him for once.

Amari growls back at him into his lips, running her hands over his naked twelve-pack abs, pecks, and around his neck. Her arms wrap around his neck as she clings onto him, in control.

Viggo thrusts Amari into him, her breasts covered in a lace bra pressed against his naked torso. Amari chuckles with pleasure. Oh, he's in trouble. Viggo picks Amari up by her thighs, staying in between them.

In the heat of it all they don't hear her office door open. Nor do they hear a knock. It's when Amari tears her lips away from Viggo's and goes for his mate mark, her eyes lock with the Asgard Lycan' king's familiar silver-gray eyes, her thighs locked around Viggo's hips and her hands on his buttocks.

Allah, the Lycan King, seems to be heartbroken, his eyes shining with tears.

"Fuck," Amari whispers as she stiffens. Feelings rush over her at the sight of her best friend, feelings that she thought she got over mixed with new ones.

Rage settles in her gut as she pushes the button on her remote to change her office back to normal, Viggo setting her down on her desk. He instantaneously turns around to face Amari's former mentor, protecting her from the man's sight. He tore her shirt and she doesn't have an extra in her desk. She used it last night and hasn't had time to put a new one in.

Viggo growls at the intruder. "What the fuck are you doing here?"

Allah has a lot of nerve showing up here after being absent for almost six years. He stayed locked away in his kingdom and never showed his face anywhere. He would only send a messenger with paperwork if needed. Coming here is a huge risk! Especially when the last time he was here he was begging for Amari to change her mind and choose him instead! When it was too late!

None of this looks good for the king! He might as well leave while he still can! He still looks the same. The only difference is the short beard he now has on his face. How long did that take him to grow? When did he decide to have one? Nevertheless, he looks good. The beard makes him more handsome than before, making Amari wish she could touch it without getting in trouble with her husband. He gets jealous when she touches other men's beards.

He wouldn't have to get jealous if he would just grow a full one or a duck tail instead of just having a full goatee!

"I know I have no place here," Allah says, his low and deep voice still sounding the same. "But I have a matter to speak with Amari. It's urgent."

Viggo tenses up and gets protective of his wife, his form rigid. "You won't set a foot closer to her," he threatens in a growl. "I want you out! Now!" Viggo barks.

"Viggo. My God." Allah turns his attention to Viggo, pressing the palms of his hands together in front of him as if he's begging for something. Maybe he is? What's going on? "Please, just give me a moment with my Goddess. I promise I won't take long."

Viggo doesn't move a muscle, staying in front of Amari and keeping her covered. He growls at the man standing in front of him in the doorway.

"Please." Allah sounds desperate. His eyes land on Amari in desperation, looking defeated.

She knows what that means. She sets her hand on Viggo's naked shoulder and he looks back at her. She gives him a slow nod. "Give us a moment, Allah. You caught us at a bad time."

"Of course." Allah steps out of Amari's office and leaves her and Viggo alone, closing the door behind him.

"Go up to our room and get me a shirt, please," Amari says lowly. "And I want you in here while Allah and I speak. I know him best. He's not one to beg and he'll probably try to seduce me to get what he's looking for."

Viggo growls in frustration and looks over Amari's head.

"Hey, I don't like it either." Amari makes her husband look at her, holding the back of his neck and thrusting his head down. Their brown eyes lock with each other. "And I don't want him here. But if he's here after six years in solitude, he's got a good reason. I just want you to help me to keep him in check. Okay? Can you do that?"

"Yeah," Viggo whispers. He kisses Amari's forehead. "I'll be right back," he says softly.

"Thank you," Amari says softly. She watches her beloved as he pulls away from her and walks out of the office. Amari doesn't wait for him for very long, hearing him outside threatening Allah before he's hurrying up the stairs. He's back down them just a few moments later.

In those few minutes, Amari is able to discard the torn shirts into her fireplace and them burned without even moving a muscle, using her powers and shifting the air.

Viggo walks into Amari's office with a shirt for her and he pulls it over her head, a new shirt and tunic on himself. His lips are on her nose as he pulls her shirt over her chin and his hands trail down her naked sides with the bottom of her shirt before settling on her hips.

"When we are done here," he starts lowly. "I'm punishing you like you deserve." He seduces.

Amari chuckles after pulling her arms through her t-shirt. She looks up at Viggo through her eye lashes.

"No, Viggo," she seduces in a breath. "It's *you* that needs to be punished after turning me on right before my meeting. I had to sit through a two-hour meeting with all the were-kind in this estate smelling my arousal. Now, King Allah is going to smelling it until we're done."

"Well, let me show you how I feel," Viggo whispers seductively. He kisses Amari and unbuttons her pants. In just a split second his hand is down her pants and panties, feeling out her wet vulva. "Just a little quickie," he whispers.

Before Amari can object to the matter her pants and panties get thrust down to one ankle and Viggo is thrusting himself inside of her, pleasuring the both of them. She moans and hangs her head back as pleasure sweeps over her, exposing her neck for Viggo to claim.

∞

The pain hits. Again.

Allah lays his head back against the wall as he sees Viggo and Amari taking care of her arousal at the back of his mind. It's a curse for him. He can't see what exactly the happy couple is doing, but he can see every caress that's shared. He can hear their moaning, see their lips meet in a gentle, passionate kiss, and he can see Viggo's hands doing the job that's supposed to be Allah's.

It's like the smell of Amari's arousal drips through that soundproof door and vanilla hits Allah's nose. He chokes on the sweet smell and tries to forget the pain by taking in Amari's scent. He opens his mouth let it take over him. That's when it hits him. The lavender. Oh, sweet mercy!

Allah feels a tug on his pant leg and he looks down to see a beautiful little girl that has one green eye and one brown eye. Ragnar growls in admiration, lovestruck. Allah doesn't blame him.

A little Amari, Ragnar howls. *She's beautiful!*

And not for you, Allah threatens with a growl.

Think about it, Allah! She can be promised to us! Betrothed! Think of all the wars we could end with just marrying her! Ragnar paces in Allah's head. *She's too young, now. But the wolf I sense inside of her. It would be a match made in Heaven's Light for us!*

You're talking about Amari's child, Ragnar! She's not the answer!

Then what is?! Amari chose Viggo, forcing us with a kingdom that's falling apart! Just admit it! This child is our next best thing!

Allah growls at Ragnar warningly, able to forget about the pain of betrayal. *We have no power here! Back. Down. Ragnar.*

Ragnar growls at Allah threateningly. *If we can't have Amari-.*

Then we can't have her child. Allah cuts his wolf off, impatient with him. *She's off limits! Back. Off.*

Ragnar snarls but he doesn't say anymore. The door to Amari's office opens and her arousal is intoxicating as it flows out. Allah plays it cool. He pushes off of the wall and turns to face Viggo, who looks at his daughter before sweeping her up in his arms protectively. This man doesn't stop! He's got to protect *everyone* from Allah!

"I'm not going to hurt your daughter, Viggo," Allah says as he starts past his god.

Ragnar snaps as Viggo's woodsy, musky scent hits Allah's nose. *Traitor!* Ragnar snarls.

"That's below me," Allah says lowly as he shakes Ragnar off.

"Good to know," Viggo replies lowly.

Allah can feel Viggo's eyes on him. *Ragnar, get a hold of yourself. Viggo is no traitor. Amari is!*

As long as I live and breathe, Amari is never a traitor! Ragnar snarls.

Allah shakes his head and pushes Ragnar to the back of his mind. Viggo closes the door as Allah's eyes go straight to Amari's mate mark. It's changed! It's not the gold wings and gold wolf head anymore! It's...

Allah's heart break at the most beautiful mate mark anyone could ever bare. His eyes meet Amari's. Viggo marked her? But why? Takals *never* mark their spouse! What drove Viggo to do it? Is it because of what Allah did?

He shudders at the thought. Allah can't not look at the mark, though. The gold wings have been replaced with a pure white cat with ocean blue eyes and the gold wolf head is now two white swords laid across each other at the cat's feet, showing a sign of peace.

Allah watches the cat flick its tail and the swords glow a pure white light. He blinks. Did he see that right? Or was he hallucinating? Does Amari's mate mark move and flicker? It's truly one of a kind if that's true!

In just a gray t-shirt and jeans, the tattoo stands out on Amari's neck with its glow. She crosses her arms and the cat on her mark sits down in front of the swords, turning into a white tiger on guard. Beautiful!

But it's weird Allah is liking the cats. He usually doesn't like them!

"What can I do for you, Allah," Amari asks, bringing him out of his trance.

He shakes his head and looks at her. Her brown eyes glow with pure white rings, replacing the green rings that were once there. Amari is at her most powerful stage with her marriage to Viggo and that makes her dangerous. Maybe he was the better choice after all.

"Your," Allah starts, trying to find his words. "Mate mark. It's... beautiful."

"Thank you," Amari replies. "Viggo has the same one."

"It's remarkable." Allah's eyes keep switching between Amari's eyes and her mark, but it doesn't change. He lets his eyes trail back to hers. "When did you... When did it...?"

"Happen?"

Allah nods. Usually, he's pretty good at keeping his cool. But this new change pisses him off, breaking his heart at the same time. He should've made the move sooner!

"The night of our wedding and Viggo's coronation. When we consummated our marriage. But the mark never stays the same. It's constantly changing."

Allah gives Amari a crooked smile as he gains back his composure. "Probably because you keep getting stronger." He compliments her.

She shrugs. Her office door opens and closes behind Allah. He knows Viggo is back in the room by the scent. "What's going on, Allah?"

"My packs. The ones I rule over… They're all at my door."

Amari shrugs, again.

"Demanding war."

"And that's my concern because why?"

"They're challenging me, Amari. Because you chose Viggo instead of me they're furious. They wanted the alliance."

"I'm sorry." Amari leans back into her desk, grasping onto the edge of it with both hands and lifting her breasts while her chest puffs out. "But there's nothing I can do, Allah. I'm happy where I am."

Allah sighs heavily. "I know. And we should break the mate bond between us. I prefer not to know when you and Viggo are getting busy." He's careful not to snap with Viggo now in the room. Allah knows the consequences if you cross a takal.

"It's fifty, fifty," Amari says, bobbing her head side to side before settling it in place between her shoulders. "Sometimes it's with Viggo and sometimes it's with Ada. Depends on who I'm in the mood for."

Allah stops a growl from rising in his throat. "I prefer if we didn't talk about this, Amari. I still don't like you fucking my ex-wife," he says in a low tone, knowing he can get away with *that*. "It's quite distasteful. And ludicrous."

"I'm sorry to hear that," Amari says lowly. "But I'll stop since you asked nicely."

Allah shakes his head. "Amari, I need a solution. If we can sit down and figure out-."

"Just because you're having trouble with your kingdom, Allah, it doesn't mean I can solve all your problems," Amari speaks over Allah, cutting him off. "I wish I could help you. Truly. But it's not like I can betroth one of my girls to you. They're too young. And they deserve to have the choice of who they love. I won't take that away from them."

Betrothal…

There it is! Ragnar snaps. *She mentioned it. Now, convince her to do it!*

I'm not one to push our Goddess, Ragnar, Allah snaps with a growl at his wolf. *Once she makes up her mind there's no changing it!*

We know her, Allah! Ragnar paces in Allah's head. *With the right push she'll change her mind!*

Like we've ever *been able to do that!* Allah spats.

The creature inside of her! I can tap into it! Convince her *to change Amari's mind!*

No! Allah keeps his eyes on Amari as he battles with Ragnar inside his head, not letting her know what's going on. But she gets the look on her face anyway. *Stand down, Ragnar! You are not ruining this for me! You have her suspicious!*

Amari shakes her head, fear in her eyes. "No. Allah. There's no fuckin' way."

"Exactly what I was thinking," Viggo growls. The blade on his arm is pressed against Allah's chest threateningly before Allah knows what's going on.

Their eyes meet as Viggo thrusts Allah backwards. His back meets the bookshelf, but he doesn't back down. Evern though he knows he should.

"Viggo, no!" Amari warns.

Viggo keeps a hold of Allah's shirt, his arm turned into a blade and pressed against Allah's chest dangerously. Viggo looks at his wife. "Amari."

"Babe," Amari drawls out, keeping eye contact with her God.

"We can't honestly let him consider it." Viggo snaps.

"We're not. Allah." Amari turns her attention to the Lycan King. He looks at her, their eyes meeting. "I prefer if you shut your wolf out. And we talk like adults do. Let him go for a run."

"Last time I did that he was gone for almost six years. I just got him back." Allah confesses, knowing the situation this puts him in. He shakes his head. "I can't be without Ragnar right now. I fought off almost a whole pack just on my way out the door."

Amari sighs and sags. She perks up, looking like an idea crossed her mind. "Then I. Amari Rose Grimert. Reject you. Allah Ammon King. As my mate."

The pain hits Allah and it tries to take over him. He fights against it this time as Viggo keeps him on his feet, his hand in Allah's shirt. Allah dips his head in a nod.

"I, Allah Ammon King, accept the rejection. And I reject you, Amari Rose Grimert, as my second chance mate." Allah gets a migraine, the stabbing pain in the rest of his body stopping instantaneously. At least he can put up with a migraine!

Viggo lets go of Allah, thrusting him off and backing up a few paces. Allah keeps his footing as Ragnar howls in pain in his head, grateful for the support of the bookshelf against his back.

It's not easy for a wolf. It's what falls in love with its mate right away. Most of the were-kind tend to mistake it as their own love for their other half. But some see past it and use their brain. Allah shuts Ragnar out to let him grieve in peace.

"Allah," Amari starts. "I don't know what to tell you. But I can only send my men that are wolves to help keep yours at bay. Just a few, though."

Allah nods. "If we can have some sort of alliance…" He trails off, unable to think of his next words.

Amari blinks and he knows what she's thinking. He was her mentor and they have some good memories together. But they usually don't get involved with each other now that she's married. They've made some mistakes. Allah should *never* have fallen in love with her. But what's done is done.

"It'll be easier, Amari," Allah puts in. "For the both of us. You're not getting the packs of my kingdom at your door, because they're afraid of you and Viggo. They don't dare to challenge you. Me, on the other hand…"

"My wife and I will talk," Viggo says lowly.

A few knocks sound on the door.

"We'll figure something out. But I can't promise you any of my men." Viggo opens the barrier behind Allah.

He keeps his eyes on Amari, his hands in his front pockets as he pushes off his support to face her. He doesn't care for who might be peering in. All he wants is to give Amari his attention.

Allah moved on from Ada. He doesn't love anyone like he loves Amari. But the scent at the door hits him, making Ragnar go crazy for it. Lilacs and wolfsbane. Oh, that smell… There's something familiar about it.

Viggo talks with the maid that's just outside the door and he says Ada's name. Allah shakes his head at Amari, keeping his mind on the war that's on his threshold.

"Amari, I'm going to have a battle with my own people if we don't come up with an alliance," he puts in, his gray eyes piercing Amari's brown ones. "This is a pressing matter. And I need you to come back with me just this one time. Maybe for a few days. Talk some sense into my packs. It'll help me a lot. Really."

"No," Amari says sternly, her eyes turning into slits of a glare.

"Look, I promise nothing will happen. I won't even touch you without one of my men or maids present. We need to get a hold of this situation and take control. Otherwise, you won't have an Asgard Kingdom for much longer. I can't take on more if all the packs decide to hit me all at once."

Amari looks at Viggo over Allah's shoulders. That's when the scent from earlier becomes intoxicatingly beautiful, wafting in the room in one giant wave. Why hasn't Allah smelt it before? He should've when he was outside Amari's office! Unless… It's one of Amari's maids.

Allah stops himself from taking a deep breath and letting it hit his lungs. Something else happens. A familiar pull makes Allah want to look and see who joined the room. But it ignores it the best he can.

What the hell?! How is another fated mate possible?! Amari nods, her eyes on Allah.

"Okay," Amari mutters at last. "We'll make a plan of attack. You can hang out here for a bit while Viggo and I talk. He and I need to go over some things before we can make a final decision."

Allah nods, grateful for his friend's change of mind. "Thank you, Amari." He scrunches up his nose as the smell hits, again. "What is that awful smell?" He covers up, acting like he doesn't like the beautiful aroma that's coming next to Viggo.

"She must need to poop." Amari looks at her husband. Wait… What?! "I will talk to Viggo while you walk around the gardens," she says to Allah. She glances at him, their eyes meeting.

Allah dips his head in gratitude. "Thank you, Amari." He turns around. His eyes lock with the little girl from earlier, her eyes innocent.

Mate!

It echoes in Allah's mind and he can't get out of the office fast enough. Fuck! If Amari finds out about this, she's going to be furious! But why is Allah now smelling it? Why didn't he smell it when the little girl was next to him?

3

Amari stares out at the scenery on the side of her estate, the green forest still having color.

She hasn't gone back to Heaven's Light yet. Her kids may like it there, being able to play with all of the animals. But there's something down here in Hallam that draws the girls here. The living life.

Clay hasn't shown much interest for the creatures down here. But he's still just a baby at four months old. He's already crawling and Amari can't believe how fast he's growing. She wishes her kids could just stay little.

She sighs and sags, leaning forward. She and Viggo talked. He isn't a fan of the idea of her going to Allah's kingdom.

"He may have accepted the rejection and completed the severing of the mate bond." Viggo tried to argue. *"But I still don't trust him. What if he tries to do something?"*

"Then I'll demote him," Amari replied. *"He'll no longer be the lycan king and god of the were-kind and Sirena will take her place as the goddess of the were-kind."*

"And who will take his place as Lycan King? His brothers are already rulers in other parts of Hallam!"

Amari looked at her beloved husband. "There won't be one," she said lowly.

"But the Moon and Lake packs around here. They'll go rogue without a king!"

"No one. Can replace Allah. I know each and every lycan and they are not fit to rule. It just simply won't happen."

Viggo nodded as he caught on. "That's the best threat to give a man like him..." He hesitated for a moment, looking into his beloved wife's eyes. "Okay. But only one condition."

"What?"

Viggo kissed Amari lovingly. "You come home right after you help Allah control his kingdom. Preferably tonight."

It was Amari's turn to nod. Then she shook her head. "I don't think it will happen. But I'll try."

Viggo kissed Amari and their lips melted together, fitting into each other perfectly.

A warm wind picks up and blows Amari's bangs back, bringing her back to the present. She's not ready to go back to Allah's place. The last time she was there...

Garrett died just a moment after he mind linked with Amari with an apology for not being able to keep his promise. She misses him. She misses his laugh and his smile. The way he was goofy with her whenever they were alone together. The way he used to make her laugh when they would just walk out of the temple after doing a session. He was it. The one.

Amari tried to ignore that in the past, not wanting to break Mike's heart. Mike... Did he make it? Is he back home? Or is he out there in the world looking for something that was already right in front of him, again?

Amari sighs, sags, then leans her elbow into her knee as she props it up, running her hand through her hair. Before she goes, she needs to make sure Heaven's

Light is guarded and ready for anything. Who knows if the Moon and Lake packs will actually go head-to-head with Amari!

Raja lies down next to her and moans.

"Hey, Raja," Amari says softly, wrapping her arm around her companion's neck and hugging her from the side. She kisses the top of her head. "I really could use your help."

Raja chuffs and rubs her head on Amari's chest.

"Allah's wolf wants a betrothal with one of my girls." She scratches her companion's ears, who enjoys them. "But I can't allow it." Amari thinks about what she might be able to do. "And I have to go to his kingdom for a while. Help him take control of it and his packs. They're wanting war, because of the lack of an alliance. But you already knew that."

Let it happen, Raja says in a mind link the she only shares with one person. She can't converse with anyone else.

Amari winces. "Let what happen?" She's afraid of the answer.

The betrothal. Give Allah the alliance he wants.

"But I can't do that with my own daughter. Emma doesn't deserve-."

Emma has a choice. Raja looks at Amari, her evergreen eyes deep in color, mocking the forest green around them. *She can choose if she wants to make that alliance. But it's not her that already has her fate sealed.*

Amari flinches. "Raja… No."

Raja lets the color of her pupils pierce Amari's as it sharpens. *I have blessed your daughters because they are meant to be somewhere else in this world. Emma will be the new Heart of Hallam after I pass. She'll be able to cross between Hallam and Homba, keep the peace between the two worlds. But Ramein…*

Amari shakes her head. "Don't say it, Raja," she warns, her heart aching for her youngest daughter.

Raja lifts her chin, meeting Amari's gaze. *She's more wolf than takal. Yes, she is like Manny. And she has a special battle form thanks to her wolf. But she is a peacekeeper. She is the calm before and after the storm. She is what will bring Hallam back to peace once more. You must let her take her place next to Allah.*

Amari shakes her head, her heart breaking on the inside. Why did Raja do that?! Ramein deserves to choose her fate! She shouldn't have to do this! "And what if I don't agree with the betrothal," Amari mumbles.

You better be ready for war. Because it will come knocking at your door when the time comes.

Amari sighs and sags, watching Raja. She knows that the tiger only means good. She's blessed Emma, Ramein, and Clay. But Amari has a feeling Raja won't be here for the birth for anymore of her kids.

Amari hugs her best friend's neck and buries her face in Raja's striped fur, starting to know why Raja is here. Her heart starts to break and shatter.

"Rest easy, my friend," Amari says softly, tears forming in her eyes. "You will be sorely missed. And never forgotten. You will always have a place in my heart."

Raja moans and lays her head on Amari's lap. *Please, heed my warning, Amari. It's my last wish for you. And Hallam. I want it to stay at peace.*

"You have my word," Amari says into the top of Raja's head. She presses her lips into her soft fur. "I promise," she whispers. "Emma and Ramein… They will fulfill your duties and wishes." Amari quietly cries into Raja's head.

Raja relaxes into Amari's arms. *Thank you.* Raja's mind link fades and Amari feels her soul leave her body. But it doesn't go far.

Amari cries into her best friend's neck as she feels her muzzle touch her head and give her one last blessing. Amari breaks down and she isn't able to hold it in, loving and mourning her best friend that was always by her side through thick and thin. A piece of her heart goes to heaven with Raja.

Amari knows Raja won't be in Heaven's Light. She won't be with Amari up there. Something else is in store for her and Amari can feel it. She just wishes she doesn't have to say goodbye to the one being that was always there for her.

Mike's betrayal, Garrett's passing, her crowning and wedding, her miscarriage, and her three kids' births. The three Raja blessed.

Raja has been there for Amari when she needed her. And now she's gone. There's no other being that can fill this hole in Amari's aching heart. And she doesn't want another companion to fill this hole.

∞

Amari walks beside Raheim as she escorts Raja's body, which is being carried by two of her biological sons. Big, strong tigers with matching stripes and strides carry Raja to her burial site. In a large casket with bars and straps that go across the bodies of the beautiful creatures, Raja gets a burial ceremony for being the Heart of Hallam. She's royalty after all.

Alafar and Kishan growl softly as they mourn the loss of their mother, their sisters behind them to continue protecting their mother until she can rest peacefully.

Her heart shattered, Amari does her best to continue forward. Even though she wants to stop and break down at the loss of her best friend. Her only companion. Her right-hand woman.

Raja was everything to Amari and it's hard to let go. She was always there for anything Amari needed. Amari leads the queen's sons and daughters to the burial site, where Viggo is waiting in his white, burial ritual Viking clothing.

The pure white wolf fur falls down his shoulders like a cape, his tunic and dragon scale shirt cling to his well-built frame, showing it off. His pants fit neatly around his hips and hang around his legs just right. His belt with the emerald stone in the middle fits snug around his waist. As much as he looks good Amari just can't think that way. And she won't be able to for a while in her mourning.

Amari stops and watches as two Viking takals take the straps off of Alafar and Kishan. They gently lay the casket down into the hole, in sync. Slowly, the casket makes its way down as Viggo starts the ceremony with the words that are meant for the Heart of Hallam. But Amari hardly hears him, her grief too much.

Raja's kin moan in mourning and grief, shattering Amari's heart. A fresh stabbing pain pierces it and she tries her best to stay on her own two feet.

Raja was the sweetest mother! She had the heart of a fighter and a mother, protecting her babies at all costs! She risked her life multiple times to save her babies and Amari!

Amari will never be able to thank Raja enough! And she will never get the chance, again! She *has* to keep her promise to her best friend no matter the cost. It's what Raja would want!

"May her spirit rest in peace," Viggo finishes up in the Russian language, Raja's language. "And may she feel the fullness of our hearts as they go with her."

Raja's family roar out, calling out to her and guiding her to the heavens. But she doesn't go there as royal azaleas and sacred lotuses fall down to her casket, releasing her spirit.

Amari's knees buckle underneath her as she feels Raja's spirit enter her and awaken a creature inside of her, the tiger roaring in response and letting her sons and daughters know that she now has a new purpose. Amari breaks down as she falls to her knees. Raja! She's here with her!

Amari wraps her heart around her best friend as she welcomes her in. She's never letting go!

This is a rare chance that Amari will keep forever!

∞

Allah watches Amari as she gets down from Ragnar's back, forcing the team of the Moon packs back.

Blue Moon, Silver Moon, and Asgard Light Moon are the ones Allah and Ragnar scent this time.

One of the werewolves takes a step towards Amari with a growl, showing his teeth and resistance. She snaps his head back with a force of wind and brown wolf lands on his back, yelping in surprise. The others look at him in disbelieved shock then look at Amari, regret over their faces.

Shit's going down and Allah likes it. He knew Amari would be able to knock some sense into the alphas when he hasn't been able to. It's a gift that she has with how stubborn she is. Amari growls at the wolves threateningly with a newfound creature stirring inside of her. Allah can even feel it!

It's awake?!

She's awake! Ragnar howls to Allah. *Her creature is awake!*

Good! Allah barks excitedly. *And Amari woke her up without our help! See what happens when you back off, Ragnar?*

No, I don't.

Good things happen, you idiot!

Ragnar snaps at Allah in his head. *I could've helped!*

Ragnar, you're an idiot. Allah snarls, repeating himself.

We'll see who the idiot is by tonight! Thinking straight for once, Ragnar shows he's finally moving on from Amari. And falling in love with her daughter.

The alphas and their betas of the Moon packs back up as they keep their eyes on Amari. The wolf she knocked over slowly gets up. He looks at her and their eyes meet.

"Go ahead," Amari threatens. "Make my day."

The wolves shift and exchange glances, looking nervous.

"I chose my mate! And I made the right decision! Whoever told you that I was Allah's second chance mate put the idea in your head that the alliance would be great. Well, guess what?!" Amari screams, making the animals in front of her whine in fear.

Allah can smell it radiating off of them as Amari's power takes over them, their whimpers louder than normal. She's absolutely amazing! This most definitely is something Allah wished he had in his hands! But in a way, doesn't he?

"There *will* be an alliance between Allah and me!"

The leaders pick up their ears, interested in the sudden alliance that Amari hasn't spoken to Allah about. She's come to a decision! It makes Ragnar pick up his ears and he gladly stands behind Amari protectively and supportively. He's interested in what she has to say.

"Just not the kind you're looking for!" Amari closes her fist next to her side and a shift in the air changes. She's challenging the packs. "You got it?!"

The alphas and betas growl at Amari, the alpha closest to her picking up his black foot as he shows his teeth. His markings are unique.

His wolf is pure white with black paws and blue eyes. He's the alpha of the Asgard Light Moon pack. The pack that killed Allah's wife. He has a personal agenda against them.

Amari looks Alpha Blackfoot, the son of a murderer, with a glare.

"Blackfoot," Amari starts. "I'm not surprised. Why the challenge?"

Alpha Blackfoot shifts into human form, not caring that he's naked in front of his goddess. He doesn't bother to put some shorts on. "Queen Amari."

"Uh, uh," Amari interrupts him, holding her index finger up.

He winces. "Goddess. Amari. Sorry. I'm not used to calling you that. But you have to consider what this looks like to us."

"You better choose your words carefully, Hapoor, or you'll no longer be the alpha of your pack," Amari warns of a threatening matter.

Alpha Blackfoot dips his head apologetically. His bright blue-green eyes meet Amari's brown eyes. "Two of Allah's omegas were killed in your estate. You once *bore* his mate mark. And my Delta heard the two of you going at it when Ada rejected him. She heard what was said and stayed downwind as she got closer to confirm her suspicions."

"Does she have no decency?!" Amari snaps. She has every right to be pissed! This is news to her *and* Allah! It's not right!

Allah growls at the thought, showing his teeth. Even if Astrid, the Delta of the Asgard Light Moon pack, was downwind he still should've felt her presence! What the fuck was she thinking?! Astrid is dead!

"She was doing her job," Alpha Blackfoot snaps, defending his cousin. "And why you're fucking our lycan king while you're so devoted to your husband is beyond reasoning!"

"The only people!" Amari gets threateningly close to him, getting a reaction from Ragnar, who growls at the alpha. "I'm fucking! Is my husband and mistress. I have no reason to have a manstress!"

Alpha Blackfoot raises an eyebrow. "Care to elaborate why you came in on Allah's back, then?" He challenges in a low, guttural, threatening tone.

His stupidity earns him a fist in the gut. He doubles over from the pain with a grunt. Amari takes a step back, making sure none of this man's scent gets on her.

That's a wise choice. Viggo doesn't like the man any more than Amari does!

"Do you expect me to walk here?!" Amari looks around the men and women that were sent to Allah's door. "It's ten miles from my estate here on Hallam and Allah came to me asking for help! Did you expect me to pass up the opportunity for a free ride without having to call for my tachala?! Let this be a warning and threat!"

Alpha Blackfoot grunts in pain, drawing Allah's attention. Amari drew claws out and dug them into the half-lycan's intestines. That's gotta hurt!

"I lost my best friend, companion, and right-hand woman earlier this week! Her funeral was this morning! You should know who it is since there was a shift in the air!"

Allah's ruling packs get nervous.

"Raja. The first Heart of Hallam."

Ears go flat and whimpers are heard throughout the kingdom. Roars of tigers, lions, leopards, and panthers are heard in the forests as a mourning for their great queen as they hear the news. Cheetahs are heard chirping and bobcats and lynxes join in on the cries.

Amari just announced to all of Hallam of Raja's death.

It's not just normal cats that are grieving. But the were-cats as well. Raja was a mother to them all. She was their queen in so many ways. She took care of each and one of them at one point in their lives.

Ragnar's ears flatten and he whimpers in fear for good reason. With Raja gone there's going to be a war with all of the cats! And Homba! All the dogs and wolves will go extinct!

"If anyone," Amari barks in her authoritative tone as she speaks to all of Hallam. "Dares to cross my kids! My daughter Emma! Who is the *new* Heart of Hallam! If you *dare* try to cause a war with my lycan king Allah! God of the were-kind! I will take you to Hell's Fire myself," Amari threatens with a growl, her eyebrows furrowed angrily. "You will be considered a traitor from then on out. Understood?"

Everything goes quiet, making the werewolves uneasy as they glance at each other and take a few cautious steps back. Their ears flat against their heads they look completely terrified.

Good.

"I said," Amari growls. She picks Alpha Blackfoot up by his dark brown hair and she exposes his neck. "Is that understood?" She threatens the man with a snarl.

He lets his eyes meet hers. He manages out a growl as his wounds continue to heal, but slowly. "I don't take orders from you," he growls.

Amari opens her mouth, her canines growing. Alpha Blackfoot smiles mischievously to show off his canines. He starts for Amari, his shaft coming to life and growing in size. Allah shifts to human form as Amari's canines sink into Alpha Blackfoot's neck. He grabs her pants to rip them.

Allah tears the two rivals apart and gets in between them, protecting his goddess and tearing her canines out of the werewolf. Alpha Blackfoot drips blood from his neck, but not for very long. His wolf starts to heal him.

It takes a few minutes since Amari dealt deadly blows. She sneers at the sight of the wound she made, happy with her work. Did she not notice what the alpha was about to do to her?

"Raping our goddess," Allah growls. He shakes his head at the alpha in front of him. "Your duties as an alpha are over, Hapoor! I strip you of your title as Alpha of the Asgard Light Moon pack and hand it over to your second born son! Hazen!"

No longer an alpha, Blackfoot now gets called by his first name. As a loner. Hapoor. He winces at his title being stripped from him, heartbreak in his eyes.

"You're now a loner. A rogue if you prefer."

Hapoor looks at Amari over Allah's shoulder, his neck bleeding from the gash she gave him. "Goddess. Amari. Please. Don't do this." He pleads.

"Your king has every right to make you a loner," Amari replies lowly. "And he has every right to strip all titles from those who dare cross one of us!" She orders for the werewolves in front of her to hear. "Since Hapoor is now stripped of his title as alpha, you can feel free to follow in his footsteps with yours being stripped from you… Or you can chase him out into the lands of the loners and rogues. Stay loyal to your king.

Your choice! But Allah and I are making an alliance to bring peace in his lands! There will be no war today! Or tomorrow! The future! You can forget it! Leave! While you still can!"

The wolves turn to Hapoor, growling and snarling at him, ready to attack. He makes a run for it and they chase after him, fear absent from his fleeing form. He shifts to gain speed, running to get to the lands quickly without further injuries.

The werewolves from other packs are hard on his tail, trying to catch up to him.

4

Amari wakes up in the middle of the night and instantly hugs her pillow, wishing she was back home with her family. She misses them. Who knows if Clay is being good for Viggo!

Hopefully, Emma and Ramein are being helpful and getting along. Now that Raja's old body is in the ground, her spirit with Amari, Emma is going to have a hard time without her playmate. She was just attached to the tiger as much as Amari.

The light of the full moon shines through the window and Amari buries her face into the fluff underneath it, closing her eyes. She moans. No wonder she woke up. All the female lycans and werewolves are going to be up, howling at the beauty outside. At least there's one upside to it!

Amari can never sleep well when it's a full moon and she has no idea why. She couldn't sleep on one when she was in Homba! Amari sighs and tries to relax into the mattress. The bedspread and top sheet cover her naked body.

She thinks about her day. Yesterday went well… Raja's funeral was beautiful and all of her biological sons and daughters were there. All the cats she saved and adopted were there as well. They all miss her. Today hasn't been easier.

In a way, Amari is still in grief. She doesn't get to hug her best friend anymore. All they get is conversations, now. All the time. Amari wonders if Raja is awake. But before she reaches out to her companion the hairs on her neck stand on end.

Don't. Move. Raja warns in Amari's mind.

Why? Amari doesn't know why she's asking that question. She knows not to question her senses!

But the question is…

Is it a who or what that's close by?

A woodsy scent hits Amari's scent glands, making her wonder who would dare to enter her room. Then the scent of sandalwood hits her.

Shit…

Rough hands glide up Amari's body as the covers get thrown back. A man straddles her. Those hands… They're not Viggo's. And they're most definitely not Allah's!

Amari stiffens, not daring to move. She's about to get raped. Who would dare do such a thing? Amari reaches out to Viggo in a mind link since she's not connected to Allah in any way anymore.

Viggo! Someone's in here! Get here quick! Please!

A rough hand sneaks around Amari's middle and takes her breast. It thrusts her onto her back, forcing her to look up at her attacker.

Hapoor Blackfoot.

Of course, it is! He's always wanted a taste of Amari's wrath, so he had a reason to do this! He always wanted a reason to punish her! They've never liked each other and constantly fought these past six years. He's such a pushover!

Amari tries to scream, but Hapoor's hand goes over her mouth, stopping her from making even the slightest sound.

I'm coming, baby! Viggo finally responds in the mind link. He sounds scared. *Hold Hapoor back as long aas you can! I'll be there soon!*

He's going to rape me! Amari screams to Viggo, scared for her life.

She loves that they share their problems with each other and know which creature they've been dealing with. It lets the other know who they're having troubles with at times like these.

Viggo growls in Amari's mind, sounding protective and ready to kill. Oh, she bet he is.

"One," Hapoor whispers threateningly. "Sound. One move." He lets out his claws on his free hand, showing them off in the moonlight. "And Hallam will no longer have a Goddess. Do I make myself clear?" He orders.

Amari nods her head, glancing at Hapoor's claws. He gets in between her thighs and wedges them open with his own. He lathers his hand with lube then sticks it inside of Amari, gaining a gasp from her.

Fuck!

Hapoor groans in pleasure as her tightness clenches around him. "Fuck, you're tight," he whispers, fucking Amari with his hand. He sucks on her clitoris to get her going.

She doesn't like it. This is so wrong on so many levels! Why is he doing this?!

Amari pants, making her breasts heave on her chest. She doesn't how to get out of this! All she can think of doing is going straight to the bathroom after this. Get Viggo to bed her to get rid of the woodsy stink of this foul man!

Amari whimpers as pleasure she doesn't want to feel hits her. She sees white and goes into an orgasm. Then it happens.

Thrust!

Amari tries to scream, but Hapoor covers her mouth with his hand, silencing her.

"What did we just agree on?" He growls threateningly, his lips right next to her ear.

Amari voices her pants into his hand, trying to look at him; frightened. He smiles next to her hair, showing off his pearly white teeth. He's going to try and mark her!

Of course!

Amari bets Hapoor is the one that rallied up all of the packs after giving them the news! She should've known he would try to pull something like this! He wanted Allah to strip him of his title so he could be free to do whatever he wants!

It was a mistake to come here! Amari and Allah fell right into Hapoor's trap!

He thrusts into her again, making her scream into his hand. But no one can hear her.

"Please," Amari begs. "Don't do this!"

"Oh, I've been wanting a taste of your body since I've met you," Hapoor growls.

Werewolves and lycans are heard outside, battling each other. Fuck! Did he plan this, too?!

"And now we're gonna have pups together, you and I."

Amari weeps into Hapoor's palm as he thrusts into her, again, his canines in her mate mark. Slam! The headboard bangs against the wall.

"And we now have a distraction to keep them from hearing you," Hapoor sneers.

"Please," Amari weeps. "God, no!"

Hapoor thrusts into Amari, again. Slam! The headboard continues to hit the wall. Hapoor gets up on his knees and he thrusts Amari's hips into him as he thrusts into her.

"Now, call my name!" He growls.

"No," Amari growls, glaring up at her rapist.

"Pity." Hapoor enunciates. "I love it when you say my first name. It just sounds so good coming from your lips." He purrs.

Thrust. Slam!

"Let go of me!" Amari begs.

"No," Hapoor growls, shaking his head.

Thrust. Slam!

"Now, what am I?!"

"Nothing!" Amari tries to screech, hoping someone hears her.

Thrust. Slam!

Amari lays her head back as she sees white and has an orgasm that she doesn't want, Hapoor somehow hitting her spot. How is he doing this to her?! Why doesn't Raja wanna fight back, now?! She did earlier!

Raja, where are you?!

I'm here! Raja calls as pleasure sweeps through Amari. Guilt hits her. *Stay with me, Mare! This will all be over soon. I promise! Just hold on!*

Amari doesn't want to hold on. She wants to kill this man, but doesn't have the nerve to lift a finger.

"I'm your alpha, Amari," Hapoor growls in her face, his breath tickling her lips. "Now, say it."

"No," Amari growls as she comes back. She glares up at him before his lips crash on hers.

Thrust. Slam!

Amari tries to thrust Hapoor off of her, but not before she bites his bottom lip with her canines out. He pulls back, putting his hand to his bloody lip. He looks at the blood on his finger before giving her a glare.

Thrust. Slam!

"You're paying for that," he growls. He slams his hips into Amari's and she screams out in pure agony, throwing her head back.

Thrust. Slam!

A crack is heard coming from the wall. The bedroom door slams open and Hapoor looks over at the intruder. He pulls out of Amari. She notices his shaft is still hard and he quickly gets himself situated before leaping out of the window, Viggo hard on his tail.

Amari gets up on her elbows, tears streaming down her face as she watches her husband. She needs him right now! He can't go after the rogue!

"I got him," Allah barks as he barges in. "You stay with your wife!" He lunges through the window just as fast as he ran into the room, diving through.

"Viggo!" Amari screams. She quickly gets out of bed and rushes over to her husband, who meets her in the middle, holding onto her tightly.

She clings onto him, scared for her life. At least she doesn't have to worry about getting pregnant this time. But she still wants Viggo to get rid of Hapoor's stink. With her new senses thanks to Raja's new gift for her, she can see, scent, hear, and feel everything even more so than before.

All Amari wants to do is be in Viggo's arm right now. She doesn't want to be anywhere else! Viggo moans in relief with his hand on the back of Amari's head, holding onto her.

Mate! Raja yells to Amari, throwing her off guard.

What? Confused, Amari starts to wonder if she's somehow a were-cat.

Amari, we're no were-cat! We're goddesses! But I always knew Viggo was your mate! It wasn't Garret, may he rest in peace. And it may have been Allah once before! But, Amari, if you were to have a fated mate, it'd be Viggo!

He's the choice I was hoping you'd make! You're bound together! And no one can break your bond! No one! Not even Allah as your second chance mate!

Amari nods at Raja as Viggo holds the back of her head.

"You're coming home," he says roughly. "Where he can't get to you."

Amari tries to laugh in relief as she clings onto the man she feels the most safe with. But it just comes out airy. "I couldn't agree with you more," she says lowly.

Viggo kisses Amari's hair before throwing her in a blanket and carrying her out of the bedroom.

∞

Ragnar's teeth sink into the neck of a gray wolf with a white patch on his chest. He reeks like a rogue and has horrible battle tactics.

Allah knows which one this is! The traitor from twenty years ago! He tried to sell secrets of Hallam to Homba! Fortunately, no one believed him.

Ragnar growls before ripping an artery out of the wolf's neck. He drops to the ground with a satisfying thump at Ragnar's feet, Allah staring at his body. That felt good. Now, for Hapoor! Where did he run off to?!

Ragnar, Allah starts. *We need to hold them off until Amari is back home with Viggo!*

Ragnar pushes forward, towards the forest that marks the border with the Blue Moon pack. *She's not safe at her estate! She needs to go somewhere Hapoor can't find her!* He keeps his eyes peeled for the rapist as he converses with Allah.

Her home is in Heaven's Light, idiot! That's where she's going until we can get that traitor killed! No one *can go there except for those who died going down the right path!*

Right! Ragnar scans the trees as he gets closer, looking for the new rogue. *That sounds better!*

Yes! Finally! Something we can agree on! Allah sounds relieved.

What about Ramein? Is she there? Hope blossoms in Ragnar's chest. Oh, he hopes his mate is safe!

She is! But not she's not old enough yet, Ragnar!

Ragnar growls as he spots pure white fur in the forest. *I just want to make sure my future mate is safe! I'm not letting this son of a bitch near her nor her mother!*

Now, we're talking, Ragnar! Those six years with that she-wolf really helped you come to your senses.

And I'm about to knock some sense into this guy, Ragnar growls. He pushes forward and uses his speed to catch up to the wolf. But it's not him.

It's a fox!

The beautiful creature looks at Ragnar and her green eyes meet his gold eyes. She's beautiful! And new! Who is she?

Get her to shift, Ragnar, Allah orders. *We need to ask her questions. Now!*

We can't. I'm sorry, Allah. Ragnar whines, wanting to obey Allah.

But they both know you can't get in the way of a new creature. They're busy being dreamt about, their actions monitored.

The beautiful fox turns around and starts for Allah's kingdom. Of course! Amari must have created her to aid in her escape!

Ragnar skids to a halt and kicks up dirt before coming to a complete stop, watching the she-fox run for the Asgard Lycan Kingdom.

She'll make sure Amari and Viggo get home safe, Allah reminds Ragnar. *Let's keep searching for this asshole.*

Ragnar dips head in a nod. He turns around to continue his search for Amari's rapist, determined to get justice for her. She deserves to see the man pay for his crimes.

∞

Madi wakes up after having a vivid dream.

Amari… Raped by a werewolf that was cast out for some reason.

It didn't happen… Did it?

Madi and Amari might not agree on a lot of things, but she wouldn't be able to live with herself if she didn't reach out. She's got to get word to her cousin in Heaven's Light somehow.

Usually, Madi doesn't care what happens to Amari. But their everyday meetings for two months turned into three meetings a month, helping Madi and Amari close old wounds, make heartfelt apologies, and move on together like cousins should. They're just not best friends like they once were. Before Mike.

Madi looks over at the clock, which is in the dark. She looks out the window and tries to tell the time by the moon. But it's useless.

When cellphones don't work here, Madi didn't bother to bring hers with her six years ago. Maybe she should've just to tell the time.

Madi slips out of bed. She quietly gets dressed in her shapeshifter clothes, black leggings and a black tank top. With these clothes on, Madi doesn't have to worry about being naked whenever she shifts. They shift with her like a second skin, disappearing.

Madi sneaks out of the estate through the back door, just to find a hellhound being chased by a Guardian cat. She shakes her head. She's glad she can create cats to help manage the hellhounds. They're always trying to sneak out!

Madi shifts into a wolf that's the same size as a werewolf. She doesn't know exactly where she's going, but she knows which direction she needs to head. Madi runs with extra speed until she's in the forest that leads to Amari's estate in Hallam.

That's when she sees it.

A beautiful pure white fox runs in the forest with two people on her back. That's them. Madi can scent them. Amari's has changed some. It's not lavender and vanilla anymore. It's tiger lilies and vanilla!

Madi shakes her head. That's odd!

She shifts into something more friendly for the couple and she races over to them. Madi looks at Amari, who is wrapped in a blanket and in Viggo's arms. Their brown eyes meet and Madi knows the dream is real.

It fucking happened.

Madi roars in frustration and races ahead. She's going to kill that bastard when she sees him! Madi can't go to Heaven's Light, but she can make sure no wolf gets in the way.

A gray werewolf jumps out from hiding and snarls as he races towards Amari and Viggo. Madi changes course, racing towards him. Oh, no you don't! The male leaps for the couple on the fox and Madi lunges into him with a roar, sinking her canines into his neck. She pins him down, putting her massive paw stripe paw on his shoulder before snapping his neck.

She makes a circle, making sure the way for the fox is clear. She bites down on the leg of a black wolf that tries to go after them, breaking it in half before continuing.

Viggo activates the doors for Heaven's Light up ahead and the forest opens up to show off a set of pearly white gates. They open as a black and white wolf gets in the way, keeping the fox from entering. Snarling. This wolf is rare. Her right ride is pure black and her left side is pure white. It's a sight to see, her right eye green and her left eye brown.

Madi races towards her with a growl, determined to end this female's life. But then it hits her. This one is pregnant! Plan B, then!

Madi can do that. She leaps onto the wolf's back and throws her to the side as Madi rolls. She doesn't throw the she-wolf too hard. Just hard enough to stun her and keep her baby alive.

Madi shifts back into human form before she rushes over to Amari and Viggo, the fox standing in front of the open gates. She takes her cousin's hand in her hand as Amari offers it.

"Tell me his name," Madi says, concerned and worried for her family since Mike. "Tell me his name and I will get on it."

"Hapoor Blackfoot," Amari replies. "His wolf is pure white with pure black paws. You'll know him when you see him. He stinks of sandalwood and pine sap."

Madi nods. "Get feeling better." She looks up at the fox. "Can she go in?"

"Yes. She's a creature that protects Heaven's Light. You should meet her human. Mack is quite foxy. She tricks you all the time. I should know."

Madi looks up at Amari in surprise. "She's a were-fox?"

Amari shakes her head. "Mack is a completely different being, actually. She's just a human that passed away. She saved her fox when she was just a pup. Mack is inside waiting for her."

Madi nods and takes a step back. "Get in before any more werewolves try to attack. I'll watch your back."

"Thank you, Madi."

Madi's eyes meet Viggo's as the fox starts forward. He gives her a nod of thanks. She dips her head with her eyes closed in a warm welcome. She turns around to face the three werewolves that are racing towards her. She shifts into a massive wyvern, ready to defend her cousin until she gets to safety.

Madi warns the wolves with a infuriating roar, her golden eyes giving them the death glare. The wolves take a step back as fear comes over them, their ears lying flat against their heads. They turn around. But they don't leave without their companions, grabbing each one and carrying them on their backs.

Madi stares after them with pride, but she knows that they'll be back.

They always come back.

5

Thrust. Slam!

Amari wakes up with a jolt and little arms are instantly around her neck, giving her a reassuring squeeze. She holds onto her daughter that just woke her up, glad to be home.

Oh, she should've come home last night. She should've listened to her husband! He always knows what's best! Why didn't Amari take heed of his warning?

Her face buries into Emma's beach blond hair as it flows down behind her back and around her neck, Amari's mouth on her daughter's shoulder. She quivers from the events of last night that also haunted her dreams all night long.

She knows it wasn't just a dream. He had the chance to finish her off. But at least he wasn't ale to get her pregnant through her dreams.

Amari clings onto her little one as she tries to come out of her nightmare, paralyzed by the intensity of it. This isn't good.

Hapoor… Cast out as a rogue… He has freedom to do whatever he pleases, now. And he's going to haunt Amari's dreams. Possibly forever!

As long as she stays in Heaven's Light, Hapoor won't be able to touch her. But he'll be able to haunt her in her sleep as much as he'd like.

Amari will have to brave going to Hallam for her meetings. She and Allah need to talk about the alliance. They weren't ale to go over much yesterday since she's been in mourning and he didn't want to bother her. He's not going to bother her today after what happened in his kingdom last night. He'll be too busy reinstating and remarking the borders. He'll also want to talk to his Beta and Delta about hiring a security a team.

No…

Amari won't go back today. She'll wait until Allah isn't busy and she's had time to recuperate from her and move on from her trauma.

Emma's little arms tighten around Amari's neck, bringing her back to the present. Viggo sits up next to her, his hand on her lower back comfortingly. He rubs it before wrapping his arm around her and kissing her hair.

"Mommy, you were crying," Emma says in Amari's ear, her caring personality showing at such a young age. "In your sleep. Are you okay?" Her little voice is sweet and soft, filled with passion and concern. Emma is truly worried about her beloved mom.

Amari lets her lips linger on Emma's little shoulder. "I had a nightmare," she says softly. "That's all."

"It was more than that, Mommy." Emma gives her mom a reassuring squeeze.

"What do you mean?"

"I saw what happened last night. I know what's going on."

Amari's heart breaks and Raja growls in her head.

I should've thought about this. Raja snaps, pacing. *I shouldn't have let it happen! I should've done something!*

It's not your fault. Amari reassures her companion. *It was your time.*

But still, Mare! I could've done *something!* Raja continues to pace in Amari's mind, clearly agitated. *Maybe I should've reached out to Emma sooner. Viggo could've gotten to us sooner!*

Is she already seeing everything, Raja, Amari asks her best friend. *Emma?*

Yes! Raja flicks her tail. *And it's all my fault! If I could've just held on a little longer… Got a boost of energy from Klauss!*

Again. It's not your fault, Raja. You were old. It was your time to go.

Raja growls in Amari's mind, continuing to walk back and forth. Amari can tell she wants to go for a run. She can feel Raja's regret and anger as her own.

Yes, but Emmaleigh is seeing everything, now! She can see it all in both worlds! Cross over!

Wait… Amari starts, knowing what this new implies. *So, that means…*

You can't go with, Amari! You and Viggo can't go with your daughter. You're both bound here!

But, Raja. Amari tries to defend herself, thinking there might be a way around the ritual that bound her here.

You died... Amari. Viggo brought you back, binding you here and making you immortal. Raja shakes her head in anger, clearly still agitated. *You can't go back ever, again!*

Amari nods. "Yes, Emma. You're the Heart of Hallam, now. Raja blessed you when you were just a baby."

"And now she's gone. Dead," Emma says sweetly, sounding sad.

Amari nods, again.

"Then why isn't she here?" Seeming to be curious and confused, Amari tries to reassure Emma with her answer.

"Her spirit took another path. She's blessed someone with it."

"I hope it's you, Mommy," Emma says as Viggo wraps his arm around Amari's waist.

He holds her close, pressing his lips on her head and listening to the conversation.

"Cause you and Raja are inseparable."

Amari raises an eyebrow. "Where did you hear that word, little Emma?"

Emma pulls back and looks at her. "Daddy."

Amari nods and kisses her daughter's cheek lovingly. "Let's get some breakfast." She hugs Emma.

"I already took care of it. And the animals."

"Well, look at you." Amari looks at Emma, proud of her. "You're taking more responsibility than you need to, Miss Emma."

"Yes," Viggo puts in. "We're proud of you."

Emma shakes her head. "No. Mommy. Daddy. I'm doing what I need to for Mommy's safety. To make sure she doesn't get hurt, again. Let me go to Homba, please. Talk to a few people. I think I can make a case."

"Homba's rules are different from Hallam's." Amari squishes Emma's cheek. "You'd be able to make a case in there, but not here." Her heart breaks, knowing that what she says is true. There's no police, EMT's, fire-fighters, or even military here.

There are no official laws, but there is still such a thing of crimes. Amari just needs to get some more ground rules for this world. Have the jobs that are of requirement and applied in Homba.

"I wanna make some changes," Emma says as she nods her head. "And I wanna make them now."

"How 'bout we wait until you're older. As of right now… your training starts. As Heart of Hallam."

Emma nods excitedly. "Yes," she breathes in a whisper. "I want that."

"I will teach you everything I know about Homba. But Lillian will take you there so you can learn more. Then when you're older and ready, you'll be crowned."

Emma squeals excitedly and her arms wrap around Amari's neck. Viggo leans in to kiss Emma's temple.

"But chores come first," he says softly.

"Aw," Emma moans in disappointment. She hides her face in Amari's shoulder, cuddling with her.

She needed this. Cuddle time with her daughter. A reminder of why she's here; Goddess of Hallam.

"Mom still gets breakfast in bed," Emma says into Amari's shoulder. She looks up at her dad. "You can have breakfast at the dinner table," she mumbles, a scowl on her beautiful face.

"Are you the cook," Viggo asks, teasing Emma in a joking matter.

"No," she draws out innocently. "But I asked him to make it extra special for Mom! I told him what happened." She keeps her arms wrapped around Amari's neck as she settles her chin on her arm, keeping her chocolate brown eyes on her dad.

Amari's chin on Emma's shoulder, she imagines her daughter batting her eyelashes at Viggo.

"I'm gonna have to min link with him and remind him who the *real* boss is around here," he teases.

"I'm the boss!" Emma beams, lifting her head.

"Yes, you are," Amari compliments her beloved daughter. "And you did the chores all by yourself." She puts her lips to Emma's ear. "Aim low," she whispers softly. "It gets him every time."

Emma pinches Viggo's belly button and he grunts in pain.

"I'm gonna get you for that," he growls teasingly. He grabs Emma and tears her away from Amari.

She screams as he lays her across his lap and tickles her belly. It puts a smile on Amari's face as the cook brings breakfast in. Ramein follows with Mack, who is holding Clay.

Amari motions for her other daughter to join on the bed. "Come on, Ramey. We're having breakfast in bed."

Mack brings Clay over to Amari and their eyes meet. Mack's brown eyes glow red, letting Amari know her fox is calling for her. "He just ate and I burped him for you." Mack's red-brown bangs fall in her face.

"Thank you, Mack," Amari replies. "I appreciate it."

Mack dips her head in a nod. "You're welcome."

Amari takes her son from her friend, who leaves the family to eat breakfast together. The cook leaves the food trolley next to them. Amari and Viggo thank him for it before he disappears.

"Alright," Amari speaks up as Viggo gets out of bed to look and see what has been brought up. "Who wants to play a game?"

"Me," Emma says excitedly as she raises her hand in the air.

"I wanna play," Ramein says, her voice sweet coated with a husky tone.

Amari nods. "Oh, it's a game for everyone. It's called I Spy. You start with saying 'I spy with my little eye'. Then you describe something that you see as well as you can. Usually, it's something in this room. But this round of the game we can include people and things in all of Heaven's Light. Does that sound like fun?"

Amari looks between her girls as they nod their heads eagerly. "Okay. I'll go first. I spy with my little eye." Amari trails off as she thinks about what she wants to describe in detail. "Something…" She looks up and squints her right eye. She thinks and thinks before she decides on her first tachala she's ever created. "Gray. With a wolf like head. But his ears are feathers." Amari looks at her daughters.

"Taran," Emma exclaims excitedly.

Amari smiles, impressed. "Very good!"

"Tachalas are easy to describe."

"Depends on who you talk to." Amari squeezes Emma's cheek. "Since you guessed it right first you get to go, sweet Emma."

"Okay!" Emma beams. "I spy with my little eye." She looks up and squints her right eye, her hands in her lap as she sits on her knees.

Taking after her mother, Amari holds back a giggle as she watches Emma think. She's so cute! And cuddly! Emma enjoys cuddling with her mom before bed. She usually falls asleep cuddling with Amari and she's usually trapped until the little one finally rolls to the other side of her twin sized bed.

"Something purple." Emma finally speaks up. "It's smooth… And can only be found in one place."

"The Heart stone," Ramein exclaims, proud that she knows that one.

Emma looks at her little sister. "Yes!" She praises.

"Good job," Amari applauds both of her daughters, rubbing their backs proudly. She completely forgot about that stone!

She knows Raja has taught Emma about it when she was here, but she didn't know Ramein knew! Flabbergasted at both of her daughters' brightness Amari continues the game as Viggo sits down on the bed with a tray of food.

"Okay, Ramey," Amari starts. "Your turn."

"I spy with my little eye," Ramein starts. She copies her dad when he's thinking, squinting both of her eyes as she stares into blankness. "Something brown. And scaley."

"Jarom," Viggo puts in as he eats a piece of French toast.

Amari looks at him. She opens her mouth as he feeds her a piece drenched in syrup.

"That dragon has attitude if you press his buttons," Viggo finishes as the goodness of maple syrup hits Amari's tongue.

∞

Lillian slides down the wolf's back. He shifts into human form.

Being called to a king's kingdom is a huge honor. Not everyone has it happen. It just sucks it has to be lycans. Lillian really isn't a fan of dogs.

Really...

She's a cat! She hates the smell! And the way they just leave things lying around. It's disgusting!

Lillian wrinkles her nose at the smell of wolves and death mingling together. Something happened here last night. She knows it's the reason why she was called.

Marcus, Allah's Beta, pulls a pair of gym shorts on before rejoining Lillian. She keeps her eyes on the silver castle in front of her, looking up at the tip closest to her.

"I'll take you to him," Marcus says. "He's been cooped up in his office trying to get things back in order. He's got the Asgard Light Moon pack and the rogues against him."

Lillian nods before following him in. The huge entry way has a white marble floor. The light gray drapes fall in front of the massive, ceiling to floor front windows to help with the lighting.

Marcus leads Lillian out of the front hall and up a flight of stairs. He takes her down a hall as it stays quiet between them. They pass beautiful décor on the way. A moment later, Marcus knocks on a door to his right.

He must've gotten the okay as he opens it to reveal a tall and broad man bending over his desk as he sits in his chair, looking at a file. A woman Lillian doesn't recognize is standing next to him, her hands behind her back as she bends over his desk. She points something out on the file as Lillian walks in. Both of them scrunch their noses.

"I thought you were human," the man puts in. He must be King Allah.

Marcus closes the door behind Lillian as she stands in one spot. "I'm the Black Cat. One of Amari's creations was created in me when I accidentally stepped into this world."

Allah looks at Lillian in awestruck worry. "That's impossible." He breathes.

Lillian shakes her head. "Everyone thought that, too. But Amelia was able to explain that before the war with Kera, the world was unstable with only spells to keep it balanced. One of those spells was one where life could cross between Homba and Hallam anytime. That's why our first dragon, Jarom, was the Eye of Hallam for quite some time before that role was no longer needed after the war."

Allah nods. "Sounds like you know more than I do."

Lillian shrugs. "I make it my business to know this world."

"Well, how would you like your business to be part of my security team?"

Lillian laughs at the insanity. A cat? Working for a dog? No, thank you!

Lillian stops laughing and clears her throat before speaking. "I don't work for anyone. And where I don't absolutely have to be here anymore thanks to the axis being fixed and there's no more spells… I don't have to work with dogs. I'm sorry. But I have to kindly decline."

"If you don't have to be here, then why are you?"

"Because I teach self-defense here during the summer. My family comes with me to visit Hallam during that time and then we go back home during the school season."

Allah nods. "Well, I'll put you down as a no, then. Thank you for coming and your time."

Lillian winces.

He didn't even fight for her!

"If you didn't want me as part of your security team, then why'd you call for me?"

"Because you have amazing fighting and leadership skills that could be used for good purposes. But cats and dogs don't get along very well around here. So, I'll let you go."

Lillian dips her head, keeping her green eyes on Allah's beautiful gray eyes. "Thank you." She turns around and starts out the door. She gets stopped when Marcus gets in her way with pleading eyes. She shakes her head at him, not wanting to stay.

"Allah, please reconsider," Marcus begs.

"Marcus," Allah drawls out. "Let her go."

Marcus shakes his head, looking at his king. "She gets to have a life in Homba. Do you know how important that would be for us?" He continues to beg, clearly distraught. What does *he* have to gain from that!

"How could that be important for us? No one can cross over willingly anymore." Allah argues.

"She and Goddess Amari have visited each other a few times."

Lillian blinks a few times.

Of course!

She hasn't done it in the longest time, but she and Amari can converse through a mind link thanks to their connection! Amari blessed Lillian's son when he was born six years ago.

She didn't make it to the hospital in Homba, unable to open the portal because of the pain she was in with labor. Amari heard about her situation and quickly came to her rescue, calling on the best midwife that could ever live in this world.

Amari got Lillian's husband here for Max's birth!

"They have a connection," Marcus continues. "One that Amari blessed Lillian and her son with. They can converse. Whenever you need-."

"Marcus, I appreciate the thought," Allah cuts off his Beta. "And while it's a good one I don't think it's such a good idea."

"But, Allah-."

"No. Mrs. Carmichael made it clear that she doesn't work for anyone. We're going to respect her wishes."

"But what about the alliance? Have you and Amari figured it out? What it's going to cost?" Marcus presses for answers.

"She's been in mourning then got raped in *my. Kingdom* last night." Allah spats. "I have to help her feel safe here before her next visit!"

No!

Lillian reaches out to Amari right away, wanting to check on her friend. *Amari, are you okay? I just found out what happened.*

"And we have to think about what's best for the kingdom. A cat like Lillian would be beneficial, but only to an extent."

Lillian snaps, turning around to glare at Allah. "At least silver isn't my weakness," she spats.

I'm not so great, but I got my family with me, Amari replies. *Please, tell Allah that I will be there tomorrow to talk about our alliance.*

Will do. Lillian lifts her chin a challenge, the king of the Asgard Lycan Kingdom in a mood. "I can withstand just about anything. I had a building fall on me and I got away with just a broken leg thanks to my small frame. What about you, Allah? Can you fit in cracks big enough for a small cat? No. Your big ass can't even fit through an elephant's asshole!"

Marcus snorts, but a warning glance from Allah silences him.

"You watch your mouth, young lady," Allah warns Lillian in a threatening tone.

"No. *You* watch your mouth." She intimidates him. "I know that Amari was once your second chance mate. I know what she did for you and you turned around to be one of the biggest assholes Hallam could ever have. Amiah Keen even said to me about you the other day 'He's nothing special, but he acts like he is'. And do you wanna know what that tells me?

Amari is a *saint* to help such an idiot like you. Because as far I'm concerned, you're not that special even as God of the were-kind!"

Allah growls as he slams his fist on his desk, trying to gain dominance. But Lillian holds her ground, not even flinching at the man's crude response.

"She even told me she just about considered you to be her god and husband, but she thought better of it, not wanting a riot from Hallam. I don't blame her. I'm surprised she still wants to agree to an alliance with you!"

"And what do you know about that?" Allah growls dangerously.

Lillian leans forward, unfazed. Her bright green eyes pierce Allah's silver-gray eyes. "She'll be here on the morrow to talk about it with you."

Allah drops his jaw in disbelief. The woman next to him looks at him before her eyes land on Lillian. She gives her a sly smirk.

"And this is why women will always rule Hallam," the beautiful woman puts in. She walks over to Lillian, standing in front of her with her hand extended. "I'm Sirena. Amari's cousin."

Lillian shakes Sirena's hand. "Pleased to meet you, Sirena." She smiles at the first siren, her hair raven black and her eyes purple. "You're absolutely beautiful."

Sirena smiles. "Thank you. So are you. Can I interest you in a different kind of job?"

"What sort of job would that be?"

"Training the newbies. I have to take into consideration your self-defense class. And how it would be beneficial for those who are in security. It would come in handy."

Lillian lifts her chin in acceptance. "I'm listening."

"Let's walk," Sirena offers.

"Gladly." Lillian follows the siren queen out of Allah's office.

They start down the hall as the two ladies talk business. "I have to say that was quite impressive. You'll be a hell of a fighter when it requires it. I bet you're one hell of a trainer."

"Thank you," Lillian replies softly, flattered by Sirena's compliments. "Now, about this offer."

"Oh," Sirena drawls out as she gets into business mode. "I don't have very many sirens, but I would love for you to train them if you've got any openings. And while Allah is a big brute, he truly cares about this world and its creatures.

He's not God of Hallam material, but he is of God of Were-kind. And his security team could use your help."

Lillian nods in agreement. "I'll see what I can do for them. But I can't promise that I can keep dogs in check."

"Oh," Sirena giggles, a trace of seduction hidden behind it. "My sirens can do that. You don't have to lift a finger if any of Allah's dogs try to misbehave."

"I'm glad to hear it." Lillian follows Sirena down the stairs.

In the big entry way, Sirena turns around to face Lillian. Standing in the middle, violet eyes meet light green eyes. "I've got to get back to my husband. I only came because Allah asked me to keep his pack away from you. They would've shredded you if they had the chance."

Lillian dips her head in thanks. "Thank you, Sirena. I appreciate it."

Sirena dips her head in a warm welcome. "And I appreciate you. I will walk with you until you're safe. Then I will be on my way."

"I'd like that. Even if I can hold my own."

"Lycans. They're more ruthless than their cousin."

Lillian nods in agreement. "I completely agree."

6

Amari pants, blindfolded while tied to the bed.

She's nervous. She doesn't know what's going on, but she trusts her husband. His lips meet her cheek tenderly before he pulls away from her.

She has to know what he's thinking of doing, because she's not so sure about this exercise. As much as she would love to make lover to her husband, she doesn't quite trust the dark just yet.

Viggo withdraws from Amari and disappears. She heightens her hearing to know what he's doing. Again, she trusts him. She knows he only wants the best for her. She's just nervous with this blind exercise.

"Ada," Viggo starts. "May. Thank you for coming."

Amari sighs with relaxation. Her mistress is here!

"What can we do for you, your highness," Ada's small, sweet and soft voice asks.

"My wife," Viggo starts. "She was raped late last night. And she wanted to do an exercise. So, I brought her here to our estate to help with it."

So, that's where they are!

"Who raped her," May asks, getting protective. "I swear to goddess, I'm going to-."

"Hapoor Blackfoot," Viggo interrupts. "And I'm afraid he's going to do it, ag-."

"That son of a bitch," May growls angrily, cutting Viggo off. "He promised me he'd leave her be if I became her maid!"

"Is he your brother?"

"Worse. I was supposed to be his Luna. But then Allah happened."

"So, this hate runs deep. Not just for Amari."

"No," May growls. "I'm afraid not."

"Amari," Ada says softly, right next to Amari and distracting her.

Amari turns her head towards her. "Ada, my sweet darling. How are you?"

Ada straddles Amari and gently touches her mate mark with a soft caress. "I'm good. While May and Viggo talk, I wanna run things over with you."

"I was just listening in on the conversation."

"Yes. Of course. Let me bring you up to speed."

Amari nods, looking up towards where Ada should be. She wishes she could look at her mistress right now.

Ada is so sweet, knowing just how to heal a person. She's part witch and part werewolf with just a little bit of lycan blood. She knows just the right spells and magic for a broken bone. A right potion to help a headache.

Ada's fingertip trails down Amari's face, starting from her covered temple and down her jawline. "Amari, I'm afraid Hapoor is challenging you and Allah. He hates the both of you and was hoping you two would marry.

He wanted it to be easier for him to take you down. With Hallam's help."

She doesn't know if she can call it a light bulb or an idea, but something clicks inside of Amari, giving her a feeling of realization. "So, wait… Could his Delta that eavesdropped on Allah and I six years ago in the forest… Could she have been…?"

"His Delta isn't part witch. Amari, Hapoor is my father. My mother is the witch that cast a spell on you and Allah. The Asgard Light Moon pack has always felt a hatred towards you two and my mother used that to her advantage.

When I came along… I was cast out because I was Allah's fated mate. I've hated my own pack ever since."

"But Hapoor. He's not old enough to have a daughter your age. He's thirty-seven years old, my age. Now, you're twenty-five years old! That doesn't make sense! He would've been twelve years old when he had you!"

"He was raped at that age. By my mother."

"Ada…" Remorse hit Amari. "I am so, so sorry."

"It's okay," Ada whispers. "Things happen."

"This world is crueler than I remember."

"And that's about to change." Ada grabs Amari's chin lightly and kisses her lovingly. "My mother worked for Allah until he fired her for malpractice. She killed his first Beta when she could've been saved easily. The Asgard Light Moon pack took my mother in after being cast out and they assigned her as their doctor.

She took care of my dad a few times because he would come in with a broken arm that needed to be reset. He was quite reckless."

"Like he is, now."

"Yes," Ada says softly in a hiss. "She trails off as though she's thinking about something.

May and Viggo are heard having the same conversation Amari and Ada are having, but in May's own words. It sounds harsher coming from her, her mouth like venom.

"Amari, my father told my mother that he owed her one of these times when he was just eleven years old. His parents weren't there because he broke his arm on Allah's kingdom near the border that marks the Silver Lake pack. She closed the door, unzipped her pants, and had him pay her that way. He got her pregnant with me.

My mother convinced Hapoor that you and Allah are bad news. She worked with Kera until she died. My mother died a few years later due to treason."

Amari nods, starting to make sense of everything.

"My father really wasn't that bad of a person until she came along. She changed him for the worst. Turned him against everyone. She even turned his whole pack against you and Allah. I'm so sorry, Amari."

Amari nods, again. "So, how do we change his mind?"

Ada sighs, heartbreak sounding in her breath. Amari patiently waits for an answer, giving her mistress all the time she needs. "I'm afraid we can't, Mare," Ada whispers. "It's too late for him. He's too far gone."

"And what about the spell? That your mother cast on Allah. Is it broken," Amari asks with hope, looking for a reason to have it in the first place.

"Because of you, yes."

"What do you mean?"

"You really weren't his second chance mate. My mother made that spell to make the two of you believe you were meant for each other. She wanted to bring Allah down. When he showed a weakness towards you, she decided to make the two of you second chance mates when you really weren't."

"Wait, what?" Panic hits Amari. So, this whole entire time… The love she felt for Allah… It couldn't be a lie! What Selena said to Amari six years ago…

"What did Selena say to you?" Ada queries.

"Ada… Get out of my head or I'm gonna have to punish you," Amari teases seductively.

Ada chuckles low. She puts her lips to her lover's ear. "I'm looking forward to it," she seduces. "But there's something you gotta do for May first."

Amari nods for what seems the tenth time. "Anything," she promises.

"May has the same rare gene as I do. But she's bi. She'll have sex with a man with no problem. But she prefers to do it with a woman. If my spell doesn't work and her real identity doesn't stay under cover, we need to count on you to give us an heir from Hapoor."

Fear strikes Amari and she shakes her head vigorously. No… She can't do it! It's not in her to do such a thing after what he did to her!

"No. Ada…" Amari starts to shake as the memories of last night come back. His touch… His smell… Amari is thrown back into the bedroom at Allah's kingdom and she panics, fear striking her. "No. I can't!"

Ada keeps her lips on Amari's ear, shushing her softly as she tries to soothe and calm her. "It's okay, Amari," she whispers. "I just need your hair. Or spit. Whichever one you're more comfortable with. I just need a sliver."

"So, this is like that Harry Potter potion. Am I right?"

"No. It's not a potion. It's not something you drink."

"Then what is it? A swap?"

Ada shakes her head next to Amari's. "No. It's a necklace. Or bracelet. Can you do that for me, please?"

Amari nods, relief flooding over her. "Yeah," she whispers. "Anything for you and May. She wants to carry Hapoor's child, right? Make a new heir to the Asgard Light Moon pack?"

"We want to help you bring him down. If he gets you pregnant, or per say May in the form of you… If the right people of Hallam find out about the successful rape, he'll be dead.

That child… will be the rightful heir to the Asgard Light Moon pack, because if anyone is concerned… It's *your* baby."

Realization hits Amari, making her glad to have Ada as her mistress. She's grateful to have such an amazing woman on her side.

"Of course," Amari whispers.

"May and I are willing to give up a few of our eggs to you just in case the necklace doesn't work. We'd hate for it to go there. But if it does…"

Amari shakes her head, fear striking her. "I hope it doesn't come down to that… But let's do the spell."

"That's my goddess," Ada encourages in a whisper. She licks Amari's cheek and stirs her down there.

"Don't tempt me, witch," Amari warns lowly, turned on by her mistress.

Ada giggles evilly in Amari's ear. "I do as I please," she says lowly.

Amari turns her head. Her lips land on Ada's. She loves how her mistress has come out of her shell. It turns Amari on more than ever. She licks Ada's lips in a seductive manner. She bucks her hips to make Ada fall into her, Ada's arms wrapping around her neck.

Amari can feel Viggo's and May's eyes on her and Ada as they get into a lip lock. She gets a growl from both of them. Getting awoken down there, their primitive instincts to protect what's theirs turns her on. She plans to use it to her advantage.

Amari moans into Ada's mouth, bucking her hips into Ada's. The woman on top of her moans into her mouth, getting the idea.

"Let's make them jealous," Ada whispers seductively.

Amari giggles bewitchingly, a smile on her face. Oh, she so's ready to do just that.

And more…

∞

Allah runs his hand through his silver hair as he looks at the paperwork on his desk.

These contracts for his security team are just not turning out right. He needs to redo them… Again… He doesn't know what else to do. There's just something wrong. He just can't figure it out.

Allah sighs and sags, closing his eyes. Amari should be coming by to talk about the alliance soon. Allah just hopes they can talk like adults. Thankfully, Ragnar moved on. And it's probably because of that she-wolf in the forest.

She's probably found a new werewolf to be with at this point! It's possible she joined Selena for a bit before coming back down!

Allah lays his head on the desk, his forehead meeting cold wood. A few knocks sound on his door before someone invites themselves in.

The smell of tiger lilies hits his nose, making him wonder who that could possibly be. Amari's daughter smells of wolfsbane and lilacs! It's not like a three-year-old is going to come looking for him, anyway.

Female hands start rubbing Allah's shoulders, getting a moan out of him. He knows exactly who it is. He's grateful that she's here.

"Wake up, sleepy head," Amari whispers in his ear. Wait… What?! "There's someone that wants to see you."

Allah moans as he sits up, laying his head back in his chair. Amari continues to massage his shoulders.

"You don't wanna say that."

"Say what," Allah asks lowly, his eyes closed as he enjoys Amari's hands on his tense muscles.

"Your security team contract. Don't ever say 'them'. It's 'he/she' with a back slash in between the two words and you wanna be more specific on the parameters and borders. Explain where they are. Don't say 'you'll know when you smell them.' You know better than that, Allah." Amari compliments.

He looks up at her and gray eyes meet brown eyes. Her lips are so close to his forehead since she's a foot and an inch shorter than him.

"Borders are never the same if you say that every time. They'll change. And you don't want that."

"Thank you," Allah puts in. "I knew something was off."

"Don't tell me you wrote this."

Allah shook his head. "No. Marcus did."

Amari grunts in disgust. "Men," she says lowly, not sounding amused. "They *never* go into details. You know it was your Beta before Marcus that wrote my security team contracts. She was the best."

"Yeah, I miss her," Allah says lowly.

"Too bad you rejected her when you found out she's bisexual."

Allah moans in disgust, watching Amari. "Don't remind me," he grumbles, not wanting to visit his reasons for rejecting his first Beta and best friend's wife.

"Alright." Amari smacks his arm lightly. "Up. I'll take care of your security team contracts. You can watch my daughter. She's been *dying* to see you, again."

Allah lifts his head from his chair. "What?" His gray eyes meet with the innocent brown and green eyes that are staring at him from across the room.

The little girl giggles at him. Oh, she's adorable.

Mate! It screams inside of Allah, again, and he's moved to stand up. He starts for the little one.

She smiles widely, throws her arms open, then runs over to him. He bends down, letting her run into his arms. He's grateful for the distraction of a little kid. He doesn't care that they're mates. Kids are kids.

"Well, hi, beautiful girl," Allah says in his baby voice. "I don't think I ever got your name."

"Ramein," she replies. She looks up at him and her green eye shines with a gold ring while her brown eye shines with a red ring. "I'm part takal and part werewolf."

"Are you, now?"

"Ramein," Amari drawls from Allah's desk. "How do you know what a werewolf is?"

"I see them," Ramein replies, looking at her mom. "When they cross over to Heaven's Light." Her little voice is so cute!

"Are you sure you're not talking about regular wolves? They seem super big to you, now. But when you get older, you'll know they're not even *half* the size of a werewolf."

"I'm positive," Ramein enunciates her words clearly. "I talked to a wolf before she went back to Selena."

"And what did *she* say?" Amari presses quizzically.

"That I got a special wolf inside of me."

Allah looks at Amari, convinced. "Amari, you have to admit. Her green eye shines gold like a royal lycan's."

Amari winces, seeming to be thrown off. "I didn't…"

"Know? You really didn't know?"

Amari shakes her head. "Not until Raja said something the day she passed."

"She blessed me," Ramein beams excitedly. "As part wolf!"

Amari looks at her daughter with broken eyes, letting Allah know something happened between her and Raja that she won't talk about. Something personal.

"Amari," Allah starts.

She doesn't hear him. It's as if the creature inside of her is talking to her. It probably is, telling her something that relates to the subject. But Allah needs Amari's attention right now.

"Amari," he says sternly.

She doesn't hear him.

"A-mar-ee," he snaps with enunciation.

She looks at him and her brown eyes show fear of realization. He winces. This isn't good. Something's going on in that pretty little head of hers.

"What is it?" He asks with concern. "What's going on?"

Amari looks at her daughter. "Ramein, sweetie. King Allah and I need to talk alone for a moment. Can you go catch Marcus and play with him, please?"

Ramein nods. "I'd rather play with King Allah, though." She protests.

Amari stands up and sooths down her slim and slick black dress. She looks at her daughter and their eyes meet. "You can play with him all you want after we're done talking, okay? We just have to have an adult talk really quick."

"About what?"

Allah kisses Ramein's little forehead out of habit, one that he has towards the women he loves and kids that he adores. "You," he teases her lightly.

She giggles before wrapping her arms around his neck. "Okay. But don't take too long. I wanna play wolves and bears. And you'll be the bear."

"Oh, I'll be the best bear you ever come across," he teases his little future Luna. He tickles her belly, getting her to squeal. It makes him chuckle.

Allah enjoys kids a lot and Ramein is no different. It doesn't matter who or what she will be to him when she gets older. He loves it when kids laugh.

Ramein pulls away and runs out of the office, closing the heavy door behind her as best she can. "I'll see you in a bit! Lover!"

Allah's eyes go wide at his nickname as they stick on Ramein's exit. He's never heard that one from a kid before! What is she hearing back home?! She sure is bold for a three-year-old!

Amari clears her throat, bringing Allah's attention to her. He stands up as he faces the woman, afraid of what's about to be said. Her brown eyes pierce his gray eyes and he braces for the worst.

"Allah, I need you to know that you can't have her until she comes of age," Amari threatens.

"I couldn't tear her from you in any way even if I wanted to, Mare," he says softly, putting his hands in his front pockets. "And why would you give her to me anyway? I don't understand where this is going."

"I think you do." Amari walks over to Allah and her scent hits his nostrils, tiger lilies and vanilla filling his lungs and bringing him comfort. She still has that effect on him. She always will.

Allah shakes his head. "You've gotta be clearer, Mare."

"Ramein," Amari growls. "She's your second chance mate." She shakes her head. "I never was."

Allah furrows his eyebrows in confusion. "What are you talking about?"

"Mavis."

Allah winces at the name.

"You remember her, don't you?"

"I try not to. But she still finds a way to haunt me."

"Did you know Ada is her and Hapoor's daughter?"

"Fuck. No." Allah isn't liking where this is going.

"Well, six years ago when we did the deed... We were tricked. Mavis made us second chance mates with a spell."

Allah searches Amari's eyes. Wait. That means... The love Ragnar felt for Amari was... Fake! Ragnar howls in agony at the news and Allah shuts him out.

"Are you sure?" He presses.

"Yes," Amari replies. "Ada confirmed it with me yesterday."

"I thought you were home, recovering."

"I was. But I asked Viggo to do an exercise with me. Where the lights were out and I had to trust him in bed."

"Amari, that's risky." Allah gets concerned.

"I agree. I got scared… multiple times… But he was there to reassure me." Amari shakes her head. "But that's not the point. Allah, I was never actually your second chance mate. My daughter is."

Allah furrows his brows at Amari. How did she figure that out?! How did she know? Allah thought he was going crazy for having a third fated mate!

"How did you…?"

"Raja. That was her blessing for Ramein. She's a peacekeeper, Allah. She's our alliance."

"Amari, you don't have to-."

"Allah, Raja and I talked about this a couple times before her time! It's her last and final wish! You're getting the alliance that you so want. And it's Ramein!" Amari points around Allah, her eyes in a glare at him. "My daughter that's your second chance mate thanks to my best friend and companion! So, you better treat her right! Cause she's your future!"

Allah shakes his head as he watches his goddess walk around his desk. "I'm not going to take her from you, Amari." He protests.

"No!" Amari turns around and sets her hands on the polished wood, her brown eyes piercing Allah's gray eyes. "You're not going to take her! I just have to figure out how I'm going to tell my husband that our daughter is mated to you! That she's the peacekeeper in all of this!

He's going to take it worse than I am! Trust me on this, Allah!"

"Then don't tell him!" Allah takes a step towards Amari, but she puts her hand up, telling him not to come any closer. He listens, staying rooted to his spot. "This stays between us! You understand me?!"

"Don't you *dare* raise your voice at me, Allah!" Amari threatens.

"Then don't *you* dare raise your voice at *me*! Amari! You came here so we could talk about an alliance! And since you're offering what I suggested before I'm taking it! Ramein is mine! At the end of this year!"

Amari growls at Allah threateningly, her motherly instincts kicking in for her daughter. He stalks towards her with a purpose.

"*She's* my mate! *She's* my future! *She's* our peace-keeper! And that gets to stay between us!" He gets threateningly close to her. "End of story!"

Amari squares up to Allah, making him admire her for her bravery. After what happened two nights ago, he's surprised she'll go up against him! She's truly a strong woman.

"That's the deal," Allay grumbles lowly as he starts to calm down, Amari's scent hitting his lungs, again. "We agree to Ramein as our peacekeeper and alliance. With no word to Viggo. I will *not* go up against a Viking takal for what's meant to be mine." Allah growls the word *not*. "Not again, Mare. I already lost you to him and I *don't* want a repeat. Especially with him," Allah growls.

"Fine," Amari growls through her clenched teeth after a quiet moment. She gets in his face. "Just don't expect it like this for very long. He'll eventually find out." She threatens.

"By then I'm hoping Ramein is seventeen and able to move in with me."

"She's not moving in with you until she's ready," Amari spats threateningly, getting on her tiptoes and pressing her breasts into Allah's chest. "You can forget it. End of story." Her eyes search Allah's.

He finds himself doing the same thing. Without warning his feelings for her resurface and the memories come flooding back with them.

His gardens. A week after Selena passed. The forest. The two days she was here… All of it is back and Allah finds himself crashing his lips on Amari's, wanting a taste of her.

She doesn't exactly pull away. Her arms wrap around his neck. His member grows hard in his pants. What is he thinking? This isn't Ragnar! His wolf is hung up on Ramein! This is completely Allah!

He wraps his arms around Amari's waist before he lays her across his desk. Soon, his lips are trailing down her breasts and unbuttoning the two top buttons on her dress. He takes her round flesh into his mouth, but he thinks twice before sucking on it. He doesn't know what he's doing. He just knows he's got to have her. Even if it's just for a moment.

"Allah," Amari whispers, holding the back his head and trapping his lips against her. "Hurry." Why is she up for this? Is she overwhelmed by all the memories as well?

…Whatever.

Allah isn't going to pass up the opportunity. He unbuckles his belt and undoes his pants. He easily slides Amari's dress up to her hips, exposing her thighs. His hand slips into her panties, feeling her wetness before her arousal hits his nose. It smells sweet and gets a growl out of him.

Amari gasps and pants with lust. Before Allah goes any further, he pulls the drapes down on his window behind him with his foot. He pulls his pulsing cock out. Guiding himself into Amari, he thrusts into her as he props himself up and watches her.

As he thrusts into her, he watches her go through a few different emotions, fear as one of them. He knows what she's thinking, holding back and not wanting to reminder her of two nights ago.

"Allah," Amari barely manages out. "Just do it."

He watches her with worry and amusement at the same time. What are they doing? It's too soon for this! Amari shifts underneath Allah and looks up at him. Her arms wrap around his torso and her hands land on his shoulders, bringing him down towards her. He stills himself inside of her as he searches her eyes. He finds fear in them. She's not ready for this.

"I trust you," she whispers.

Allah shakes his head and starts pulling back. "No, this was…" He clears his throat and Amari sits up with him, taking his lips with hers and holding his neck.

He happily obliges, closing his eyes and letting his lips melt into hers. He loves this woman. More than anything. He'll do anything to keep her safe. Allah brushes Amari's bangs back, tucking them behind her ear. He so wants to be the man by her side.

"I love you," Amari whispers into his lips. "Just as much as I love my husband."

Allah looks into her eyes.

"I just made the wiser choice for Hallam."

"But… six years ago."

"We were basically still kids, Allah. The choices we made… And the spell we were under thanks to Mavis…" Amari shakes her head. "We weren't thinking clearly when we around each other back then."

"Amari," Allah says lowly. "It's too soon for you. The rape…"

Amari brushes her nose against Allah's. "Then let me go," she whispers.

He shakes his head, his heart breaking. He can't do that! She's his best friend!

"It's me or Ramein, Allah. You can't have both."

"Can he…?"

"Feel this?" Amari shakes her head. "No. He has no idea when I'm doing it with Ada. And you still want her to give you pups, don't you?"

Allah shakes his head, able to tell Amari the truth at this point. "I'm over her by now. It's you I want." He brushes her temple with his thumb.

"Then show me."

At Amari's seductive tone, Allah can't hold himself back. He kisses her tenderly as he holds her face in his hand. Wanting her now more than ever he lays her back down. He guides himself back into her, thrusting into her and watching her throw her head back and orgasm. He lets himself go, gliding his hand down her side. He grabs her hip and pulls it into him, deepening his thrusts and making her orgasm, again.

"Allah," Amari whispers. She clings onto Allah and her fingertips dig into his shoulders. Her tightness envelopes him and pulls him in as if she's accepting him as her mate all over again.

But they both know she's already made her choice. So has he. Allah buries himself inside of Amari, letting her take him in fully. He wants this. He wants her. He wants a life and future with her.

Allah will marry Ramein when the time comes. But until then… He's making love to his best friend. Soon, Allah's cullions leap and he spills his seed inside of Amari, filling her up as they both orgasm together.

In sync, their panting mingles together. Amari shudders in Allah's arms and he holds her close, getting protective of her all over, again. He's not letting her get hurt in his kingdom ever again!

That's a promise he's planning to keep.

7

Amari wakes up on her side and look at the dresser, her back to Viggo. He snores lightly next to her, lying on his back.

She loves waking up next to him. It's part of what made her fall in love with him. Amari sighs and relaxes into the mattress, closing her eyes and snuggling her face into her pillow. She thinks about what she did with Allah yesterday.

As much as she trusts him, she just can't sleep at his kingdom anymore. Not after the rape. To trust him yesterday… The sex… The confession! She can't believe she did that! Amari tried to deny her feelings for Allah in the past, when she thought he wasn't real and she couldn't have him; letting herself fall in love with Mike and Garrett instead.

Six years ago, her dreams became reality. She's been in denial with her feelings for Allah all over again. Amari sighs and sags, sinking into the comfy cloud underneath her.

She hates herself sometimes. Falling in love with two men at a time… It's why she was able to move on from Mike so fast in the end. She was in love with Garrett before he ever left! Now that her old life is gone Amari now has the life of her dreams in a different world. She never has to worry about bills.

Viggo stops snoring as he starts to stir. He rolls over into Amari and his arm drapes over her flat stomach. She's lost more weight ever since she's married to Viggo, going on adventures with him. He pulls her into a protective hug and kisses her naked shoulder, making her fall in love with all over again.

Oh, why does she have to be so in love with two men at a time? Why can't she just get over Allah and focus on her love for Viggo! He's her husband and the father of her children! She chose *him* to be the god that rules beside her! Not Allah!

"You know, it's weird that you don't wear your garments anymore," Viggo says lowly. "But I also love it." He kisses Amari's hair and moans into it. "Good morning."

"Morning," Amari says softly. She leans back into Viggo's chest and looks at him, taking his goateed chin in her hand. She strokes it, loving the feel of it in her hands.

She's glad he grew it back out. He shaved it off a few years ago and scared Emma when she was just a baby. She didn't recognize him, making Amari reassure her that it was him. Whenever Amari kissed Viggo while it was prickly bothered her and kept pricking her chin. She didn't like the feel of that.

Viggo looks at Amari, their brown eyes meeting. "I'm glad you got the alliance worked out with Allah. His packs should leave him alone, now."

"Except for the Asgard Light Moon pack. And Hapoor. They're going to be a nuisance until May can give them a better heir than Hazen," Amari says softly, watching her beloved husband.

"He's sixteen, almost seventeen. Once he's of age, he should be able to find the right Luna for the job."

Amari kisses her beloved husband. "I hope so," she continues softly. She slides onto her other side and lets her naked breasts press into Viggo's chest, skin pressing against skin. "Cause if he's anything like his father, he'll be cast out."

Viggo kisses Amari and their lips mend together, fitting into each other perfectly. "More like killed," he says gruffly.

Amari wraps her arm around Viggo's torso and lays her head flat on his spine, looking at him with soft eyes. She loves this man more than anything. She would do anything to keep him by her side. He means everything to her.

"No more talk of this. Let's do something else."

Viggo shakes his head. "Amari, you're... It's too soon, don't you think? The rape is still..."

She holds his face in her hands, pressing her lips into his. "I wanna be reminded of what it was like before him. Please."

Viggo sighs and relaxes into the bed. He searches Amari's brown eyes. "Okay. But just know I wasn't liking you loving on Ada two days ago. And it's still fresh on my mind."

Amari smiles sweetly at her husband. "I love it when you get jealous."

"Oh, it makes me do crazy things," Viggo says lowly.

"I know it does," Amari seduces. She and Viggo kiss, getting lost in each other.

Tongue meets tongue. He rolls on top of her, caressing her hip and swallowing her whole. She enjoys his touch and loves it when he pulls her thigh into him.

Amari wraps her arms around Viggo's shoulders, pulling him into a tighter hug. He groans into her mouth, turned on. Then it happens.

Slam!

Fear strikes Amari at the noise and she pushes Viggo off to sit up straight, her eyes widening. "What was that?" Nervous, her voice shakes.

Slam! There it is, again!

"I don't know," Viggo starts. "But we're about to find out." He and Amari slip out of bed and dress quickly.

Slam!

Amari's fear turns worse as the noise sounds way too similar to a headboard slamming against the wall. Her beloved husband takes her hand in his. He leads her out of their bedroom.

Slam!

Who won't it stop? Is there a couple doing it without a care in Heaven's Light? Usually, the people that die are pretty good at not sneaking into the castle and having sexual intercourse! They keep it in their own homes!

Slam!

Amari jumps as the sound gets closer and she hides behind Viggo, memories of her rape flashing right before her eyes. Why is this happening? What's going on?

Slam!

Amari buries her face in Viggo's arm and he protects her, knowing what she needs.

"Mack," he exclaims. "What the hell is going on?!"

"I'm so sorry," Mack says, sounding concerned. What is she doing in here?

Slam!

Amari jumps and tries to get away from the noise, burying herself into the nook of her husband's side. She knows he can keep her safe.

"Some drapes came loose so we're putting them back into place." A hammer! But why does it sound so similar to a headboard slamming into the wall?

Slam!

Amari continues to jump from each sound. She whimpers into Viggo's chest, shaking and trying to get away from the memories that are haunting her.

"Well, can it stop until we're outside," Viggo asks in an orderly fashion. "My wife is still going through a traumatizing time and the sound of your hammer against the wall is way too similar to a headboard banging."

"Oh." Mack trails off. "I am so sorry, your majesties. We will stop right away.

Slam!

Hapoor is above Amari, again, thrusting into her with a cruel purpose. She screams out, not knowing if she's screaming in the memory or if she's hearing herself out loud. Either way, she wants it all to stop and give her peace. Viggo tightens his hold on Amari protectively.

"Stop!" Mack snaps. "Stop the slamming! You're scaring our poor goddess! After what she just went through!"

"Sorry," a few men say in unison, sounding sincere.

Amari shudders at the sudden silence, grateful for the noise to stop.

"Now," Mack says quietly. "Let's get you guys breakfast and take it outside. It's a beautiful day."

"Thank you, Mack," Viggo puts in. He gives Amari a reassuring and comforting squeeze as he keeps her close, protective of her. "We appreciate your help through this. It helps a lot."

"My pleasure. Amari, dear. We just had a new human join us. He was a clothes designer and I'm sure you can find him a new role as your fashionista. He's very good."

Amari peers one eye out from the comfort of Viggo's side, looking at Mack. Her brown hair that's almost red shines in the sunlight that made its way into the corridor. The sun penetrates Amari's dark thoughts.

She shakes her head. "I'm not... Quite interested in one."

Mack nods. "Okay," she whispers sweetly. She rubs Amari's upper arm. "But let's get you out of here."

Amari nods. Viggo keeps her close and lets her cling onto him as they walk out of the hallway and down the stairs to the kitchen, where Emma is learning to make an omelet.

"Emma," Amari starts. "Sweetie. What are you doing? You know you don't have to learn how to cook."

"Oh, but it's a joy!" Emma beams. She looks at her mom and her chocolate brown eyes meet Amari's hazel brown eyes. Emma looks so much like her dad, but with long blond hair instead of brown. "And I wanna learn how to cook for whenever I cross over to Homba."

Amari nods. "I need to talk to Lillian about taking you to Homba with her sometime."

Emma tilts her head in curiosity. "Who's Lillian?"

"The Black Cat." Amari replies sweetly.

Emma gasps as excitement dances in her eyes. "Yes! Oh, please! Oh, please!" She repeated herself. "Mommy, that would be the *best* thing ever!" She squeals at the exciting news.

Amari nods, lending her hand out to her daughter. Her heart gets the comfort and serotonin that she so desperately needs. "Let's leave the cooking to our cooks that we have for the day. And go take care of animals."

Emma nods and leaves the bowl filled with whisked eggs. She walks over to Amari, who cleans her face with a wet rag, getting down to her daughter's eye level.

"Your face is filthy."

Emma giggles before Viggo decides to pick her up.

"A takal that gets to cross into Homba," he puts in, looking at his beloved daughter. "Now, that's an honor."

Emma nods and wraps her arms around Viggo's neck, his lips landing on her cheek lovingly. Amari stands up and walks out of the kitchen with them.

∞

Madi thrusts her sword into the rogue's chest. He chokes on the pain. His blue-green eyes meet her brown ones. She then thrusts her weapon out of his heart.

Men… They're worthless! Well… Not all of them. Just the rogues. They never give up any information! Madi *has* to find this Hapoor guy! For the sake of Amari!

Madi may have once wanted her cousin dead and released Kera out of Hell's Fire six years ago, vengeance on her mind. But she has learned to love Amari, again.

Madi lets go of the man as he falls to the ground. She knows where he's going and there she will be able to interrogate him with any kind of torture she desires to use on him.

Madi sends her sword back to her armory in Hell's Fire with just her mind. She walks towards a tall man with a well-built stature. Who is he? Why is he watching her?

"Out of my way," Madi snaps as she bumps into him on purpose. She doesn't have time for this. She has to get to the bottom of her cousin's rape!

The man grabs her upper arm and stops her. She looks up at him, his silver-gray eyes meeting her brown ones. "I don't think it's wise for you to treat me that way."

"I don't know you. And I have no means to get to know you." Madi retorted.

"Good. Cause I'm only here for one reason." He snaps.

Madi glares up at the sixty-year-old man. Or is he in his fifties? "What?"

"Get off my land," the man threatens. "You're upsetting everyone here. Me… The most."

"And why's that?" Madi shrugs out of his hold and starts into the forest.

"Because you killed my son," he spats angrily.

Madi stops dead in her tracks. No… It can't be!

"And he was my only heir. Why Amari gave you Hell's Fire no one will know. You've killed half the population here and made the lieut extinct. You're not quite welcome here."

Madi looks back at the lycan king over her shoulder, hiding behind it. If she continues to snap at him, she won't live another day. Her kids would grow up without a mom!

"It's a good thing I'm leaving, then."

"Good. And Madison."

Madi takes a step forward, but she stays in place, staring ahead.

"Tell Ryker his sister is here to visit. She hasn't seen him in so long and I'd hate for them to miss out on a reunion."

"I'll let him know."

"Are you going to clean up your mess?"

"I can't shift the elements. That's Amari."

"Then I guess you better get to it."

A shovel lands next to her and she looks down at it. He's gotta be kidding!

"I don't want him reeking up my kingdom. I've got enough on my hands."

Madi growls before picking up the tool. She waits until King Allah has left then turns towards the rogue she just killed. She drags the dead body into the forest, finds a little hole made with stones and tree branches, and looks inside for traces of life.

She throws the dead human body in it then covers it up with dirt. It takes her an hour, but she gets it done. She leaves the shovel next to the hole. Madi shifts into the form of a golden eagle and takes off, flying for Hell's Fire on the other side of the forest. Near the Silver Lake pack border.

She twirls in the air and dives down a few times just to climb back up towards the sky, enjoying her flight. Letting the wind flow through her feathers. It gives her that thrill she enjoys as she flies for home.

∞

Viggo covers Amari's body with his own, laying on top of her with his hands on the ground above her head.

Two squirrels throw nuts at his head, making him growl. Squirrels… Why did Amari have to create squirrels?! She smirks up at her husband as he glares at her. But the glare isn't for her and she knows that. She just likes to tease Viggo.

He shakes his head at her. While he enjoys being in the forest with her, these critters are a nuisance. In Heaven's Light, they don't have to worry about Hapoor. But they got other beings to worry about. Those who have passed and made it here.

Viggo's chocolate brown eyes search Amari's hazel brown eyes, the green rings around the brown turning silver from the creature inside of her. He could smell it the day it was awakened. Raja's funeral. He wonders if it's her. It would make sense as to why she isn't here.

Even though Raja had a choice to go to Heaven in Homba, Viggo knows she would *never* leave Amari. They were super close and did anything for each other.

"Squirrels," Viggo starts. "You just had to create squirrels."

Amari searches his eyes. "Blame Madi. She and I were talking about them when we were younger. It's what brought on the dream of them with their flaming acorns."

Viggo snorts and smiles. "I guess I'm going to have to punish you for it," he seduces before kissing her.

Her hand sneaks around the back of his neck. "Make it quick. Because I can hear someone coming for us."

Feet stand near Viggo's and Amari's heads. "That someone is already here."

Viggo and Amari look up at Klauss's father, Viggo's cousin.

"And I just wanted to ask. Why the two of you are alone in the middle of the forest for everyone to see?"

"King Nikolas," Amari says. "I find the forest quite calming."

"As do I. But I don't just bang my wife in the middle of it. I find a place that no one knows about."

Amari giggles as Viggo's eyes meet Nikolas's blue ones.

"I don't mean to pry, but," Viggo starts. "I'm sure that's where you just were. With your wife. Having the time of your life," he teases. He winks at Nikolas.

"Yes, well," the takal king starts. "At least my wife and I keep it private," he teases. "We like it that way."

"Everybody does."

"But not you, apparently." Nikolas's English accent makes him sound cold with his tease. But he could never be cold towards anyone unless it's his enemy, who died a long time ago and is now in Hell's Fire.

"Shockingly, I wasn't about to fuck my wife." Viggo puts in. "We got two squirrels chucking their nuts and acorns at us. I was just merely protecting my wife's fragile noggin."

Nikolas laughs and a tear escapes his eye. He wipes it away diligently. "Oh, those two squirrels. My wife and I named them Nina and Fred. They did that to us just the other day. They don't like royalty it sounds like."

"Point us the way of your secret hideout and Amari and I will take us there."

"Oh, it stays a secret. You'll have to find your own." Nikolas turns and walks away, starting for the village that's a few miles away.

Viggo looks at his beloved wife and an acorn meets the back of his head. "Should we get out of here?"

Amari brushes her nose against Viggo's. "I thought you'd never ask," she whispers.

Viggo gets up, taking Amari with him. He carries her in his arms, her arms wrapping around his neck. Their brown eyes meet. "I'm not letting you down," Viggo defends himself before Amari can say what's on her mind.

"Then I guess you better find a spot for us to hide. Cause you're turning me on," Amari flirts with a seductive tone. She hits on her husband, knowing she can get away with it.

"A place where there's no memory of you know who? I couldn't agree more." Viggo starts away from the clearing and deeper into the forest.

"Viggo, I…"

He looks at her.

"I can't believe my luck. You're the *best* thing that's ever happened to me. I enjoy having you by my side and I love that I get to rule Hallam with you. You're truly amazing."

Viggo steps over a tree root then turns to his right down a trail. "I'm happy to be here with you, Mare." He stops at an oak tree and knocks on the door that was built in it. "And I'm more than happy with you."

The door opens and Viggo ducks his head to walk inside. Amari holds Viggo's cheek and kisses the other.

"I love you," she says softly.

He looks at her. "I love you more," he replies softly. He lays her down on the bed and the earth fairy before Sunni walks in.

"Ah," Sahara says. "Glad you two could make it."

Viggo looks back at her, her leaf green eyes meeting his chocolate brown ones. "We're happy to come. Amari doesn't get this treatment enough."

"Don't worry. I will check how Ada's and May's eggs are doing in Amari's ovaries and make sure they're being accepted as I give her the full body massage. She should start feeling better soon."

Viggo nods. "Thank you." He looks at his beloved wife. "Do you want me to stay?"

She looks up at him and their eyes meet. "If you're busy, I understand."

"For you, Amari…" He leans over her and gives her a kiss, not wanting to leave so soon. "I'm never too busy."

Amari moans and kisses Viggo. "Then stay."

He groans. "Gladly."

8

Amari relaxes in Sahara's hands, which were massaging her neck and then her shoulders. Naked, Amari only has a white towel to cover her lady parts. She knows she can trust her late earth fairy.

She needed this. The massage.

With Viggo not too far away, his scent envelopes Amari. Cedar wood shavings fill her nostrils and she wonders where the fresh scent of the pines went. But she doesn't think much of it. Viggo has two colognes that he tends to put on and it seems he only put the one on. Amari wonders why he did just the one, but not too much. It's rare, but sometimes Viggo will go without cologne! When he puts one on, though, Amari is right there to smell it on him. She'll press herself into him and get on her tiptoes to put her nose to his neck. She did that today and he must have forgotten to put his other cologne on after she left with her serotonin boost he often gives her.

Sahara trails her hands down Amari's sides then back up for a moment before she continues back down and rubs a knot out of Amari's left side. Amari moans as a sharp pain hits her and she enjoys the feel of it easing little by little.

Does he know, Sahara asks Amari in a mind link.

Does who know what, Amari replies with a question, in a relaxed state.

Ada's egg is fertilized. She's going to have a baby.

Amari winces and looks up at Sahara's. *It's not my husband's.*

So, whose is it? Sahara continues the massage and her leaf green eyes stay on Amari's side as she works her hands on it.

Allah's. I guess he's going to be a father.

Sahara nods. *I suggest you give Ada's egg back. You don't want to carry so soon. Your body is still healing from Clayton's birth.*

It's Amari's turn to nod as she watches the fairy. *I will call on my mistress.*

Sahara nods and continues the massage. She doesn't speak for a bit, letting it go quiet for a while. *You're in love with him… aren't you?* She speaks up after a few quiet moments.

Who? Allah?

Sahara looks at Amari and her green eyes say enough. Amari sighs and sags.

My downside is I'm always in love with two men. In this case, it's two men and a woman.

Don't get too comfortable with your situation. The first earth fairy warns. *You're going to have to choose just one at some point.*

And I'm ready to make that decision when it comes to it.

Sahara disregards Amari's comment, moving her eyes to her goddess's body. She runs her hand down Amari's thigh then lifts Amari's leg in a stretch, pushing

Amari's thigh in towards her own stomach. Sahara keeps her thigh pressed against her stomach for a moment then lays it back down.

She's already massaged Amari's feet and legs. She's just about done with the massage! And it has felt so good. Amari comes to Sahara whenever she's ready for another child, wanting the elf fairy to help her body relax. But this time it's just to help her destress and help her body heal from that stress that was put on it the past few days.

You will get pregnant, again, Sahara says in Amari's mind. Their eyes meet. *With May's baby. Give Ada her child and she will carry. It belongs to her and Allah anyway.*

Amari nods. She knows fairies can't see the future dead or alive. But their healing powers are so strong, any living thing can thrive with them.

And then you will have to do the same thing with May. Please, come to me when he gets his way with you. I will help you heal quicker for the transfer.

Amari gives Sahara acknowledgement and then lets her head and neck relax, closing her eyes.

"Viggo," Sahara starts.

"Yes, my fairy," Viggo asks teasingly.

"Usually, I want the couple out of here before they do it."

"Okay," Viggo drawls out. "I don't know why we would. Amari needs time to heal from the rape. It's why we came."

"She should be okay to do it, now, if you prefer. Just don't get her pregnant. Her body isn't ready for that trauma, yet."

"We'll wait until later. I don't wanna push it."
Viggo sounded sincere.

"Of course." Sahara gets on the other side of
Amari and massages it. She stretches the goddess's other
thigh out. "She had a lot of knots in her body due to the
stress of the rape. But she should be good, now." Sahara
pulls away from Amari, who slowly sits up. "I'll give you
two some time alone."

Amari looks at her beloved husband and their
eyes meet. He gets up with her clothes in hand and looks
at her lovingly.

"Do you want me to put these on for you?" He
flirts with a teasing tone, talking softly.

Amari gets off of the massage table and sets the
towel aside, letting him see her naked. She trusts him and
knows one day it's literally going to bite her in the ass. His
teeth will literally be in her buttocks when she least
expects it. He's done it before.

Amari lifts her chin and throws her bangs back
with her head. "I prefer it when you take them off of
me," she flirts through a seductive breath. "Cause I hate
barriers." She walks over to him and into his tall frame,
wrapping her arms around his torso and looking up at
him.

He moans, kissing her lovingly. "Don't tempt me,
beautiful," he warns lowly into her lips.

"We can go." Amari sets her chin on Viggo's
chest, looking up at him with her lips barely brushing his.
"Or we can stay. Your choice."

Viggo starts bending at his knees, keeping his eyes
on Amari. She watches him as he slowly glides down and

quickly pick her up by her knees, throwing her over his shoulder and getting a short scream of surprise out of her.

Her breasts press into his back and he slaps her ass, a sting hitting her there a moment later. Well, it's a good thing he's never changed!

"I'm taking you home," Viggo puts in. "And we're getting some work done." He starts for the door, Amari's clothes in hand.

"Viggo," Amari starts as her arms dangle above her head, getting her husband into trouble. "Amar. Grimert. I'm gonna beat you when I get the chance."

"Oh, but that's not gonna happen."

"You're taking me outside naked!"

"Am I?"

She looks up at him with a glare. "Our powers don't work like that."

"But we can shift the air and make it look like you're *not* naked."

Amari shakes her head. "Don't you dare," she enunciates.

Viggo nods. "Oh, I dare." He dips his head to get through the door and steps outside into the warm, fresh air.

"You're lucky it's warm," Amari drawls out slowly.

"Oh, but I prefer it to be cold," Viggo flirts. He winks at his wife.

"Only because it makes my nipples harden and press into your back!" Amari can't believe he's doing this… again!

"You better believe it." Viggo smacks Amari's naked ass, making her backside sting.

"Viggo," she screams in frustration.

He chuckles and ignores her protests. He did this before they conceived Clay! The miscarriage before him was tough on her and she came to talk to Sahara about a possible solution to keep her from having anymore.

That's when Sahara suggested the full body massages and stretches. To relax Amari's body and help it heal faster. She needs to come for those more often. Viggo starts for the pure white castle and Amari looks at the ground in disbelief.

"Here we go, again," she says lowly. She shifts the air and she's able to use it to her clothes from Viggo.

"Hey!" He stops where he is. "You're cheating."

She looks up at him as she puts her bra on while she's upside down. "Only because I don't wanna be humiliated. Remember last time?"

"Oh. Yeah. Nikolas saw right through the disguise and saw more than he should've."

"What do you expect? You takals are hard to manipulate."

"Fine." Viggo gives up. "But only the bra! Give me the rest of your clothes." He hesitates for a moment. "Please," he adds nicely.

"Since you asked so nicely." Amari gives the rest of her clothes back to Viggo and he gladly takes them.

"Thank you," he drawls out before starting forward, again.

"You're welcome." Amari looks at the ground as Viggo takes her to the castle. She prefers to live in a farmhouse with acreage, horses, dogs, and cats. A chicken coop not far from the house would be nice, where the kids can collect eggs and feed the chickens. Maybe chase them and catch them whenever they feel like they haven't gotten enough wiggles out.

Then the kids could make their way over to take care of pigs and then the goats. As much as Amari hates goats, they have a few up here. Of course, in Heaven's Light no animals are harmed in any way. If somebody wants bacon or any other kind of meat, Amari or Viggo have to go down to hunt the creature that sounds delicious at the time.

Viggo throws Amari against him, reminding her of her situation and she comes back. Oh, she wants that farmhouse with a couple hundred acres. It sounds so nice right now!

"Better than my current situation," Amari says with a growl, looking up at Viggo. He looks back at her.

"What is?"

"That farmhouse I so want. I only tell you like every single day."

"Fine." Viggo acknowledges a few people, who look at Amari funny. She acknowledges them with a wave and a 'hi' then continues to look down. Then it hits her.

She furrows her brows. "Babe…"

"What?"

"Did you shift the air before we came in?"

"Uh," Viggo drawls out. He sounds uncertain.

"Viggo!" Amari looks up at him. "You gotta be fuckin' kidding me!"

Viggo looks back at Amari with a sly look, a sly grin on his face and his eyes devious.

"Ooo, I hate your acting skills."

"I could've led you on for longer." Viggo winks at his beloved wife, a sly grin on his face that reminds her of the man she created Viggo in the image of.

"Viggo." Amari looks at the ground with her hands in clenched fists. "Amar. Grimert. You're in fuckin' trouble!"

"Am I?" Viggo gets inside the castle and he instantly heads for the west wing. "Or are you just saying that because you thought I let everyone see you naked?"

Amari punches Viggo in the back of the thigh and he stumbles. But he doesn't fall, catching himself before he can. "Ow!" He hisses.

"You're lucky you remembered to shift the air," Amari drawls out threateningly.

"No." Viggo quickly goes up the stairs. "You're lucky I remembered. We're both lucky I remembered. And why would I do that to you anyway? I would never embarrass you like that." Viggo opens the door to Amari's office and takes her inside, closing the door behind him.

"I'm lucky to have you, Viggo."

He snorts. "You're lucky. I'm lucky! That you chose me! Klaussof was a-."

"Is a best friend and already taken," Amari interrupts Viggo before he can say Klauss was a better option. He's not! While Amari loves Klauss, she can only love him like a brother. She saw a future with Viggo while

Allah was pushing her away and going through things with Ragnar.

While Amari would have loved to help Allah with Ragnar, she knew that Hallam needed someone that's already stable. And Allah needed some time alone. Amari just didn't think he would take six years.

Viggo pushes Amari's comfortable rolling chair away and sits her down on her desk, standing in between her thighs and putting her clothes on her desk. She looks up at him and their brown eyes meet.

"And you're the better choice anyway," she says softly. Viggo leans in, letting his lips feather Amari's lips.

"And why's that?"

Amari looks at Viggo's lips, tempted to kiss and make love to her best friend that she also calls the love of her life. "Because Allah made decisions that I wasn't happy with. And I couldn't just let them slide. Also." Amari looks into Viggo's chocolate brown eyes. "You're older and wiser. And more stable. And I just love… Older men." Amari seduces softly.

Viggo chuckles with a smile on his face and then his lips are on Amari's in a passionate kiss. She cups his neck as she breathes in the scent of his cologne, cedarwood shavings and vanilla filling her nostrils.

∞

Emma plays with Booties, at the estate. She snuck away with Mack's fox, but not without telling Mack and one of the cooks where she was going. She didn't want to leave her parents too worried. They'll come looking for her eventually. And they'll know that she's safe. They went to talk to Sahara after what happened and Emma doesn't blame her mom. She went through a lot the other night and Emma wonders why Hapoor did that to her poor mom.

She deserves much better treatment! Why is Hapoor so obsessed with her anyway? And mean to her at the same time? Emma tries to shrug it off. She hates that she already understands some adult situations. But she guesses it's a curse that comes with her blessing.

Emma puts up a little course for Booties that's easy for him and his old bones. She knows he's getting there. But soon he'll be passing into Heaven's Light and he'll be young, again. Just like what Emma's mom wants. While Booties can still be a Guardian, he's just too old for it now, his bones becoming brittle and his strength weakening. He can't shift anymore.

Emma looks at Booties once she's done with the small course for him. "Okay, Booties," Emma says. "Go ahead."

Booties meows. He gently goes through the course, happy to oblige. He weaves in between the sticks, steps over a small bundle, and then he curls up in Emma's lap and gets comfortable. She looks up in dumbstruck disbelief. She heard her mom talk about it before. She can't move, now!

Emma's stuck like this until Booties decides to move! How long is that going to take! Emma looks around the gardens, looking for something to do. The maids and manservants for the estate are out for the day, staying with their families in the village close by. Emma doesn't have another play date except for Vixen, Mack's pure white colored fox with evergreen eyes. Maybe she should've thought this through.

Emma looks down at Booties as she starts to wonder if she can just somehow carry him. But the moment she decides to grab him, he decides to start to purr. Ah, shucks! Now, she can't do anything!

A low male chuckle comes from the other side of the hedge and Vixen gets up from her spot that she was just curled up in, showing her teeth in a deep growl. Emma freezes at the sudden male presence. And he sounds familiar.

She looks up at him as he comes around the corner and he looks handsome as ever. Why does he have to be the most gorgeous man in Hallam?! Emma's chocolate brown eyes follow the man as his bright blue-green eyes shine at the sight of her. This isn't good. And it's going to end badly by what Emma starts to see in her mind. She should've stayed in Heaven's Light.

"Well, look at this," he growls softly. "Isn't this precious?"

"What do you want," Emma snaps, glaring at the evil man that raped her mom.

"Just to talk. If you'll let me."

Emma shakes her head. "You don't wanna talk. You're here looking for my mother."

Hapoor bends down at Emma's eye level and it pisses her off, making her clench her little fists. "And you look like your dad. For the moment." He purrs.

Emma clenches her jaw as she watches the man that's insanely good looking, it should be illegal for a criminal like him. "Buzz off. You're not welcome here."

She threatens. She pets Booties as he sleeps in her lap, keeping her chocolate brown eyes on the man in front of her.

"Now, I can't honestly do that. Emma."

Emma freezes her hand. How does he know her name?

"And if your mom isn't going to show up at least I got you."

Emma smacks Hapoor's hand away as he reaches for her, but he doesn't listen. He grabs her by her beach blond hair and he yanks her towards him, Booties getting dropped out of her lap. She screams and Vixen barks at him. Hapoor throws his fist into Vixen's muzzle and she yelps before taking a step back.

Hapoor holds Emma up by her hair and the pain of dangling in his hand stabs her in the head like little needles. This is not good! What does he want from her?!

"You're going to be absolutely beautiful when you come of age," Hapoor threatens with a growl. "Too bad your five years too young." His tongue glides over his pearly white canines as he shows them off. Emma stares at Hapoor in horror. "I don't rape children. Just your mother."

Emma screams a growl and lashes out at Hapoor with her nails, furious with him. But all her nails meet is air. A loud thud is heard from behind her and then a wolf knocks Hapoor back, making him drop Emma. She lands on her hands and knees and she stares at the ground for a moment before looking up to see King Allah sliding on his paws in wolf form and turning to face Hapoor.

Emma falls in love with King Allah and his wolf, Ragnar, instantly and she watches him as he growls at her mom's rapist, showing his teeth. He looks absolutely beautiful. God-like with his protective stance in wolf form. Vixen steps above Emma, protecting her and thinking King Allah is going to hurt poor Emma.

But his eyes are on Hapoor, who gets up and gives King Allah a sneer look.

"You're going to have to do better than that, Allah," Hapoor sneers with a growl.

Allah snaps his teeth at Hapoor, ready to kill. Emma quickly climbs on Vixen's back with Booties on her shoulders and she gets settled as Allah chases after Hapoor, who runs and shifts mid run, his clothes tearing apart. Emma puts her hand to Vixen's neck and looks at her, ready to get out of here and somewhere safe.

"Let's get home, Vixen," Emma says in a panic, scared for her life and her mom. "We've got to tell Mom."

Vixen nods her head, then races into the forest the opposite direction from King Allah and Hapoor. Booties slides into Emma's arms as she holds on and he gets comfortable with her. Vixen races through the forest, the wind buffeting Emma's small face until the entrance to Heaven's Light is seen. She uses her hands to open the forest and the pearly white gates open for her.

Vixen slows down a little, but she doesn't stop until she's in the safety of Heaven's Light and the gate closes behind her.

"Emma," Amari screams in fearful relief. The tone of her voice makes Emma scared, wanting to cuddle with her mom and wait for her fear to subside. Emma slides down Vixen's back with Booties in her arms and her dad catches her, holding her close in a bear hug.

His squeeze starts to get a little too tight for her to breathe and she's gasping for air. "Dad," Emma barely manages out.

"What were you thinking," Viggo asks, getting protective and only slightly letting up on his grip on Emma. "You could've been killed. Dear gods… I would've killed myself if something happened to you." He sounds frantic. And scared.

"I wanted to play with Booties," Emma replies sweetly. She pulls back as Booties slides off of her shoulders and onto the ground. He instantly starts looking younger and his fur starts to glisten with light once again. He was waiting for Emma to come and get him!

"I'm sorry." She looks at her beloved dad. "I won't do it, again. I promise."

Amari grabs onto Emma and pulls her into a hug. Amari's arms wrap around her daughter and she kisses her temple. "I better hope not. Oh, my baby." She moans as she clings onto Emma. "We were worried sick."

"I saw King Allah."

"And?"

Emma settles her arms on her mom's shoulders and looks at her, their brown eyes meeting each other. "He saved me from Hapoor."

Viggo growls from behind Emma. "He was at the estate?!" He blows up. But not on Emma. On the news.

Emma nods. "He was looking for you, Mom."

It was Amari's turn to nod. "I'll have a talk with him," she growls. She pulls Emma into another hug. "Right now, I just wanna love my baby."

Emma hugs her mom's neck. "I want that, too. I just wanna love my mother. Who is the best goddess in the world."

Amari chuckles. Booties mrows and she stiffens at his familiar meow. "Booties," she breathes. She looks down at him. "You're here. That means…" Booties meows, confirming Amari's suspicions. "Oh, love. At least you went peacefully. Just like the first time."

Booties leaps onto Amari's shoulder and Emma scratches his head. Emma has always felt a pull towards Booties and now she gets to play with him up here in Heaven's Light! She doesn't have to sneak away ever again!

Now Booties gets to cross between Hallam and Heaven's Light, being a guardian of Heaven's Light.

9

Ragnar takes Hapoor's wolf's neck scruff in his jaws and he throws him to the ground. The white wolf rolls, blood on his fur, and Ragnar chases after him.

Hapoor's wolf gets up and meets Ragnar in the middle, their front claws on each other's chest and their jaws snapping at each other in snarls. He's not getting away this time! Khnight and Hapoor are dead!

Ragnar shoves Khnight down, delivering a nasty gash to his chest. Ragnar gets on all fours and growls at Khnight as he circles the wolf. Khnight watches him, keeping his piercing blue eyes on Ragnar as he heals quickly. Khnight shows his teeth in a snarl, challenging Ragnar. He accepts and lunges at the white wolf with black paws. They tumble and roll around, Ragnar's teeth sinking into Khnight's shoulder and Khnight sinks his teeth into Ragnar's shoulder.

They snarl and bark at each other, trying to throw the other one down. But neither one of them backs down. Ragnar pulls out of Khnight's hold and his shoulder screams in pain. But he pushes through it and head butt's Khnight's side, throwing him back.

Let's bring out, Asgard, Allah orders in a yell. *He's both of us put together! He can talk and fight!*

Why would we want to talk to this son of a bitch?! Ragnar snaps. *He's better dead! He won't be able to touch Amari if we kill him!*

I have a feeling that if we kill him, we won't get any answers! Mavis may be dead, but there's something fishy going on!

Fine! Ragnar sinks his teeth into Khnight's leg and starts dragging him.

Khnight yelps and tears out of Ragnar's hold before taking off, bleeding and limping.

He won't get far, Allah starts. *Get him!*

With. Pleasure. Ragnar snarls in delight. He pushes forward and chases after Khnight. He catches up in a mere second and he leaps at the injured wolf, shifting into Asgard mid-leap.

The lycan grabs Khnight's neck with his hand and digs his claws in. He rolls with the wolf before getting up and slamming his back into a tree, getting a yelp out of Khnight.

"Who's behind this attack," Asgard orders, glaring at the struggling wolf. "Who turned you?!"

Khnight yelps in fear and he claws at Asgard, slashing his face. Asgard growls in frustration and tightens his grip on the wolf's neck, making the wolf gasp for breath.

"Is Mavis behind this?!"

Khnight whines a yelp, fear striking him as Asgard's power rolls over him and paralyzes him. Asgard continues to press Khnight into the tree, waiting for Hapoor to shift and give him answers. But a black wolf leaps into him and throws him off of Khnight, sinking her teeth into Agard's neck. Asgard thrusts his palm into

the rogue's shoulder, throwing it back, and she tears away
from him.

She lands on all fours and runs off with a limp,
running alongside another black wolf that has taken
Khnight onto his back. Who was that?! Asgard gets up
and glares at the two wolves that are fleeing with
Khnight. He needs answers! And he will get them!

Asgard begrudgingly shifts into Ragnar and
Ragnar runs back to the kingdom, knowing he won't be
able to knock any sense into the rogues.

∞

Amari stares out the window of her office as she
watches Emma play with Booties. She's glad her daughter
is safe. But Hapoor is still out there doing who knows
what.

Amari doesn't know what she's going to do if he
succeeds in raping her, spilling his seed inside of her
when all the eggs May and Ada have given her have been
flushed out. They didn't give her very many and she's
already given Ada's egg back. Amari seduced Ada at the
estate this morning and gave her the egg back, telling her
she's going to have a child with Allah. Ada wasn't very
happy about it, but what's done is done.

Ada will forgive Amari in time. She knows Ada
doesn't like Allah. And because of that Ada is furious to
have a child with him anymore. She once bore with the
thought, only wanting the best for him. But now she's
dedicated her life to May and can't stand the thought of
baring Allah's child. At least Amari didn't hide the truth
from Ada. Her mistress took her egg back for her health.

Amari watches Viggo walk over to Emma and bend down to her eye level. He talks with her and Amari enjoys the view. She loves her husband so much! She doesn't know what she would do without him! She has no idea how she managed before him!

And then there's Allah… Amari has been in denial of her feelings for the lycan king for years and she's finally owning up to them. But she doesn't regret her decision. Amari is in love with Viggo and she vows to stay with him. Even when she gets killed and moves onto heaven, she will always remember him. But she doesn't want to go to heaven. She prefers to stay here in Heaven's Light. Maybe when she's bound here, she'll stay here. And be able to be with her beloved husband.

Clay speaks up from his play pen and lets Amari know he's frustrated with his toy.

"Let me help you," Ramein says. She's heard climbing into Clay's play pen and then she's playing with him. She's such a little athlete at three years old. She'll be perfect for Allah when she comes of age! But will Amari be able to let her daughter go through with it? She's in love with Allah but his wolf calls Ramein his second chance mate. They're meant for each other, but yet Amari doesn't know how she feels about it.

If she could, she would change Ramein's fate. Let her have a choice and be with whoever she wants. Amari isn't quite sure of her daughter being part werewolf. And she has no idea how it happened.

It's for the better, Amari, Raja says in Amari's mind.

But is it really? Amari doubts Raja's plans and blessings. What if she's meant to have two husbands?

No, Amari! You can't have Allah! He's not meant for you!

But I'm in love with him. Amari's eyes fill with tears.

Stay away from him, Mare! I'm telling you! You made. The right. Choice.

Amari sighs with a sag, tears in her eyes. She knows that. But sometimes she wonders what it would've been like if she pushed through Allah's stupidity and chose him instead. Would Hapoor have treated her differently? And what about the takals? Would they have accepted Amari as their goddess if she chose Allah instead? Or would this all be turned around with the war being between the takals and Amari? Would Viggo have turned against her?

I know it's tough. I had a choice to make and choose between two amazing mates. It was hard when I loved them both. But I chose my king in the end and I couldn't have been happier.

Viggo's brown eyes meet with Amari's as she talks with Raja.

"But do you miss the other," Amari asks lowly so Ramein can't hear, barely moving her lips so Viggo can't read them.

I think about him from time to time. But I was able to move on from him after he became happy with a new mate.

"Yeah, that'll be years from now," Amari says lowly.

You need to start taking Ramein to Allah once in a while. Let them get to know each other. It'll help you move on from him. I promise. Raja's voice is filled with love and passion, showing Amari that she still cares.

Amari nods. *I'll start that today.*

That's my girl. Raja sounds pleased, smiling in Amari's mind.

Amari looks back at Ramein to find her playing with Clay and helping him figure out his new toy. Clay sings into his brand-new microphone that the inventor of Hallam made for him and Ramein encourages him. She smiles at him and it warms Amari's heart, Clay's voice echoing in the toy microphone. She had one of those when she was little!

"That's beautiful singing, Clay," Amari coos. She walks over to the play pen and pulls Clay out. He drops his microphone into the play pen and she holds him, kissing his cheek.

"Mommy," Ramein starts. "Is everything okay? You look sad."

Amari looks at her beloved daughter, who sits in the play pen. "I'm fine, sweet girl. Thank you for asking." Amari is grateful to have two daughters who care greatly for her. They have the biggest hearts and they get it from her. She just hopes nobody tries to take advantage of their caring hearts like they did her. Amari has had it happen to her way too many times back in Homba.

"How 'bout you and I go see King Allah," Amari asks as she helps Ramein out of the play pen. "You like him."

"I do!" Ramein exclaims. She looks up at Amari, her feet against the play pen and Amari's leg while holding onto her hand. Her eyes dance with excitement. "Can we go see him? I know you don't really like him."

"Oh, don't say that." Amari drawls out slowly. "I like him."

"But I've caught you glaring at him. And I know when you're teasing." Ramein shakes her head at her mom. "You never tease Allah."

"Maybe because he's been stupid in the past."

Ramein giggles. "Stupid for you," she flirts teasingly.

"Oh, you are such a tease." Amari lets go of Ramein and she falls onto her butt in the play pen. "I'll let you get out of there yourself if you're going to be like that." Amari teases, challenging her daughter to a nice and playful game.

Ramein screams a laugh, a big grin on her face, while she holds herself up with her hands behind her and she looks up at Amari. "I bet you I can get out myself!"

"Oh yeah?" Amari drawls out, amused and teasing her daughter.

"Yeah!" Ramein drawls out, keeping eye contact with her mom. Her eyes are one of a kind and rare. With her right eye green and left eye brown she looks so much like a hybrid. But she looks a lot like her great grandma from Homba.

Amari's grandma on her mom's side. She so wishes the two could've met. Amari holds Clay's calf as she gives Ramein a challenging look. "Let's see you do it."

"You might wanna back up for this."

"Okay, then." Amari drawls out. She takes a few steps back and she watches Ramein look around the play pen before grabbing onto one of the legs.

Ramein walks up the leg of the play pen, holding onto the net with her hands. When she gets to the top and leans over Amari puts her finger to Ramein's forehead teasingly. Their eyes lock and Ramein shakes her head.

"Don't you dare," Ramein warns.

"Or what?" Amari dares to challenge her daughter.

"Or I won't do chores for a week!"

Amari chuckles. "You think you have a choice?"

"Of course, I have a choice!"

"Ha! Chores are mandatory. They're not a volatile thing."

"Then… I won't make breakfast for you!"

"We got cooks for that."

"Then…" Ramein growls as she can't think of anything else to threaten Amari with.

"I'm just kidding, Ramein." Amari offers her arm for Ramein. "And trust me. As you get older, you'll grow with your training and learn new tactics on how to threaten others. Your own mother included."

Ramein looks at Amari's arm for a moment. Then she gladly takes it and Amari helps her out.

"Good choice." Amari sets Ramein down on the ground and Viggo comes walking in with Emma. Amari looks at him and their brown eyes meet.

"Emma wants to go see Allah," Viggo says.

Amari winces. "Oh?" She looks at her five-year-old daughter and Emma gives her puppy eyes. "And why's that?"

"Because. And I quote."

Amari looks at her husband.

"She's in love," Viggo says with flirtatious enthusiasm in a high-pitched voice. He flutters his eye lashes with his hands clasped together and close to his chest.

Amari laughs. "We can go. Ramein wants to see him, too."

Viggo winces, his eyes on Amari. He lets his hands down at his sides. "Why?" He drawls out.

"Same reason."

Viggo shakes his head. "If any of our daughters winds up with that man, I better hope it's Ramein. She has the wolf and would be a perfect Luna for him."

"Something we can agree on, my love."

"No," Emma objects loudly. "I'd be a perfect Luna!"

Amari and Viggo look at their oldest child. "Emma, sweetie, you have a different path from Ramein," Amari says sweetly.

"But I wanna marry him," Emma whines. Her chocolate brown eyes meet Amari's hazel brown eyes. "He saved me! He's hot! And perfect for a young lady like me!"

Amari snorts and holds back a laugh. "I'm pretty sure he was in wolf form when you met him."

Ramein walks over to Emma. "And he's nothing like you want. He's a god. And king. And he deserves a queen like me to rule beside him. A wolf." Ramein clasps her hands together and puts them to her chest as she gives her older sister attitude. She walks out of Amari's office.

Viggo snorts and smirks, shaking his head and stifling a laugh. "It's things like this I wish we could record somehow."

Amari gets an idea. She has journals for her kids.
Maybe she can use them for stuff like this! Amari gives
her husband a smirk and he looks at her.

"What?"

"We can."

"Oh, good. Just what we need. Technology." He
doesn't sound thrilled.

Emma, who was dumbfounded, finally follows
Ramein out and they start bickering about who gets to
have Allah. Amari walks up to Viggo and her breasts
brush against his rib cage.

"Journals," Amari says. "Babe. We got journals
for them."

Viggo nods. "That I can do."

Amari nods. "Let's take our kids to see Allah.
He'll enjoy them. And we do have to thank him for
finding Emma yesterday."

"I couldn't agree more." Viggo puts his hand on
Amari's lower back as she walks past him and out the
door. He smacks her ass as he follows her out and closes
her office door.

∞

Allah goes over the contract for the security team
and it finally looks perfect. Amari was right. Those
changes needed to be made. She was trained and looked
after well.

Leah knew what she was doing with Amari. But
while Allah misses the way his first Beta did things
around here, he doesn't miss her. He'll always stick by his

opinion. The LGBTQ community is not welcome in his kingdom. But Amari is different.

Amari… Allah closes his eyes as he starts to think about her and he goes back to a couple days ago when she came and made an agreement on their alliance. Her black dress hugged her figure, making her look irresistible. While Selena's dress made the same effect on Amari, the dress she wore when she was here reminded Allah that she was in mourning for a loved one. And the lust he felt towards her had to do with the moment and nothing more.

Guilt hits him in the gut as he wants to feel her, again. He wants her underneath him, feeling every single inch of her skin. He wants to feel her lips on his lips and he wants to remind her why he would've made a better choice for her. Not only does Amari's body fit perfectly with Allah's body. But he also trained her. He was her mentor and knows her like the back of his hand. Which is why he knew he was going to have to fight to be by her side when it came to her coronation.

He wound up completely failing, but he still did his best. Allah goes back to six years ago when Amari relieved him from his pain. The feel of her skin was intoxicating. Her lips were seeking for his approval. His member pulsed inside of her and she accepted him as her mate. He was ready to commit to her when the time came. And now he'll never have her. He should've convinced her. Given her a reason why he would've been a good fit for her. They could've had everything. And each other… Allah will always regret not trying harder. But at least in fourteen years he'll have his real second chance mate to fight for and keep. It's just the matter of moving on from Amari.

It's going to be tough. He knows this. Allah had a tough time moving on from Ada. And then he's gone six years. In love with Amari and unable to get her off his mind. How long is it going to take to get over her? Six more years? Allah sighs and hangs his head. He hates himself for pushing Amari away.

He should've succumbed to his love for her when she was here and he had the chance six years ago. A couple of girls are heard in the hallway and they sound way too familiar. Allah lifts his head and stares at his door. Could they really have come to see him? Or is he hearing things?

"He's mine," Ramein is heard screaming. "King Allah is my betrothed! Not yours, Emma!" She sounds distressed.

Allah gets up, eager to see Ramein, and he starts for the door, hearing Ramein and Emma fight over him. It makes him laugh. That's adorable. Allah strides out of his office and he finds Amari with her family. His eyes land on hers and she looks defeated. She's tried to stop her girls' bickering over him, but with no success.

Allah strides over and sweeps Ramein off her feet, picking her up and holding her like a baby while managing to get a growl from Viggo.

"You're too young to fight over men," Allah puts in, looking at Ramein. "You better stop fighting with your sister over it or this man will have no interest in you or your sister." He warns his future luna.

Ramein giggles up at him and then throws her little arms around his neck. "I was just trying to explain to Emma that wolves stick together. But she thinks lycans and wolves have mates other than each other."

Allah hugs Ramein. "It happens." His eyes meet with Amari's. "But it's rare."

Viggo growls and takes a step towards Allah, but Amari stops him with her arm across his chest. Viggo looks at her and backs down. But his chocolate brown eyes don't waver from Allah.

"Ramein, sweetie," Amari starts. "Would you believe that Allah once had a human mate?"

"No," Ramein drawls out, pulling back and sitting into Allah's arms. Her brown and green eyes shine with jealousy.

He nods his head at her. "I did. But she wound up marrying someone else."

"Were you in love with her?"

"That's not important," Amari puts in way too quickly, not giving Allah a chance to answer her daughter. She clears her throat. "Anyway."

Allah looks at Amari and their eyes meet.

"We wanted to come and thank you. For finding Emma yesterday." Her baby boy asleep in his carrier on her chest, Amari looks like a mother that's ready to take on the world.

Allah puts Ramein down, keeping eye contact with the woman he so loves. "Of course," he breathes. "I would've done it for anyone in need."

"When she disappeared, we didn't know until it was too late. Mack told us not long after she left with Vixen. But by then she was already missing."

Allah clears his throat, knowing the panic Amari and Viggo felt. He's been there with Zack. "She was at your estate. Like you said in the message."

Amari nods. "Mack told us that's where she was headed. To be with a cat of mine that just passed away recently. He was old," she says softly, patting her son's bottom, the soft look on her face speaking volumes.

Allah nods his head, knowing which cat Amari is meaning. The cat that chose to be her guardian. Booties. "I'm so sorry for your loss. But I'm sure you get to enjoy him up in Heaven's Light."

"Yes." Amari looks up at Viggo and he clears his throat.

"Emma loves him," Viggo puts in. "He's her favorite cat."

Allah looks at Viggo and their eyes meet. "He was Amari's favorite as well."

"He's more than that with her. You and I both know this."

"Yes, of course." Allah feels a tug on his pant leg and soon Ramein is climbing up his leg while Emma climbs up his back.

The girls giggle as they hang on him, thinking they're being super sneaky. The look on Viggo's face changes and his tone of voice changes with it.

"And my girls know no boundaries," Viggo starts. "Girls!" He snaps, sounding annoyed with his daughters.

"No, no." Allah starts, trying to reassure Viggo. "It's okay. I'm used to this anyway." Truly, he is. Asa's kids always climbed all over Allah, jealous when one of them got all of his attention.

Viggo raises an eyebrow.

"Please," Amari puts in. "Do tell."

Allah shrugs. "My sister. Her kids used to climb all over me. And now her grandkids do it."

"How is your sister? I haven't heard anything about her."

"She isn't doing very well. Cancer. It's taking a toll on her."

"I am so sorry," Amari says softly.

"Yes," Viggo puts in, sounding heartbroken.

Allah doesn't blame him. Viggo was Asa's fated mate before they severed the bond for his marriage to Amari. He probably feels guilty for not staying in the loop of Asa's health and whereabouts. "Our apologies. How much longer is she expected to live?"

"Just a few weeks."

"I'm so sorry," Viggo says lowly. He looks down at the floor and he goes quiet. He seems to be regretting some things.

"I swear," a female voice starts down the hallway behind Amari and Viggo. "You're like a fox in a hen house when it gets caught. Amari!"

Amari's brown eyes gleam and she turns around. "Lillian! So good to see you!" She and Lillian hug as Allah and Viggo start to visit, talking about the war that's upon them and where Hapoor might be. "Emma! Lillian is going to take you to Homba for the next few days."

"So, that's why you packed my bag!" Emma slides down Allah's back as he continues talking with Viggo.

"I tried to get answers, but he wouldn't shift," Allah continues. "A black wolf attacked and took off with him and another black wolf."

"I find that odd," Viggo puts in. "If he's been working with the rogues all this time, then this war is strictly between you, Amari, and them. But why would he work with them?"

Allah shakes his head. "I have no idea." He puts his hands in his pockets. "But I have a feeling Mavis started it all."

"Mavis died. Madison can confirm that. She and Amari meet up three times a month and she reported to Amari about Mavis's arrival."

Allah shakes his head. "Witches. Never get involved with them in any way. Mavis raped a few wolves in the packs I protect. And I wouldn't be surprised if they're all rogues, now. She has that effect." Allah shakes his head in disgust.

"Hapoor is one of them."

Allah winces, looking at Viggo in shock. "What?"

"Mavis raped Hapoor when he was just twelve years old. Ada is the result."

"Fuck," Allah whispers. Ada was his fated mate! How did he not know this about her! "I didn't..."

"Know? Neither did we."

Allah nods. "Well, the only one that knew everything was Raja. She was the Heart of Hallam anyway."

Viggo nods. "And the Heart saw everything." He shudders. "I feel bad for Emma." He watches his oldest as she climbs up Allah's back and wraps her arms around his neck, giggling softly. "Becoming the Heart of Hallam at such a young age. She deserves a normal childhood."

"And she will. There will just be some things that she will see and they'll change her. It'll be tough. But she'll get through it." Allah looks at Emma as she snuggles into him.

Emma presses her lips into Allah's cheek as he looks at her. "I have to go. But I want you to know that I will be thinking of you."

"Don't think of me too much. You gotta do well in your training."

Emma nods her head and then her little lips are on Allah's lips. His eyes widen, shocked at how bold Emma is.

"Emmaleigh Rose Grimert," Viggo snaps, sounding protective but angry at the same time. "Get your hands off him!"

Allah pulls away from Emma and she giggles. She slides down his back and then takes Lillian's hand, going with her to one of the portals to get to Homba. Allah looks at Viggo and their eyes meet. Viggo shakes his head in angered disbelief. Allah doesn't blame him. Emma is being quite bold!

"I will have a talk with my daughter," Viggo starts. "I am so sorry." He apologizes.

Allah rubs his lips, getting rid of the memory of little lips on them. He doesn't want that to happen again! It's too weird! "She's bold. I'll give her that."

"Hopefully she grows out of it."

"Homba will do that for her," Amari puts in. "When I was there, I was nervous to be bold like that when I got older. You get in trouble for things like that there."

"Were you ever," Allah starts. He doesn't dare ask if Amari was ever abused for being bold. But he still tries.

Amari shakes her head. "Not physically. But I have an ex that emotionally, mentally, and verbally abused me whenever I tried to be bold." Amari trails off and shudders. "Hallam helped me forget that and now I'm myself, again."

Allah nods in understanding. "Well, that man's dead next time Lillian crosses over. I'll put a hit on him and she'll take care of it."

Amari snorts and bites back a laugh, a smirk on her lips as they press together. "Better than prison."

Allah snorts as Viggo chuckles. Ramein giggles as she climbs up Allah's back and wraps her arms around his neck from behind.

"Hi, handsome," Ramein beams in Allah's ear. He looks at her.

"Hello, beautiful!"

Ramein giggles as she kisses Allah's nose. Now, this is what he could get used to. His little future luna kissing his nose is appropriate for a girl her age. On the lips is too much.

10

Emma watches the weird metallic moving things with wheels as they drive down the street in awestruck disbelief. What are those things? And what's with the weird bikes that don't have pedals?

Emma watches the weird things in horror. This can't be happening… This is Homba?! But why is it so weird? And the houses! They're nothing like what Emma is used to! A dog barks and familiarity hits Emma. Lasodo… Oh, he's a good dog up in Heaven's Light. But he tends to bark, playing with other dogs. Emma wants to go back home. Play with the dogs and be wrapped in her dad's arms as he protects her and plays with her. Help the cooks prepare food for the day. Take care of the animals and help the people with their chores. Play with Ramein and help with Clay. This world is too much.

Emma misses her family right away. What was she thinking! She should've waited a few years for this! Lillian's son that's just a year older than Lillian takes her hand in his and she looks up at him. He's tall for his age and his dirty blond hair has a red streak in it, his green eyes shining bright with softness.

"It's okay," Max says softly. "It's a lot to take in. But you'll get used to it fast."

Emma shakes her head, her beach blond bangs falling in her face. "I don't think I will."

"Pffft." Max gives Emma's hand a reassuring squeeze. "I wasn't used to all of this at your age." Emma gives Max a suspicious glare. "But I was able to get used to it really fast."

Emma shakes her head. "But that's you. I'm different.

Max nods. "Well, come on. I know just what to do to help you get used to everything."

Emma nods. "And what's that?"

Max smiles, showing off his pearly white teeth. "Skates. They're not like the cars or bikes. But they're a lot of fun and you can get around on them."

Emma nods, again. "Okay. As long as I can go my own pace. Let's go."

"You can use my mom's old ones when she was your age. I'll wear mine and we can go together." Max leads Emma into the house and they go down to the basement, where he starts rummaging through weird looking boxes with lids.

"What are those?"

"They're called totes. They're quite convenient when you wanna move. But we mainly use them for storage."

"Food storage?"

"That and more."

"Kids," Lillian calls from above. "I'm making lunch! Mac and Cheese should be ready in ten minutes!"

"Mac and Cheese?" Emma looks at Max after looking up the stairs, curious to know what that kind of food is.

"Yeah," Max replies. "It's super good."

"What is it?"

"Macaroni noodles in a cheese sauce. You'll like it. It's really good," Max says as he nods his head at Emma. His green eyes dance.

Emma moans, her mouth watering as she remembers how hungry she is. And the food sounds delicious! "That sounds delicious."

"Oh, it's so good. But you can't have it without a glass of milk. It's a must."

"Is there any goat milk? I'm lactose intolerant."

"Oh. Shit." Max looks at Emma in disbelief. "Does my mom know that?"

Emma nods in confirmation. "My mom told her. But it's possible that she forgot."

"Mom!" Max starts for the stairs, in a panic.

"What?" Lillian calls.

"Emma can't have dairy!"

"I know! I'm using almond milk as a substitute! And sharp cheddar instead of the packet! Amari said the cooks use them in food all the time!"

"What about goat milk?"

"I couldn't find it at the store, so I bought milk that has the lactase enzyme! She'll be able to drink that!"

"Okay!" Max drawls out. "Thank you, Mom!"

"You're welcome!"

Max looks at Emma and their eyes meet.

"Hey!" Lillian stands at the top of the stairs, looking down them and at the kids. "After lunch you should take Emma out on the skates! It'll be good for her! Her training starts tomorrow and we want her to get comfortable here."

"Already on it, Mom." Max smiles brightly at his mom.

"Good! Thank you, Max! You're the best!"

Max nods his head and smirks at Emma. "Wanna play something while we wait for lunch?"

Emma nods for what seems like the tenth time. "Sure. What do you have in mind?"

Max laughs evilly. "Only the funnest game ever." He starts for one of the rooms in the basement and he opens the door. He looks at Emma. "Guess the toy. I have to blindfold you and then you run your hands over the toy to figure out what it is."

Emma nods her head, excited to play the new game. "Let's do it!"

Max walks into the room and comes out a moment later with a black blindfold. He puts it over Emma's eyes and she holds her hands out. He instantly puts a spikey toy in her hand, but the spikes are dull.

"Is that a toy mace," Emma asks.

"Close," Max replies. "Try again."

Emma feels out the spiked ball that seems to be on a plastic chain and plastic handle. She nods her head. "That's a mace on a chain."

"That was too easy." Max takes the toy from Emma and replaces it with something smooth. She feels plastic and her hands go over a few grooves before finding a nub. "That's a baseball bat."

"You're good at this."

"Give me something harder," Emma challenges Max.

"Alright."

Emma sets the bat down and Max hands her something that's smooth in some spots and with holes. She feels the ends, finding out there's a hole on one end and an oval shaped tip on the other end. Emma nods her head. She has one of these!

"It's a type of flute," Emma replies.

"You're super good at this," Max says sounding impressed. He needs to give Emma an even better challenge if he wants to stump her!

"Give me something else." Emma drops the flute and waits for the next thing.

Max puts something a little weighted in Emma's hand and without hesitation she blurts out what it is, feeling the smooth wood and metal.

"A pocketknife!"

"How did you know?"

"Max, my mom has quite a few of these. They come quite in handy."

"Alright." Max takes his pocketknife back. "Then guess this." Max slaps Emma's hand lightly and something wet hits her hand.

"Ew," Emma drawls out in disgust. "Is that your spit?"

"No. It's a thing!"

Emma curls her fingers around something slimy, wet, and sticky, which is in the form of a ball. Oh… This is a tough one! Emma twists her lips as she tries to think about what she's holding. She's never felt anything quite like it before. "Slime?"

"Yep," Max drawls out proudly.

Emma instantly takes her blindfold off and looks at the green slime that's in her hand. Seeing it for the very first time, she gets drawn to the Homba creation.

"I wasn't done!"

"But this is the first time I've ever seen or felt slime," Emma breathes. She watches the slime as she squeezes it with her fingers and it slips in between them.

Max giggles. "There's a first with everything."

Emma nods. For once, she's liking Homba. Her mom has put down ground rules at the kingdom of Heaven's Light. And she once mentioned banning slime. Emma didn't know what she was talking about. But now that she has a visual on the stuff, she can now see why it's banned. This stuff will get everywhere! And Emma likes it. She giggles as the ooze sticks to her fingers and tickles them.

∞

Ramein climbs onto Ragnar's back as he lies down and helps her up with his muzzle. He could easily have her as a little snack if he wanted.

Amari came to Allah's to let Ramein visit with him. They need the time together and it gives Amari a break. But she sure wasn't expecting Viggo to come with her, making it impossible for her to have some time alone. Amari watches Ramein and Ragnar together as he gets up and lets Ramein ride on his back. She gets jealous, wanting a ride on his back once again. But she doesn't get too jealous.

She remembers the feel of the wind on her face as it blew her golden-brown hair back, Ragnar racing through the forest to Allah's kingdom. Amari remembers the feel of his silver-gray fur in between her fingers. His gray fur glows silver in the moonlight and casts a beautiful shine in it. It makes his fur look even softer.

Amari can see Ragnar in the light of the moon at this moment and it steals her breath away. She instantly misses the feel of his fur. She watches him as he shakes out his neck fur and makes Ramein scream and giggle, clinging onto him. Viggo's arm wraps around Amari's waist and he watches Ramein with Ragnar.

"She's his mate," Viggo says lowly. "Isn't she?"

"What?" Amari looks at Viggo with fear. If he figured it out that fast, the truth is going to come out sooner than planned!

Viggo looks at Amari. "Ramein. She's Allah's third fated mate." His brown eyes search her brown eyes. "Isn't she?"

Amari nods her head hesitantly. "Yeah. Which is why he hesitated back in my office. He was fighting with Ragnar about it."

Viggo sighs and sags in defeat. "Guess the betrothal is back in question. Well, more like… The solution."

"Viggo," Amari drawls out. "What are you getting at?"

He kisses her temple. "As much as I wanna protect our daughter from such a fate it seems it's what Raja gave her."

Raja growls in Amari's head. *He better not imply what I think he's going to imply.*

"And I wish she didn't. Ramein deserves to choose her destiny."

"Viggo, Raja was just doing what's best," Amari says softly, defending her companion and best friend. *That's right!* Raja growls, clawing at the ground impatiently.

"But do you honestly believe that Ramein should be the peacekeeper between us and the were-kind?" Viggo presses. "I mean… We can figure something else out."

"It's not like we can reverse your coronation and give it to Allah, Viggo." Amari searches her beloved husband's eyes before he looks away. "You'd be back to a normal Viking takal! Is that what you want?"

"No!" Viggo barks. He looks at Amari and his chocolate brown eyes bare into her hazel brown eyes. "And how can you say such a thing? If we reversed the coronation, our marriage would be out the window." He shakes his head. "And the six wonderful years we've had together would be memories."

Amari sets her hand on Viggo's cheek. "And nothing more." She kisses him then rests her forehead on his forehead. "I don't wanna reverse the coronation. Or end our marriage. I'm happy with you. And I don't wanna give Allah that power, knowing the lycans and wolves would take advantage of it and hurt many people."

Viggo kisses the palm of Amari's hand and then her lips. "This is why I love you. Even when you're in mourning you think clearly." He shakes his head at her. "And I could never live with myself if I let you think otherwise." Viggo kisses Amari's forehead, letting her know how much she means to him.

She gives him a side smile as their brown eyes meet. "Only because you were technically my only option and I would've chosen someone that's not supposed to rule beside me." She teases, knowing she's about to get into trouble.

"I'll make sure he knows you said that." Viggo lays Amari down on the grass as Clay takes a deep breath and sighs, sitting next to Amari. Viggo kisses Amari before looking at their son, who makes a sound of jealousy. "What's your problem?"

Clay looks at Viggo and his blue eyes shine bright. Clay moans in longing and keeps eye contact with his dad. Viggo makes a protective barrier with his arms around Amari as he continues the stare.

"She's mine," Viggo warns. "You get your own girlfriend."

Amari laughs. "He better not be a momma's boy or I'm going to be disappointed in you." She teases.

Viggo looks at Amari and their eyes meet. "I'll be the one disappointed in you for letting him become a momma's boy. You're the one that can do something about that. Not me."

"Oh, it goes both ways." Amari teases. Her hand slips down to Viggo's tribal belt and she unbuckles it, keeping her eyes on his eyes. "And I'm not letting you get away with that remark."

"Amari, you can't even reach. I'm taller than you by a foot. And you have short arms."

Amari smiles and she sneaks her hand up Viggo's chest underneath his shirt, now that she's able to get to it with his tribal belt off. "Who says that's what I was going for?" She teases seductively.

Viggo growls. "You're intoxicating."

"And rightfully so," Amari seduces softly in Viggo's ear. She feels him get hard against her thigh and he thrusts his hips into her as a warning.

"Don't make me take you away from here," he growls warningly in her ear.

Amari giggles evilly, her smiling lips against Viggo's ear. Oh, she plans to do just that. She grabs onto his loose shirt and thrusts him into her. "You might wanna do just that," she whispers seductively.

Viggo growls in Amari's ear and his teeth are on her shoulder, clamping down in a lustful warning. She laughs and moans in his ear, wanting him.

∞

Viggo lays Amari down on the bed and she instantly rolls on top of him, straddling him.

Oh, he doesn't get to have his way with her. She gets to be in charge for once! Viggo watches Amari with his hands on her hips and she takes each one in turn to secure them in the handcuffs above his head. He moans, his voice filled with lust. She can tell he likes the change. And maybe. Just maybe… This change will help her move on from the rape. Amari kisses her husband and their lips melt into each other. She holds his face in her hand and she licks his lips. She wants to take this nice and slow.

With Allah a couple days ago, it was fast and over with quickly. But Amari had flashbacks to the rape. Luckily, she didn't let them overtake her, but she still had a hard time pushing through with it. It was Allah, though. And she loves and trusts him. Amari trails her lips down Viggo's neck and her lips land on the mate mark. It's time to upgrade. Again.

Amari lets her canines grow and she sinks them into the mate mark, getting a grunt from Viggo. He growls with lust as Amari's canines do the work, making the mate mark handsome with protective powers. No one will be able to lay an offensive hand on Viggo. And when Amari is done with him, he can upgrade her mate mark to do the same for her. She needs this. She needs him.

Viggo moans in Amari's ear as she makes the finishing touches on the mate mark. Then her lips are trailing down his naked chest. She sucks on his well-toned peck and gives him a hickey. She decides to give him hickeys all over his chest. And she doesn't leave a single inch of skin on his torso untouched by her mouth. She lets her lips linger over every inch, marking Viggo's abs delicately with her mouth.

He growls lustfully and he tugs on his restraints. He wants to touch her. She can tell. But it's not his turn yet. Amari pulls Viggo's pants and boxers down and she takes them off of him for him. She kisses the skin right above his shaft before taking its massive head into her mouth. She strokes the half that she's not able to deep throat as she takes on the rest, taking her sweet time.

Amari lets her fingertips lightly brush Viggo's massive member and she can't think of a better time to punish her husband for earlier at Allah's kingdom. Her free hand massages Viggo's cullions and she feels them lurch. She instantly pulls away from Viggo's shaft and it shoots its semen onto the bed sheets. Viggo groans and Amari watches him throw his head back. He shudders as she grabs onto his thighs and gets between them, spreading them out. He tenses up as she quietly gets her strap-on put on. She wants to see how Viggo likes it in the ass.

Amari takes his shaft into her mouth and sucks on it as she gets lube on her strap-on. He relaxes and she puts some lube on his asshole. She thrusts her strap-on dildo into it and gets a yelp out of him.

"Fuck," Viggo yells. "Amari. What the hell?" He looks up at Amari as she keeps the dildo deep inside of him. Her brown eyes meet his brown eyes and she raises an eyebrow at him.

"You asked for it."

"Oh," Viggo drawls out in a chuckle, shaking his head. He doesn't seem to be really thrilled with this, but he plays along. "You're in trouble," he warns lowly, watching Amari with his brown stare.

Amari thrusts her hips into Viggo and he throws his head back. She watches him and it turns her on more as he moans. "You're the one that's in trouble." Amari thrusts into Viggo and watches his reaction at the dildo in his ass.

She can tell he's not so sure about it, but she
continues to thrust into him.

"Amari!"

Thrust. Slam!

Amari has a flashback as the headboard slams
against the wall, but this time she feels as though she's in
control, getting Hapoor back. This is a change! Yes!

Thrust. Slam! Viggo groans and looks up at
Amari.

Thrust. Slam! He rests his head back and takes it
from her, knowing the look in her eyes. She needs this.

Thrust. Slam! Viggo makes an unsure sound and
then he grunts.

Thrust. Slam! Amari sees herself above Hapoor
and making him take on her own penis instead of a strap-
on.

Thrust. Slam! Hapoor cries out in a plea in
Amari's mind and she makes him beg.

Thrust. Slam! Hapoor looks at Amari with scared
and pleading eyes.

Thrust. Slam! *Wench!* Amari can hear Hapoor call
her names.

Thrust. Slam! He calls out, pleading and begging
for her stop. She's able to rest, knowing that this is what
she needed.

Thrust. Slam! Relaxation comes over Amari as she
sees and hears Hapoor whimpering in the dark.

"You have no idea how hot you look pissed off,"
Viggo growls, bringing Amari back to him.

Amari looks at him with loving and seductive
eyes. "Then take me," she seduces in a growl. Amari

swiftly takes the strap-on off as she pulls it out of Viggo's ass and she takes his hands out of the handcuffs.

Viggo instantaneously takes Amari into his arms and he rolls on top of her, their brown eyes meeting. He searches her eyes. "Are you sure," he asks lowly.

Amari wraps her arms around Viggo's torso and lets her lips brush against his. "I trust you… Love." It's true. Amari trusts the man that she calls her husband and the love of her life. She would be lying if she said she didn't.

Viggo's lips crash onto Amari's and their tongues spar. It isn't until a moment later his lips trail down her neck and his canines sink into her mate mark, upgrading it with the protective powers. Viggo tears Amari's shirt in half and pulls her breast out of its barrier, sucking on the nipple and then marking it. He thrusts her pants and panties off her then gets in between her thighs. She looks up at him and their brown eyes meet. With just his eyes, he asks for permission, again. She gives him a nod.

Viggo guides himself into his beloved wife and fills her up completely, making her gasp in relief. She pants as she takes him in. He lowers himself on her and her arms wrap around his torso as he thrusts into her. She doesn't have flashbacks to the rape, but the memory of it is still there. Viggo protects Amari, creating a barrier with his arms, and they take their time with each other. His caress on her arms and sides lasts and she lingers her lips on his shoulder.

Amari wraps her legs around Viggo's, intertwining them. She doesn't let go of him and doesn't let him let up. She wants him. She wants the man she loves to know that she wants him and loves him. Making love as if they're newly-weds and consummating their love for each other, Amari knows this is the first step to moving on from Allah.

She couldn't be any happier with Viggo. He has always made her felt so safe. And while Allah has the same effect on her, with Viggo it's different. His touch ignites something inside of her. And when he waited for her to be ready to take him, again, she can't help but admire him.

Amari and Viggo make love like they're newly-weds all the time. But this time is different. This time they're falling in love with each other all over, again. And Amari couldn't ask for a better husband since there isn't one. Viggo is the best man and husband anyone could ever ask for. He's so sweet and caring with his kids, but he also disciplines them when it's right. Amari will always love him. And with her eyes open to see everything that he has done for her, she's making her decision. She chooses Viggo. And she will always choose him.

Viggo thrusts into Amari and she throws her head back as she sees white. She orgasms as he holds her hand, not letting up. He continues to thrust into her until they finally orgasm together and he spills his seed inside of her.

Amari lets her free hand fall down his back and she thinks she's got a play to derail Hapoor at a time like this. He'll think he's won her over, but, in reality, she's beaten him at his own game. She's ready for action.

Amari will have to set a trap for him. It won't be easy, but she can think of something. Viggo moans in her ear, bringing her back to him. She clings onto him, shaking from her orgasm.

Their panting mingles together before Viggo finally pulls out of her and kisses her, holding both of her hands with their fingers entangled.

<u>11</u>

Viggo is startled awake he has a nightmare, sitting up instantly and looking for life in the bedroom that shouldn't be in here.

His blades are out of his arms, ready to slice through anything. He knows he's in Heaven's Light, but you never know if a witch has made her way here with manipulation. It's mainly warlocks that are welcome here.

Because of what Kera has done, witches go to Hell's Fire as a technicality whether they're good or bad. Amelia will go there before coming here, Heaven's Light.

The thought of a bad witch manipulating the system still enters Viggo's mind, though. He looks around the room and lightning strikes outside. His eyes settle on two sets of little human eyes and he lets his blades into his arms, relaxing. It's just his kids.

Clay is heard whimpering and Emma steps forward. "Daddy, we're scared," Emma whispers, her eyes filled with tears.

"Come here," Viggo whispers soothingly. "Come get in bed with us. It's okay."

Emma and Ramein rush over to the bed. Viggo takes Clay from his oldest before she climbs in. He wraps his arm around Amari and kisses her shoulder tenderly to wake her up before letting Emma and Ramein climb in between them.

Amari rolls onto her side and her eyes meet Viggo's in the dark as he lays down with Clay. "Thunderstorm," she asks softly, her voice barely breaking the silence.

Viggo nods. "Yeah," he replies in a whisper.

Amari sighs and pulls her nearest daughter into her. Ramein. She kisses her shoulder. "They're always so scary when you're young. You get used to them when you're my age, but you still would rather have the company of at least an animal when there's one."

Ramein nods then rolls onto her back, looking at her beloved mom. "So, this is normal?"

"Of course, baby." Amari looks at Viggo. "I don't know if it's true about Vikings... But."

He nods in confirmation. "I was afraid of them when I was a kid," he said in a low and soft tone. "I didn't outgrow of it until I was almost nineteen."

Amari snorts. "At nineteen, I was bringing Booties into the house with me because I would get nervous." She opens her arm towards her beloved husband and son as Clay starts to fuss and roll on his side. "Gimme. I wanna love on my son."

Viggo picks Clay up just to hand him to her. She gladly takes him and soothes him with a song she knows from Homba, singing softly. Viggo looks at Emma as she snuggles into him, Amari starting to hum the tune.

"Your mom is a beautiful singer," Viggo says lowly.

Emma looks up at him and he notices her tears are gone, seeming to be comforted. "She knows just the song to sing and hum. It really helps."

"I agree," Ramein speaks up. "Phil Adams is a brilliant man for writing it."

Viggo looks at her. "How do you know who wrote that song?" He challenges sweetly.

Ramein's brown and green eyes meet his brown ones in the dark. "I asked Mom and she told me the man's name. I had no idea he's from Homba."

Viggo nods. "She's very much into music."

"And made a career out of it," Amari puts in, talking softly and lowly. "I was a manager for a famous singer back in Homba before I was bound here. But I still see her around."

"How?" Emma looks back at her mom.

"Well, she's been able to travel between both worlds since she's apparently Lillian's cousin. She has a connection to them, but she can only come through the portals when Lillian or Adam activates them."

"Where is Adam? I haven't seen him in a while."

"He's back in Homba. His mom has been sick, so he hasn't been able to come to Hallam."

"Is she going to be okay?"

Amari shakes her head. "I don't know. I haven't heard from him."

Emma nods then snuggles back into Viggo's side, her little arm wrapped around him the best it can be. It takes his breath away and he's reminded of how much he loves his family. He would never give them up for a place in Homba nor for this world. He's already had both. He's happy where he is. He will always protect what's his and what he loves. He's not even done creating what he loves! He plans on having more kids with Amari once Hapoor is dead. Viggo wants to be the one to put his blade in Hapoor's chest. Or better yet, his head.

Viggo wraps his arm around his eldest and kisses her forehead. He looks at Amari and their eyes meet as their kids start to fall asleep. It's been a few weeks since the rape and Hapoor hasn't surfaced anywhere. Viggo wants to go out searching for him, but he and Amari talked to Allah about having him and his lycans looking for him while on patrol.

Viggo knows that Ramein is Allah's second chance mate and the reason for the alliance. He had suspicions before the conversation with Amari. As much as he hates the idea, he can't go against Raja's wishes. She made Ramein the peacekeeper between the were-kind and Amari and Viggo for a reason. There's no breaking of that blessing.

Viggo will *always* protect his daughter, though. The moment it gets ugly for her, he's pulling her out and calling off the betrothal. He *won't* let her get hurt! Ramein will *always* be his daughter!

What are you thinking, Amari asks in a mind link.

The moment it doesn't look good for Ramein, Viggo starts, his eyes on his beloved wife. He's happy to have her back. She's almost her complete self again after what happened.

Viggo, you don't wanna take her away from Allah's wolf, Amari warns. *He'll try to kill you.*

He can try all he wants. But she's my daughter.

And she's mine, too. Amari sighs as her shoulders relax. *Look. Viggo. I'm not telling you to not pull her out of danger. But Allah will protect her. You can trust him.*

I know that. But–

But you still doubt him. Amari cuts Viggo off. She sighs, again, and sags into the mattress.

Viggo raises his brow at Amari. *Can you blame me?*

Amari shakes her head. *No. I see where you're coming from.*

Then let me do what a father does best. Protect.

I'm not going to win this one, am I? Amari asks in defeat.

For once? Viggo shakes his head at the love of his life. *No.* He searches her eyes in the dark. *You're not.*

Amari sighs, searching Viggo's brown eyes. *Just promise me you'll trust his new security team. They're some of the best and Lillian is personally training them.*

Viggo nods. *You have my word, Mare. I trust Lillian. She's been good to you.*

She's my best friend, Amari says in a low tone.

Viggo smirks at her. *And you're mine,* he says in a growl. If he could, he would kiss his wife without waking up their three kids in between them. But since he can't he gives her a promising look, one that says he's kissing her the moment they all wake up in the morning.

And he's not going to let the kids stop him because they're grossed out.

∞

Amari wakes up hugging her pillow, Viggo's lips landing on her shoulder.

She's so glad she decided to wear a nighty last night. Thunder and lightning storms rarely make it into Heaven's Light. But when they do they light up all around the kingdom. It's amazing to watch.

Sad thing is it scares all the kids up here. But the adults always comfort them and let them know they can't get hurt up here. They're safe. Amari's kids on the other hand… They can get injured from the lightning if they're not careful since they're not dead.

Viggo snuggles in with Amari, but Clay protests, screaming in Amari's ear. She instantaneously buries her face in her pillow and Viggo pulls away from her. She imagines he's giving their son a look of disbelief.

"Why do you have to be so jealous all the time," he asks his son in disbelief. "Can't I snuggle with my wife?"

"No," Clay screams.

Amari throws her head back laughing, looking up at the wall. "There's his first word!"

"At six months," Viggo asks in disbelief. "I don't think so, Mister!"

"No," Clay screams as Viggo tries to snuggle with Amari.

He looks at him. "Hey!"

"No." Clay orders.

"Clayton Bjorn Grimert," Viggo says in a disciplining tone.

Amari giggles into her pillow as she listens to the conversation between her husband and son.

"She's my wife. And your mother. You can share."

Clay leans over Amari's back and tries to push Viggo off of her.

"Hey!"

"No!"

"Alright, calm down," Amari puts in. She flips onto her back and looks at the two boys bickering over her. "There's plenty of me to go around. Okay?"

Viggo and Clay look at her, their eyes in a bickering mood.

"No," Clay says softly after a moment, leaning over and putting his hand on Amari's breast.

"Oh, is that you want? Are you hungry?" Amari queries.

Clay nods, his blue eyes piercing Amari's brown ones.

"Well, at least you're not crying this time." She sits up and grabs him. She pulls her nighty down and offers him her nipple.

He takes it greedily and gives Viggo an evil glare, knowing he won this round. Amari laughs in astonishment, looking at her husband. Their brown eyes meet as Clay suckles on her breast.

"That's not fair," Viggo puts in, sounding heart broken.

"Life's not fair," Amari puts in. "Now, is it?"

Viggo moans in disappointment. "Your boobs are mine tonight."

"You had them last night."

"And they're mine, again, tonight."

Amari giggles at Viggo. "Where are the girls?"

"They were getting dressed then going out to do chores."

"I love those two. They've taken responsibility at such a young age."

"I have a feeling all of our kids are going to be like that."

Amari moans, a small smile on her face and love in her eyes. "That's because they have you as their father," she says as she squeezes Viggo's cheeks.

"And they have you as their mother," Viggo says in between squished cheeks, looking at her.

She kisses his lips. To tell the truth, Amari can't see her kids being any other way other than responsible. While they would take it with Allah as their dad, it just wouldn't be the same. They would be wilder and harder to tame.

Takals take pride in doing their chores right the first time and they start at an early age to learn discipline. Given they have decades to learn since they're immortal thanks to their lineage, they still don't like to veer very far from their paths.

They'll be wild. Yes. But they're not hard to tame since they aim to please and want to do the right thing. They weren't trained to be that way. They were born with it in their veins.

A tachala, part-wolf, part-tiger, and part-eagle, is heard calling out in the rolling hills nearby, welcoming a loved one. Amari pulls away from her husband to look at him.

"Sounds like someone just joined us," Amari says lowly.

"Let's go see who it is," Viggo replies lowly. He gets out of bed and the girls scream in the doorway at his nakedness. He jumps and covers himself up with the covers.

"Dad," Emma screams. "Ew!" She drawls out.

Ramein gags, being over-dramatic.

"Oh my gosh." Amari laughs, a smile on her face. She looks down at the covers and shakes her head. She feels bad for her girls walking in on their dad, but it's still funny! "This is going to be an eventful day."

"Dad, cover up better," Ramein orders, covering her face in horror. "I can still see your pee pee!"

"I'm so sorry," Viggo says apologetically. "Just turn around, please, and I'll get some boxers on."

"Make it briefs," Emma orders. "I don't wanna see your bulge! I try to block you and Mom out of my head as much as I can already!"

Amari snorts and bites back a smirk. She forgets the Heart of Hallam sees everything. Throughout the years the Heart trains to just focus on the important stuff and block out the rest. It gets easier with time.

Luckily, time is on Emma's side. When she's part takal she's immortal. But instead of her aging stopping at thirty like most takals, it'll stop at forty since she's also part human. Amari looks at her beloved daughter with a sympathetic look.

"How are you doing on that, by the way," she asks.

Emma looks at her with her hand up to block her peripheral view of her naked dad, who is going through his sleek, farmhouse dresser. "Raja has been helping me thanks to you. I'm grateful for your connection."

"What connection," Viggo asks. Amari feels his eyes on her, but she keeps hers on Emma.

"It hasn't been too much of a hassle, has it," Amari asks her daughter. "Getting to her?"

Emma shakes her head, seeming to be grateful for the distraction. "No. She's easy to communicate with thanks to the blessing."

Amari nods. "Good. I'm glad."

"Amari," Viggo drawls out, getting his wife's attention.

Their eyes meet.

"What connection is Emma talking about?"

Amari tilts her head as she gives Viggo a side smile. "She never left me. She blessed me the moment she died. I've had her as a part of me ever since."

"That explains your scent changing to tiger lilies."

Amari nods in confirmation. "I don't wear lavender and vanilla perfume anymore. It's tiger lilies and vanilla and I've never felt so close to her before."

"Can we go see Kishah, now?" Emma interrupts.

Amari looks at her daughter with disbelief. "Who?" She asks in shock. Her tachala she created on paper is here, now? The one she chose to ride?

"Kishah! He just stepped through the gate! He went from *really* old to *very* young."

Amari throws the covers as Clay finishes up and she hands him to Viggo without a thought. "Take him," she orders, eager to see her very first tachala to call her his rider.

Viggo catches Clay in his arms with just pants on as Amari quickly grabs her pants. She puts them on as she hurries out the door. She replaces her nighty with a white t-shirt as she continues to rush. Her kids follow her from behind, Ramein trying to catch up.

Amari absolutely loves tachalas! They're like a big house cat with their demeanor towards their human if they have one. But it's rare for a tachala to adopt a person. They mainly stay with their mate and younglings, teaching their cubs how to fly when they're old enough.

Tachalas are amazing creatures. They have a wolf-like head that's more like a fox, but a short snout. Their ears are covered with feathers, poking out on the top of their heads. Their wings are massive, one being the same length as a bus. They're magnificent creatures, some having stripes of a tiger and some being a solid color of a fox with other markings. They're truly one of a kind.

Amari pushes off of the top of the stairs with her powers, shifting the air as she flies down the stairs. She helps her daughters fly down gracefully and Viggo follows with Clay in his arms.

Dressed in only pants, you can see how he has a body of a Norse God. Think Thor from the Marvel series. Viggo is loaded with muscle and abs. Thanks to Amari yesterday, his torso is now covered in hickeys. She smirks at the thought as she walks out of the castle and greets her old friend.

Kishah looks her way, his white feathered body with black stripes glistening in the sunlight. He looks absolutely beautiful with his front feet as claws and back feet as tiger paws.

"Kishah!" Amari smiles. "Good to see you, old friend." She wraps her arms around his neck and he hugs her with his head. Their minds link right away from the touch.

It's good to be here. He sounds grateful. Relieved as though he's been hurting.

Is everything okay back home? Amari lets the conversation carry in the mind link.

Yes. I was just in a lot of pain. My family laid me to rest.

Well, your parents are waiting. I heard Taran call out.

Kishah chuffs in Amari's ear. *Then I must be off to see them.*

Let my kids and husband greet you first.

Of course. Kishah finally lets Amari go and looks at her family as she takes a step back.

"Kishah, meet my kids," Amari starts. "This is Emma." She sets her hand on the top of her eldest's head. "She is the new Heart of Hallam and my oldest. Cats are her absolute favorite animal."

Kishah blinks his eyes slowly, letting Amari know what he's saying without the mind link by just the look on his face. *She gets that from you.* He steps forward and presses his face into Emma's little body so he can say hi to her. After a moment he pulls back and looks at his rider.

"This is Ramein." She puts her hand on the top of Ramein's head next, keeping eye contact with him. "She's our peacekeeper and has a great role ahead of her to keep the peace between us and the were-kind."

Ramein beams at the idea, a big smile on her face. She hugs Kishah's head as he presses his face into her little body to give her a formal hello. Amari waits a moment and watches Kishah with her daughter.

They take a bit and Amari knows they're having a conversation about how big of a responsibility she has in this world. After a few more minutes Kishah finally pulls back. Amari grabs Viggo's upper arm as he stands next to her, looking at the tachala.

"This is my husband, Viggo," Amari starts. "And our son, Clayton. But we call him Clay for short."

Kishah dips his head at Viggo in a hello. Clay grunts in awe, showing his personality already.

"Welcome home, Kishah. We hope you find your permanent home to your liking."

Kishah looks at Amari before he walks over to her. He folds his wings in and rubs up against her body, letting their minds link. *It already is,* he says lowly, sounding grateful for her. He purrs before taking a few lunges forward and taking off in the skies, towards the rolling hills that are specifically home for his kind.

12

Hapoor paces, looking at Khnight's big black paws as he stays in wolf form.

Stupid Allah just about paralyzed him when *he* was in Lycan form. Hapoor had to stay as a wolf to let his spine heal correctly. Now that it is, Khnight won't let him shift back.

You've had a few days to recover, Hapoor snaps at him, angry with his creature. *A few days! And now you won't let me shift back! What's wrong with you!*

May, is the only thing Khnight will respond with.

What about May? She was our fated mate and we rejected her when Allah marked her as a sick joke!

Because that's what he wanted! Khnight snaps. *We're his biggest rival!* He growls.

Hapoor growls back. *So, what are you trying to get at!*

What if we went after her? Found her and asked her what Amari's next move is. She's our second chance mate's best friend after all. She might help us!

It's Ada that May is best friends with! Not Zara! Ada and May are second chance mates!

Khnight growls as he stops pacing, glaring at the ground and curling back his lip. *Don't say that!*

You still feel something for May, don't you?

Just a sliver! I mean… It's hard to forget your first fated mate!

Hapoor sighs in frustration. *So, what do you want me to do?*

Distract her. She's bi, so it won't be hard. Once you get her going, I'm sure she'll spill secrets about Amari.

And if she doesn't?

I'll think of something, Khnight snarls.

Hapoor growls in frustration this time. *Khnight, we need to do this. Get Amari to lean our way. Give us pups. If she doesn't, our bloodline dies with us.*

Yes, I know! I can't believe Allah made Hazen, who is dead, the alpha of our pack!

He doesn't know that both of my sons died in the hands of Mavis! And neither does Amari! They need to understand our pack is without an alpha! We need those pups! Zara is too weak to have another.

It's Khnight's turn to growl in frustration as he starts pacing, again, his heart yearning for the love of his life. Amari is their only chance at this! They risked becoming a rogue over this! If there's any way for them to regain their throne as alpha, they would do it!

Wait… Khnight stops pacing and picks up his front right paw, looking into the forest. *Hapoor,* he starts, trailing off.

What? Hapoor is eager to know if Khnight is thinking the same thing as him.

May could give us pups. I know they'll be bastard children, but at least they'll have alpha blood in them. And our daughters! They'll be perfect lunas!

Hapoor claps his hands in Khnight's mind. *Yes! Just what I was thinking! But I'm not giving up on getting Amari pregnant, either! That baby will be the alpha of the Asgard Light Moon pack the moment it's born!*

Khnight nods before he starts towards Heaven's Light, dead set on bringing Amari out. *Let's do this.*

Can I have my body back, now, Hapoor asks impatiently.

You'll want me to get us there before I let you shift.

Hapoor growls in frustration, his eyebrows furrowed. *I miss my body!*

And you'll get it back! Just hang on!

We need clothes first! We wanna be polite this time.

Khnight nods then walks over to Hapoor's bag. Zara came out with it for him, knowing something happened. She knew he needed to stay away for a while.

Khnight takes off with it and races through the forest, towards Heaven's Light. He now knows where it's located thanks to the scouts that attacked the couple to slow them down. They weren't planning on Madison intervening ad only leaving two alive, though.

Hapoor made sure Fey was given a funeral so her family could say goodbye. Khnight's white fur gets slicked back as a slight wind picks up. It's warm, making him slip his tongue out and pant. He runs in silence as Hapoor thinks about his next plan of attack. Since he never got to finish Amari off in person, she's not pregnant. But it was her that visited him in the dream, letting him finish the deed.

A beautiful white fox comes out of the gates of Heaven's Light as they open up ahead. A few minutes later, she's running past Khnight with Amari on her back. Khnight skids to a halt and watches after her.

He breathes in the scents of the forest and searches for Amari's to make sure that it really was her. Who is he kidding? No one can leave Heaven's Light unless they'realive and just bound there like Amari and her family! Tiger lilies and vanilla hits Khnight's nose and soon the fox is right beside him, circling him with her and Amari's eyes on him. He watches her.

"Well, look what the dog dragged in," Amari drawls out with a sneer. Her eyes show a sliver of fear, but her demeanor is cool and calm. "Funny seeing you here, Hapoor. Were those wolves scouts? Just to hold us back a little so you could maybe catch up and follow?" She doesn't wait for an answer. "Clever move if I must say so myself. You're finally going to strike, aren't you?"

Khnight shakes his head in denial.

"Oh, don't deny it, Hapoor. You came to finish me off." Amari's vixen stops right in front of Khnight and blue eyes meet brown eyes. Amari shakes her head at him. "News flash, Hapoor." She leans in towards him, letting her breath tickle Khnight's nose. "I'm going to finish you off," she threatens lowly, making Khnight pull his ears back and growl at her, his lips curled back.

"And your wolf is going to be mine. To ride. And to claim."

Khnight snaps at Amari, barking and snapping his teeth at her. He lunges towards her, dropping Hapoor's bag. Her fox leaps out of the way with ease and shoves him in the shoulder. Khnight falls down to the ground and the pure white creature stands on his shoulder, growling at him as she keeps him pinned.

As much as Khnight wants those pups with Amari he won't put up with her attitude! Just like how Hapoor won't! Khnight looks up at the fox with a snarl, curling his top lip back. Amari peers around her.

"By the way," she starts. "This fox?" She shakes her head. "Not mine. She's Mack's. Remember her? She was a human with a rare gift. Giving life back to those who never got a chance at one. This fox is one of the first ones she brought back. Awesome thing is each one gets to come and go through Heaven's Light. It's quite remarkable. Don't kill her," Amari threatens lowly. "Or I will personally kill you myself."

The animal gets off of Khnight and Hapoor takes control, shifting back to himself and holding his bag in front of him as he begs for Amari to stop her attitude.

"Amari, for once, stop with the attitude and listen to me," he starts hurriedly. "It's urgent."

"Was it urgent when you raped me a few weeks ago?"

Hapoor winces. How is he supposed to answer that? "I…" He hangs his head. "I'm sorry. But my pack is without an alpha."

"What are you talking about?"

"My sons…" He looks up at her. "They were killed."

Realization hits Amari in the face. It looks like she starts conversing with someone, her eyes hazed.

"By Mavis."

Amari holds her one moment finger up and listens to someone as they mind link with her. If that's Raja somehow, Hapoor hopes she's telling the goddess of Hallam the whole entire story. The beautiful white fox shifts underneath her as she turns away from him. A few moments later she looks at him with remorse.

"Hapoor, I'm so sorry," she starts. "But it's no reason for you to rape me."

"If you can just give me a chance," Hapoor starts, getting cut off by Amari.

"I will think about reinstating you as the alpha of the Asgard Light Moon pack," Amari snaps. "But the rape will be on your head. You honestly think that it gave you the right to force an heir on me?" She glares at Hapoor with disgust. She truly hates him and he doesn't blame her.

"Heirs," he corrects her. He steps forward and sets his hand on the side of the fox's neck opposite from him as he gets close, standing at the front of her shoulder. "I need them, Mare."

Amari shakes her head. "You don't have the right to call me that!"

Hapoor lets his hand drop from the fox and he looks down. "I'm sorry," he says softly.

"At least you're finally being honest with me. How long have the rogues been working for you? And doing your dirty work?" She presses.

Hapoor looks up at her, his deep blue eyes meeting with her hazel brown ones. "I help them, M…" He stops himself. He lifts his chin as he keeps his eyes on her. "Amari. A few of my wolves in my pack have families with them, afraid to claim them as their mates. We know how bad it looks to the other packs and we don't want to be bullied by them since the rogues come from them. They're rejects from when they were omegas and fated to a higher class like an Alpha, Beta, or Delta."

Hapoor shakes his head. "I've been trying to make Hallam a better place for them, but it doesn't help they're constantly bullied."

Amari growls at the news and she turns her friend away from Heaven's Light. "I'll see what I can do." She urges the animal forward and that's when Khnight creeps into Hapoor's mind.

Do you think she bought it? Khnight sounds hopeful.

"I hope so," Hapoor responds, watching Amari race away. "Because it's the truth."

The world has been the harshest to us, Hapoor. It's amazing how you've stayed sane.

"You as well, Khnight. I don't know what I would do without you."

Die in a hole and let your whole entire pack go rogue.

Hapoor snorts. "Yeah, that's a little extreme for me. And you for that matter."

Let's get home. Maybe Zara will be waiting for us.

"I agree," Hapoor throws his black duffel bag into the air and lets Khnight catch it in a leap as he shifts. They race home to find their Beta and Gamma struggling to keep the wolves at bay.

Hapoor knows he has his work cut out for. This is going to be a long day. And some wolves have funerals of their loved ones fresh on their minds from all of Madison's recent attacks.

This is going to be tough.

∞

Hapoor looks at the papers on his desk, hovering over it with his hands flat on the top of it.

This can't be right.

Mavis dies a few years back and she leaves the Asgard Light Moon pack with nothing, making them look like they abused her, while Ada gets everything. But that's not the worst part!

Their rival pack is threatening to expose their secrets about their alliance with the rogues! Make them look like the bad guys that they're not! So, Hapoor made a mistake with Amari! And while he would do it again to get a few heirs out of her, he still thinks highly of her! He's attracted to her!

He wants his scent all over her to send a message to her husband and best friend. She's his! No one else's! Hapoor looks at his Beta.

"You're sure," he asks with hatred, his eyebrows furrowed towards the bridge of his nose.

"I couldn't make this up even if I wanted to," Zane says, drawing his first two words out. His light brown eyes show off his emotions. He feels betrayed. Alone. When he doesn't have a mate because his chosen was killed by Madison, he wants nothing to do with all of this right now. He wants to grieve.

Hapoor sighs and sags, letting out a breath that puffs out his chest. "Okay." He stands up straight. "Zane, I'm so sorry you had to deal with this. You deserve to grieve for your loss right now. Go. Take care of your kids."

Zane looks down at the polished floor. "It's not just that." He mumbles.

Hapoor slowly blinks. "What's going on?"

"I found my fated mate."

Hapoor blinks, again, uncertain if he wants his suspicions confirmed.

"She's the Beta of the Silver Lake pack." Zane meets Hapoor's blue gaze. "Our rival pack."

Hapoor growls in frustration. This isn't happening! Zane deserves better! "Please, tell me you rejected her."

"No." Zane looks back down at the floor. "I couldn't bring myself to do it. And neither could she."

"She's not mated to another, is she?"

"I'm afraid she is. Chosen mate. And I'm going through the pain of betrayal right now."

Hapoor slams his fist into the desk, making Zane wince from the sound of cracking knuckles. "She doesn't deserve you!" He snaps. "Sever your end! Now!"

At his cold hard order, Zane shivers from where he stands, looking at his former alpha. "Alpha?"

He points at his Beta threateningly. "If this is how she's going to treat you, you need to get rid of her." He growls.

"I… I can't."

"You can. I know you can. The pull is just too great right now for you to think clearly."

Zane's pained brown eyes search Hapoor's angry blue ones. "Hapoor, I'm…"

"Hurting." Hapoor finishes for him. "I know."

Zane sighs and relaxes, showing the betrayal is over. "I need you to end it for me. I can't lay a hand on her and I can't bring myself to sever my end."

Hapoor sets his jaw, closing his teeth together. He nods, ready to defend his Beta. Oh, it's going to happen. And it's not going to be pretty. Zara prods Hapoor's mind and he lets her in.

Hapoor, my love, Zara starts in the mind link. *I'm so sorry to be a bother.*

You're never a bother, my love, Hapoor starts. *Please. Tell me what's going on.*

I just got back from the doctor. And I'm afraid I have bad news. Fuck… Hapoor can't lose his second chance mate at a time like this! She's the love of his life!

I'm on my way. He starts for the door. "Take a break, Zane. Go mourn with your kids. They need you more than I do."

"Yes, Alpha," Zane puts in before Hapoor is out the door and meeting his wife in their bedroom.

He quickly gets in it, which is just a few strides from his office. When he turns around his wife and second chance mate gives him a welcoming hug. He wraps his arms around her and holds onto her.

"Zara," Hapoor says roughly. He breathes in her bluebell scent that gets to him every time, but it's mixed with a cancer smell. No… "Honey. No."

She looks up at him and her lips brush against his. "It's okay," she whispers. "We don't know how much longer I'm going to live."

Hapoor shakes his head in denial. "It can't be back. We got rid of it."

"I'm afraid it came back. With a vengeance."

"I was only gone for a few weeks. How can it be back so strong so soon?"

Zara shakes her head. "Doctor said it never left. He did a cat scan. They missed another lump while I was under surgery a few years ago."

Hapoor shakes his head and Zara caresses his face, her blue eyes filled with love.

"I prefer to spend my last moments with you, anyway," she says softly and sweetly.

Hapoor presses his lips against his wife's forehead, squeezing his eyes shut as a tear escapes his eye. He lost his family to Mavis. Now he has to lose the only thing he has left. He bets this is Mavis's doing! She cursed his mate to have bad health and killed his sons after she raped them!

Hapoor is lucky to be alive! Mavis tried to kill him when she raped him at the age of twelve, but he stabbed her with a pair of scissors then got away. He wishes he could go to Hell's Fire and make her pay for her crimes, torturing her and make her writhe in pain himself.

Madison's hellhounds and wyverns get to do that, instead.

"I prefer that, too," Hapoor finally manages out from his tight throat. He huffs, stifling his tears. "But I also prefer you not being succumbed to sickness. I want longer with you." Heartbreak envelopes Hapoor at the thought of losing his wife so soon.

She nods, her strong demeanor left down and letting Hapoor see how tired she really is. "Me too." She says in a weak tone. "Me too, babe."

Hapoor shakes his head. "He said you could go any day?"

Zara nods. "Yeah. It could be weeks. It could be months. Or it could be days. But either way… Hapoor, I want you to be here when I go."

"Of course, baby. I'm here. I won't leave your side. Astrid's got this. She can be in charge while I care for you."

Zara nods. "Thank you," she whispers softly.

He kisses her forehead then holds her close and tight, not wanting to leave their room and just stay here with her.

13

Amari sits on Vixen's back, her legs straddled across the fox's back as she stares at Allah.

She just caught him coming back from patrolling and looking for Hapoor. Well, she knows where he is!

But the questions is, does she dare tell her lycan king and husband that Hapoor found Heaven's Light?

As much as she trusts Allah and Viggo with her life, she's not sure she can trust them with the fact that the infamous rogue has found her. And wanting heirs since his sons were killed. Raja confirmed his claims to her. She saw it. All of it.

She even let Amari see it all. Mavis raped and killed Hapoor's sons, leaving him with no heirs. She knew Zara had cancer since the poor woman went to her doctor about the first lump. What Zara didn't know was she had a second lump that the doctors didn't catch. But Mavis did. She just never said a word, wanting Hapoor and his pack to crumble into nothing. They always treated Mavis well.

Amari is not going to let that pack cease to exist. They deserve a better life! But if she tells Allah and Viggo everything she knows, they might use the information against Hapoor. That's why Amari has got to leave some details out.

Allah walks over to her after getting a pair of jeans on and he looks up at her, past Vixen's head.

"What brings you here," Allah asks, seeming to be not very happy that he hasn't found a trace of his current enemy.

"I need to talk to you," Amari replies. "In your office."

"Are you sure you want to do it behind closed doors? Or…" He drawls the word 'Or' out, hitting on his best friend. "Let the lycans watch from the rooftop." He winks at her.

She laughs shortly. "Ha! Real funny, Allah." She swings her leg over Vixen and starts sliding down.

Allah catches her and pulls her into him with his hands on her hips, Vixen behind her and not giving her an escape route. Uh oh… "Look."

"Don't you dare," Amari warns, pointing up at him.

He takes a moment of consideration, but he continues anyway. "Look."

Amari snorts, crossing her arms in front of her chest.

"I need you to stop coming in on a white fox."

Amari searches his eyes to see a teasing, but serious side of him. She's seen this before. And it's always a hoot to watch it all unfold.

"Or my Beta and Gamma are going to tease me about having my queen coming in on a white fox. You have no idea how this looks for me."

"Vixen is my only ride at the moment. What do you expect me to do? Walk?"

"No," Allah says as he relaxes into Amari, looking to his right. "But you look pretty damn hot coming in on her." He looks at her. "And my pack has already started asking questions about it. Why my queen is riding in on a white fox with her family." He shrugs. "It looks bad for me."

"You should tell them your *'queen'* is none other my youngest daughter, Ramein." Amari air quotes *'queen'*.

"They're not gonna believe me," Allah says as he shakes his head.

"Well, then they got issues."

"You got issues. Loving two men at once."

"Oh, like it's a habit." Amari starts for the doors of Allah's castle, slipping out of his hold. Vixen lays down in the warm sun.

Allah follows Amari. "Well, you did love Mike and Garrett at the same time."

"Oh." Amari blew a raspberry at him, sticking her tongue out as she continues forward and keeps her eyes on the castle doors.

Allah opens the door for her and their eyes lock. "I'd close that pretty little mouth of yours if I were you. Or you're going to be in my bed." He seduces. He winks at her flirtatiously and Amari moans in teasing disgust.

She walks through the open doors. "You better hurry, then. Cause I got a man to get to so he can knock me up with Ada's baby."

Allah stops where he is as Amari continues to his office.

"Are you coming?"

"Yeah," Allah drawls out. He catches up to Amari as she walks up the stairs. He clears his throat. "Who wants a child with Ada? And why do you have her eggs, again, to begin with?"

"Well, you're having one with her since we didn't use protection the other day."

"Great," Allah drawls out lowly. "Just what I need. Who's the other lucky bastard?"

"Office. Now." Amari orders.

"Yes, ma'am," Allah says lowly. He hurries ahead and waits for her at the door of his personal space, his hand on the doorknob.

They keep eye contact and there's a teasing look in their eyes as they have a quiet conversation. As much as they love each other, they both know it's not going to happen, Allah and Amari making their final decisions. She chose Viggo, her god and husband. He chose Ramein, his fated mate and future wife.

But the god of were-kind and goddess of Hallam can't stop themselves from teasing each other in a harmless flirtatious way that only compliments the other. As Amari reaches Allah, he opens the door for her.

"Thank you," Amari drawls out as she walks in.

Allah smacks her ass and makes her stop, questioning his decision. He puts his lips to her ear. "You're welcome," he whispers in a teasing but seductive tone. He closes the door behind him and walks past her. "Now." He heads over to his desk and leans into the front of if with his silver-gray eyes on Amari. "Who's this lucky bastard that's going to have my ex-wife's child? It

better not be Marcus. I'll kill him if he's touched you."
Allah growls.

"No," Amari says, shaking her head. "I've talked
with Viggo about the plan. Ada and May came to help me
out the day after the events here. We were at my estate.
And we talked about Hapoor. Did you know Ada is his
daughter?"

"He had her when he was twelve years old. Mavis
raped him. Your husband told me." Allah confirms.

Amari nods. "Well, May and Ada gave me a few
of their eggs. We figured Hapoor would try, again. And
after talking with Raja in Heaven's Light I found out why.
You left his pack with no alpha."

Allah blinks in disbelief. "You gotta be kidding
me."

Amari shakes her head. "Mavis raped and killed
his sons. And his wife is on her death bed. He's losing
everything and it's driving him mad. He's wanting an heir
to his throne so he's raping me so that his baby is an
automatic alpha no matter its age if something happens to
him. He risked everything for an heir."

Allah winces. "And I just left his pack defenseless
without an alpha."

Amari shakes her head, her eyes on Allah. "His
pack doesn't know that. But the Moon packs do since
they were there at his demotion. Blue Moon and Red
Moon. Allah, Hapoor needs his title back as alpha, so the
Asgard Light Moon pack isn't defenseless."

"I can't just give it back to him," Allah snaps
slowly. "He raped you!" He motions his hand at the
woman that he's in love with.

"Yeah, well, I can. And I'm giving him the title back. With. Your. Permission."

"Fuck, no!"

Amari glares at Allah.

"Amari, I love you! And I'm not just gonna give you my permission to promote your rapist! It's absurd!"

"Look, I don't like it either," Amari snaps. "But that pack is defenseless without an alpha and they don't have *anyone* with alpha blood at the moment. He needs. To get. Promoted."

"Manny." Allah motions at Amari. "Your manservant, Manny. My nephew. He's got alpha blood. Royal. Blood. Give it to him. He even has an heir already."

Amari winces and Allah sets his hand back on his desk, his eyes on her.

"Please, Amari. I can't give Hapoor the alpha title of the Asgard Light Moon pack back after what he did to you!"

"Give it back to him or our alliance is gone. No more Ramein, Allah. And you're back to square one."

Allah winces. "You wouldn't."

Amari holds her hand up next to her head as if she's holding a piece of paper. She shifts the air to activate the contract that both she and Allah signed for the alliance, the contract coming to life by a flame of Heaven's Light. Allah watches in horror.

"What are you doing," he asks lowly.

"Destroying it," Amari replies. She takes the contract in both hands and Allah speaks up in a panic.

"Wai-wai-wai-wai-wai-wait!" He holds his hands up in caution. "Let's not do anything irrational."

Amari looks at him in disbelief. "I'm being rational." Her brown eyes bare into his gray eyes and she couldn't be more serious about the situation.

Allah shakes his head warningly. "Don't do it. Please."

"Then give him his title back. Once you do, I'll force myself on him and make him get me pregnant with one of his daughter's eggs. Get back at him for what he did to me."

"But he's always wanted you." Allah defends. "You and I know this. It's why you two fight like cats and dogs all the time. He feels sexual intention with you and you don't like it!"

Amari starts ripping the paper.

"Okay!" Allah stutters. He lurches forward and takes the parcel ripped at the top. His eyes meet Amari's in a glare. "I'll do it."

"Right now, please." Amari watches as she notices a shift in the air.

Allah creates a mind link that goes out to the packs he's a king of. It's hard to do for someone that's not of his status. But for him it's easy. Amari waits patiently and her daughter prods her with a mind link. She opens up to Emma right away.

Emma, sweetie, not now.

I know what you're doing, Mom. Emma replies. *And I'm proud of you for giving Hapoor his pack back. It means a lot to him. And me.*

Amari looks down at the floor. *Emma, you're still so young.*

But you should hear Hapoor rejoicing right now. He's able to celebrate with his wife before she goes.

Thank you, Emma.

You're welcome.

Now, get back to training. Amari orders. She cuts off the mind link before looking at Allah. Their eyes meet.

"It's done," he says lowly. "He's alpha, again."

Amari dips her head. "Thank you."

"Now." Allah walks around his desk and grabs the tape, starting to repair the contract.

Amari starts for him.

"What else did you need?"

Amari sneaks in right next to Allah, sitting on his desk and repairing the contract with her magic with a swipe of her hand over it. "You to spank me." She leans into him as she gets seductive. "Because I've been a naughty girl," she whispers.

He looks at her just in time for her to give him a wink. "Oh, you don't wanna tempt me," he moans, drawing out the first word.

"Good thing we're moving on, right?"

"Are we?"

"I have Viggo. And in twenty years you'll have Ramein."

"Fourteen. Years." Allah tries to correct Amari.

"Well, find an omega you can fuck with to help your urges for the next eighteen years. You're gonna need it." Amari seduces.

"I don't need an omega."

"Oh?" Amari raises an eyebrow at him.

"I have you." He looks at her lips before he moves in. His lips crash on hers.

She breathes in through her nose, taking in his blood orange scent. She knows she shouldn't, but he's the one that moved in. The kiss is filled with longing, but it doesn't last very long, Amari pulling away before it can turn into more. She rests her forehead on his.

"Allah," Amari whispers, wanting so much to do more with him, but not wanting to betray her husband. He deserves better.

"I love teasing you," Allah says lowly.

"Oh," Amari breathes before slapping Allah's arm, knowing why he said that.

He kissed her to get a reaction! Well, two can play at that game! "Ow!"

"You asked for it." Amari looks up at Allah as he pulls away from her.

"Seriously, though. Did you come for anything else?" Allah presses. He looks his second fated mate up and down, his eyes quickly roving over her.

Amari throws her bangs back with her head, her brown eyes on Allah's gray eyes. "Ramein will be five in two years. And she'll be old enough to start her training as your future luna. I only want the best."

"I know someone. I just got word she's cancer free after a miraculous and successful treatment."

"Don't tell me."

"Sunni. She gave my sister a full body massage and other treatments. She's going to live for another ten years or so. However old she wants to be."

Amari smiles at Allah. "I'm excited."

He rests his forehead on hers as he has a moment of weakness. "Me, too," he says softly.

Amari's eyes fall to Allah's lips. He pushes his rolling chair away to get in between her thighs, settling his hands on her hips as they have a tender moment.

"I'm still irrevocably in love with you," he whispers after a quiet moment. He shakes his head. "I know I shouldn't... I have Ramein. But... I love you, Mare. And I always will."

Amari lifts her chin and her lips brush against Allah's. "I feel the same way," she whispers into his mouth, wanting nothing more for him to know the truth.

He brushes his fingertips over her temple. "I just want you to know the effect that you still have on me." Tender with her, his eyes soften.

"Believe me, Allah," Amari says lowly. "If I could, I'd take you as my second husband. And be your luna."

Allah moans and kisses her. Their kiss is passionate and tender. Amari can taste brandy on his breath, knowing he's already been drinking.

"I just..." He says lowly into her lips. "Wanna resign. As your king and god."

"No!" Amari pulls back and looks up at him. "You can't, Allah. For the good of Hallam."

"Why?" His voice low and husky he couldn't be more irresistible, awakening Amari down there.

She runs her fingers through his hair. "Because no one is as good as you. And I need you. Here. Not in Hallam as my manstress."

"Yeah, but being your manstress is what I want right now, Amari. I'm never going to love Ramein the same as I love you."

Amari grabs Allah by the belt loops of his pants and thrusts him into her, making his body flush with hers. "You don't want me as your luna. I'd bug the crap out of you. Just ask my husband. He can vouch for me."

Allah snorts and smiles. "You'd be my bug." He flirts teasingly.

"On the wall. On the shelf." Amari starts to tease. "On your desk. At the dinner table." She continues.

"Oh, now you're getting technical," Allah says with a smile.

Amari nods. "And in bed."

"So, it'd be an everyday thing."

Amari feathers his lips with hers. "And an all-night thing."

He presses a soft, sweet, and tender kiss on her. "Your daughter will be no different from you," he says lowly into her lips.

"Way to turn me off." Amari retorts, the mood ruined.

"Well, let me get you going," Allah seduces. "Cause you're gonna need it for Hapoor."

Amari smiles into him. "Make me come, gorgeous," she seduces.

He moans into her mouth before slipping his hand into her yoga shorts. He rubs her clitoris in circles. She moans in pleasure as it sweeps over her and she rests her forehead on his shoulder as he gets her going.

14

Hapoor gets woken up in the middle of the night, making him reach for Zara.

But then he remembers.

She passed away just hours earlier, Hapoor only having a day with her. She withered away so fast the moment he came home. He misses her terribly.

All she did was lay down for a nap with him. When he awoke, he could no longer feel the mate bond. He can't think straight and he doesn't want to be with anyone right now. He just wants to be left alone.

Hapoor closes his eyes with a sigh, a tear trickling down. At least he was able to say goodbye and love his luna for just a few hours. Zara was so headstrong. She knew how to run a business and she was the perfect luna, taking a watchful eye on the pack. She only did what was good for them. Whenever her brother teased her, she would grab his hand and twist his fingers back. He loved her like a brother should.

Hapoor hated to be the barer of bad news earlier. He just couldn't do it. But his presence at his brother-in-law's place was enough. He knew right away, cussing and throwing furniture in the house. He broke windows. He screamed to cures the moon goddess and Hapoor couldn't help but empathize with him. He lost his sister to Madison when he sent her out to scout for Heaven's Light's location.

Hapoor still beats himself up for sending his sister to her death. So much of it… And for what? Madison shouldn't have a place in this world! All she does is bring pain to everyone here! What was Amari thinking?!

Zara's scent lingers on her side of the bed and Hapoor breathes it in, letting the smell of bluebells overtake him and send him into flashbacks. All the times he spent with his wife, not just the love making. But the nights they spent with their sons in bed while they told ghost stories. Hapoor seeing Zara on their wedding day, her black hair cascading down her back in curls with half of it pinned up. Her light-brown eyes dancing in the sunlight as she smiled her beautiful and contagious smile, lighting up anybody's day.

The colors of the zinnias and lilies in her bouquet against her white mermaid cut dress with a slit between her breasts that showed off some skin of her slim torso. Hapoor can see himself put the bluebell he found just for Zara in her hair, moments before their first kiss as husband and wife. Luna and Alpha.

Hapoor rolls onto his back and he's thrown back to the times Zara's skin was fair, kissed by the sun. She only tanned and never burned. He can see her in her favorite bright yellow bikini, laying out by the pool while she got her tan on. Her backside to him while he swam and snuck up on her to scare her.

Zara was very calm and down to earth, while she was also independent, stubborn, kind, and sweet. She's the type of woman you don't want to mess with. Another tear escapes Hapoor's eye as a woman straddles him.

He instantaneously opens his blue eyes, ready to throw his omega off. He knew she would come to cheer him up at one point. But he looks in the eyes of Amari instead. Well, it's good to know that Jennifer, the always horny omega, knows when to keep her distance.

But what is Amari doing here? And how did she find Hapoor? He growls up at her, warning her not to do anything funny. He's not in the mood for sex. He's grieving for crying out loud!

"Need a hand," Amari asks softly, her scent covered up. Did she do that so no one knew she was here? Or was she dreaming this?

"Amari, what the fuck are you doing here," Hapoor asks with a growl. He's not in the mood for her! He wants to mourn in peace!

Amari's hand trails up Hapoor's naked chest, her brown eyes on him. That's when her eyes light up, letting him know that she's actually here. Her arousal hits his nose and he's instantly disgusted by her motives.

"She just joined me," she says softly. "I went back to Heaven's Light after running some errands and convincing Allah to give you your alpha title back." So, it was her! She convinced Allah to give Hapoor his pack back!

He guesses he owes her after all.

"When I got back, there she was," Amari says lowly, drawing circles on Hapoor's chest. "Waiting to be greeted and welcomed into Heaven's Light. I guided her to your moon goddess myself. She's safe. And healthy. Zara wanted me to tell you that she misses you already."

"So, what are you doing here?"

Amari glides her hands up and she wraps her arms around his neck as she lowers herself on him. Her lips feather against his. "I'm here to cheer you up," she whispers seductively. "I know what it's like to lose to the love of your life."

Her soft brown eyes bare into his grieving blue eyes. She kisses him gently and he instantly shoves her off, rolling on top of her. He pins her hands above her head with his own, against the bed.

"Don't," Hapoor growls threateningly. He's not having it tonight!

"What?" Amari sounds offended. "Comfort you?"

"I feel no mate bond with you. And you have no power over me! Forget it!" Angry, Hapoor is ready to cast this bitch off of his property.

Amari wraps her thighs around Hapoor's legs as she opens up, thrusting his hips into her and letting him know that she intends to do it with him. "But what about your threat towards me. Hmm? Don't you want me to have your pups?"

"It's not just about my pups anymore," he threatens as he comes up with a new plan. He's still in mourning for his beloved luna and wife, but he's not off his game! This is his moment to choose a mate and he's taking it!

"I'm making you my luna once and for all," he growls, glaring at Amari. He shakes his head at her.

"You're mine. And you will demote Viggo and divorce him. I'm your god, now."

Amari lifts her head and shoulders off the bed, brushing her lips on Hapoor's. "Then claim me," she whispers, throwing him off. What did she just say?

He winces. He knows Amari! This isn't her! This is some trick! Some spell! Hapoor can only think of one witch that would do such a thing. And she's part lycan thanks to his lineage. He's part lycan! It's the most powerful gene in the were-kind! His sons had it! His daughter got the gene as well. His only daughter.

"What's wrong," Amari asks. Or should Hapoor say… Ada. Why would his own daughter bed him?! She's a lesbian! Not to mention her naked body is all wrong! There's something about it that's familiar.

Hapoor growls and it all starts to make sense. Amari has no idea where his pack house is, but two people that were once part of his pack do! He notices the necklace around her neck, knowing what it's for. He'd recognize that stone anywhere.

Hapoor thrusts it off of the woman's neck and he watches her appearance change, her golden-brown hair turning a shade darker and her brown eyes turning green. Of course! Ada's second chance mate! And Hapoor's first fated mate.

"May," Hapoor growls as the mate mark on her neck changes. "Who's doing is this? Yours?!"

May's eyes go wild as she realizes her plan is derailing fast.

"Answer me!" He shakes her. His first fated mate. Is underneath him. Hapoor's wolf wants to dominate her and remind her of the mate bond they once shared. His cock springs to action.

"Yes," May manages out in a stutter. She quickly gains her composure and her demeanor changes back to before. "I conversed with Ada. And she and I agreed that this would be a good plan. We just had to get Amari and Viggo onboard."

"And you thought it was going to work?!" His hand instantly wraps around her neck. He tightens his grip on her.

"It was a good plan. Until you saw right through it."

Hapoor holds Ada's necklace up by his head. "I know this necklace. It's a witch's pendant. My daughter's to be exact." He chucks it next to May's head, making her wince.

"Well." May says formally, knowing she can't argue with her once alpha way too well. "Now, that our plan has gone to Hell's Fire what are you going to do, now?"

"I'm having fun with you," Hapoor growls. His eyes go to May's mate mark. "Mate."

"No!" May drawls out as she screams.

Hapoor's mouth goes straight to her mate mark and he sinks his canines into it, changing it to his own. She screams and he covers her mouth with his hand. He gets to have his way with her once, again!

Hapoor swiftly pulls his cock out of its barrier and he thrusts it with guidance into May's wet opening. Having her at the same height as him, he gets to thrust into her while making out with her. He does just that.

Furious with her, Hapoor thrusts into May hard and fast, raping her as he puts his lips to hers. She screams into his lips, but she knows it's useless. The Asgard Light Moon pack's men love it when their women scream! It helps them their vengeance when they were raped as kids by their witch and survived!

May bites Hapoor's bottom lip and draws blood. He thrusts into her harder, making the headboard bang against the wall. May throws her head back as she screams and begs for this to stop. It drives Hapoor to rail into her, her screams and begging making his primal instincts kick in. Her tightness envelopes around as he grows inside of her. Her body takes him in, accepting him as her chosen mate. His hands hold onto her hips and he thrusts them into his own, pumping into her.

Mays screams of begging for a release from this turn into panting screams of pleasure, her spot seeming to be getting hit with every movement. Her arms wrap around Hapoor's torso and her hands lay flat on his shoulder blades. He doesn't let up. He continues to have his way with his first fated mate. While she will be his breeding machine Amari will be his luna. *She* will be the one to give him his first heirs! May is just a backup!

Hapoor can see it, now. His wedding with Amari. She will be dressed in a slim off-white dress, her belly showing through it to show everyone Hapoor's new heir. Amari's golden-brown hair will be curled and the done the same way Zara had her hair done for their wedding. Amari's makeup will be done to show off her eyes and mate mark made by Hapoor. She won't have any trace of Viggo, who will be demoted. She will live with Hapoor.

He can see all their pups around her as they grow up, continuing to pump into May with all his strength. A baby is in Amari's arms every time. Hapoor gets lost in his thoughts as he continues to have his way with May, deep inside of her with every thrust. Her tightness gets tighter with every movement. Is he going to get stuck?

Hapoor drives May to her ecstasy as she digs her nails into his shoulders and chokes on an intense orgasm. He spills his seed inside of her, but continues to thrust into her until he's pleased with the outcome and he's run dry.

∞

Amari uses a makeup brush for foundation to lightly apply some to May's bruised neck and face, who is shaking uncontrollably.

She was raped for the first time and she's taking it much harder than Amari did with her rape. Why? May never thought Hapoor could be so cruel. She may have begged Hapoor to thrust into her harder. But she didn't expect him to enjoy it so much and backhand her when she challenged him with the question.

Is that all you got?

Amari can't believe May is so daring. But it is May. She pushes people to their limits and she wasn't going to pass it up with Hapoor. She's pregnant with his pup for sure. There's no doubt. But when everyone finds out that Hapoor got her pregnant, there won't an immediate heir to take his spot when he dies.

He *will* die. He's not getting away with this. Amari made a mistake. She should've agreed to Allah's suggestion and made Manny alpha of the Asgard Light Moon pack. It's not too late. All Amari has to do is kill Hapoor.

She can promote Manny after that. Another idea hits Amari, but she dismisses it. That idea is stupid. And it wouldn't work anyway. The baby wouldn't have a choice either way.

But it works, Raja puts in.

Amari continues to pain May's face with makeup as she converses with her best friend. *Raja?*

Manny can train the baby, Amari. Think about it! Raja sounds too excited.

I'm not having Allah's child. It'll be too weird. My daughter is his second chance mate!

You're already having sex with him! Raja retorts.

And I don't see you stopping me! Raja. It's not going to happen. End of story. Amari puts the foundation brush down. *Besides. I prefer to have my husband's kids.*

You can't with Hapoor still out there. And while you're fertile right now he's not going to be on his best behavior with you.

Oh, like how I was the other night? And what about May last night? Was she fertile then? Amari challenges her companion.

Raja sighs in her mind. *Yes. And yes.*

Amari slips and drops the eyeshadow, making it go all over the place. "Fuck," she says lowly. She bends over to grab the case and what's left inside. *How can I be on my period, again, already?*

You haven't had a normal cycle in quite some time, Amari. You bleed more than normal.

Since when?

Since you've had covid seven years ago.

This time Amari drops the eyeshadow in her hand on purpose, realization hitting her. She moans and puts her face in her hand.

"What's wrong," Ada asks as she rubs her second chance mate's shoulders to try and relax her.

"Oh… just… my animal." Amari looks at Ada. "I have a creature I talk to in my mind."

"Raja."

Amari blinks, in shock. Ada shrugs, looking at the first woman she's ever loved.

"It only makes sense."

"How did you…?"

"Emma let it slip that Raja isn't in Heaven's Light. I figured she blessed you with her spirit to talk to."

Amari nods her head. "Just don't tell anyone. Please."

"Of course."

Amari bends over and grabs the empty case. She throws it in the trash then starts cleaning up her mess, bent down with a rag.

"So, what's Raja saying," Ada asks.

"Oh," Amari starts. "Just how irregular my periods are anymore."

"Talk about it," May says lowly. "Ever since I had covid a few years ago I have periods that last for a month! And then I don't have another until a few months later. It's so weird."

"May, have you gone to the doctor for that?" Amari stands up.

"No. Maybe I should've mentioned it while I was there getting a rape kit done earlier."

"It's okay. What's done is done." Amari shakes the rag over the garbage can then throws it in the dirty hamper.

"Which speaking of."

"May, don't." Amari looks over at her. "Don't do that to yourself. Trust me. I did the same thing."

"It's just the things he said."

"Well, Ada remarked you and the doctor gave you the morning after pill so you don't get pregnant."

"He's going to try, again."

"And I'll be prepared for it. I'm going to him."

"Mare." May trails off. "He's cold. And brutal, now. Zara is… gone. In Heaven's Light."

Amari grabs a new case of red eyeshadow and she starts for her mistress's mate. "I've dealt with cold and brutal before. Allah was… all over the place when Selena passed."

"I remember," Ada mumbles. "I was young. Just a teenager. But the way he was with his Beta that one day." Ada voices her shudder of fear. "It's part of the reason why I feel safer with women."

"You're lucky I'm on your side," Amari says lowly. She starts doing May's eyeshadow and her breath tickles the werewolf's eyelashes. "When someone hurts somebody that I love…" She shakes her head. "You don't wanna get in the crossfire. I will kill your ass with no regrets."

Ada snorts and giggles. "I've seen you do that before," she says softly. "Well… sort of."

Amari looks up at her mistress. "When?"

Ada shrugs. "I was probably like… Ten years old." She continues to rub her mate's shoulders. "But in a dream of yours I was walking by when you were protecting Garrett from a werewolf that threatened to end his life. You yeeted a poor cat that was just crossing the street it wailed in surprise as it flew high."

May burst out laughing.

"Oh my gosh," Amari drawls out, putting her hand to her mouth in horror. "Is it okay?"

Ada nods. "Saphira caught her mid-flight and kept her from becoming a squashed pumpkin."

"I'm so glad she was there."

"You're lucky your air fairy has wings."

"Of an angel," Amari says enthusiastically, batting her eyelashes. She gets back to doing May's makeup.

"Anyhoo." Ada trails off. "I'm sorry you're having bad periods."

Amari grunts in disgust. "I got I-U-D removed quite a while back and I haven't bothered to get another. It didn't help me with my periods so why get another. Y'know?"

"I couldn't agree more."

"How irregular are your periods," May asks. "As bad as mine?"

You have more days where you're fertile, Mare, Raja says in Amari's mind. *And periods that last even longer.*

Amari finds herself repeating Raja. "More like I'm fertile for much longer and my periods last longer than before."

"No wonder you've been able to have kids whenever you want," Ada says. "And why Allah got you pregnant."

Amari grunts in disgust, again. "Don't remind me."

"What are you ladies talking about," Viggo asks as he walks into the room. He stops when he sees the state May is in. "May, who did this to you?"

"Hapoor," May replies. She opens her eyes and Amari moves onto her hair. "He was rougher with me than planned."

"What happened?" Viggo gets protective right away, even though May isn't much of a friend and more of an acquaintance.

"I got raped. What was supposed to be a rape on him wound up turning around after he noticed the necklace and thrust it off me. I'm sorry, Viggo."

"Don't say it," he threatens lowly.

"But I'm afraid Amari is going to have to go in and get pregnant after all."

Viggo growls as Raja speaks up. *Amari, Ada's baby! What do you mean,* Amari asks.

It's Allah's! And technically it was in you! You could say it's yours, but you couldn't carry with Clayton so young! Raja suggests. *Our people would buy that!*

Amari shakes her head. *Yeah, but everyone would know it's not mine once they see it has Ada's traits instead of mine. What was once a fool proof plan isn't so fool proof, now.*

Raja sighs. *You're right.* Her tail lashes in disappointment.

"Amari," Viggo snaps, bringing his wife out of it.

"Sorry, what?" She looks at him.

"Can we talk? In private, please?"

Amari nods. She lets her hand gently land on May's shoulder reassuringly before she pulls away and follows her husband to her office. He doesn't come with her to Hallam very often, staying in Heaven's Light with Clay anymore while Amari has her meetings with Madi alone and lets Ramein and Emma play with the maids' and manservants' kids and Madi's son.

But this time it's different.

Amari left Viggo with the kids once she got the news May was brutally raped and didn't plan on meeting her husband here. He holds the door to her office open for her before following her in, closing the door behind him.

"Raja hasn't given you any of these ideas, has she? Agreeing with May and Ada's plan? Coming up with alternatives if it doesn't work?" Viggo presses.

Raja growls in Amari's head as she winces from his question, dumbstruck. *How can he think that?! He knows me!*

Yeah, but Raja you've been awfully quiet. Do you care to share why? Amari presses. She looks up at her husband and their brown eyes meet, getting no answer from her companion.

"No," she replies. "It's all them and me. Raja's been awful quiet and only coming to the surface when she feels it's necessary."

Viggo sighs and sags. He takes Amari's hands in his as he keeps eye contact with her. "Please, don't go through with this," he says lowly. "I can't stand the

thought of Hapoor touching you." He seems genuine…
Protective.

Amari gets on her tiptoes and kisses him lovingly.
"Don't worry," she says lowly. "He'll be tied up. And
dead by the time I'm finished with him."

Viggo searches Amari's eyes. "I'd feel better if it
came from Allah."

It was Amari's turn to search his eyes, this time in
confusion. "What do you mean?"

"I know you need an alpha for the Asgard Light
Moon pack. And as much as I'd prefer my son to be that
alpha, he's meant for somewhere else. Somewhere
greater."

"Thank you for supporting that idea," Amari says
softly. "But I think that's what we'll do."

"Get pregnant, Mare," Viggo says lowly with a
growl, making Amari wince.

She pulls her head back. "What?"

"You still have Ada's and May's eggs. Get
pregnant. With Allah's child. And carry. It's the only
way."

"I'm not doing that to you," Amari says a little
too softly, stepping into Viggo's firm body. She holds the
back of his neck.

"But you already are."

Amari furrows her eyebrows in confusion. "What
are you talking about?"

"Amari, with our mark I feel everything. I know
when you're doing it with Ada. And I know the last two
times you've had sex it was with Allah." Viggo shakes his
head. "Not her. She never went with you."

Amari wildly searches Viggo's brown eyes in dumbstruck disbelief. He's been putting on an act this whole entire time?! Why didn't he just tell her right away?! She would've stopped having sex with her mistress!

"I know I'm your last choice," Viggo mumbles.

"No." Amari shakes her head. "Viggo, you're not."

"Amari, if I let Allah speak up at your coronation six years ago, he would have you right now," Viggo says firmly. "Not me." He searches Amari's eyes. "And none of this would be happening. I know this."

"Viggo, don't do that to yourself."

"I wanted you to choose for yourself, Amari. Not me." Viggo searches Amari's eyes lovingly. "I didn't want you to be persuaded by anyone. Especially Allah. He was never a potential suitor and I saw your mate marks. So, did Klauss. He and I both knew we couldn't let Allah speak up so he took his place as a potential suitor. He held Allah back as best he could without causing a scene."

Amari gets happily frantic hearing this news. Viggo truly wanted her to be happy! She was right to choose him! And she's so glad she did!

"Just please tell me you'll let Allah get you pregnant and claim it as your own to the world. I don't want another man touching you. But I know I can trust him to treat you well."

"Viggo, I…"

"Just let it be the last time you have sex with him," Viggo says softly, almost in a whisper, as he trails his fingertips down Amari's face, tracing her golden-brown bangs. "And I want you to be done with him. Romantically. It's all I ask."

Amari searches Viggo's sad chocolate brown eyes. "I can't betray you like that, Vi. I don't have it in me."

"You didn't have a problem with it the other day," Viggo says lowly.

"The conversation got heated."

Viggo glares at Amari. "And yesterday? Your little visit to him got heated then, too?"

Amari shakes her head. "No. You couldn't be farther from the truth!"

"Then why did I feel the pains, Amari?!" Viggo snaps. "I felt them clear as day! You were fucking him! And loving him!" He shakes his head at her. "Just get pregnant with his baby and be done with it! Please! I don't want you involved with him romantically, anymore!"

"Viggo, it's hard to get over a man overnight. It's impossible."

Viggo takes Amari's hands off of him, stepping out of her reach as he glares at her with betrayal. Betrayal that runs deeper than veins. "You're in love with him?" He breathes, sounding heartbroken.

"It's my only downfall, Viggo. I swear. I was in love with Mike and Garrett at the same time. And now I'm in love with you and Allah. I'm so sorry." Amari's heart is hit with a pang of guilt as a hammer drives a nail into it. She doesn't like this conversation... She doesn't *want* to have this conversation!

"How can you do this to me?" Viggo glares at Amari in silence for a moment, his lips parted. "No. Let me rephrase that. How can you fall in love with a man like *him*? After six years!"

"I've been in love with him the whole entire time!"

"You and I have three kids together, Amari! Three!"

Amari jumps, flinching at Viggo's harsh tone.

"Kids! And I'm wanting more kids with you!" He sounds heartbroken and she's not sure how to tread around this. But she does the best she can.

"Viggo." Amari takes a step towards the love of her life, but he holds his hand up, making her stop in her tracks. Her heart breaks\at the sight of his in his eyes. She wants to fix it and move on from this. "I want more kids with you as well. It's you, Viggo. Yes. I'm in love with Allah. But not as much as I'm in love with *you*. It's *you* that I wanna have kids with! It's *you* that I feel safest with! It's *you*. Viggo. And it has been for six. Year. And it always will be you."

"Yeah," Viggo says softly. "Ever since Garrett died." He shakes his head at Amari, disgusted and heart-broken. "He should've found a way to somehow survive." Viggo turns his back to Amari and starts for the door.

"Viggo, no!" Amari takes a step towards him, but she has no idea how she can fix it from here. "Don't go," she pleads. "Please… Don't leave me. Or our kids. We love you." Her throat starts to tighten as tears threaten to fall down her face. She can't lose him! She's in love with him!

He's the best thing that ever happened to her! He's shown her what true love really is! She feels it with him! She'll *always* have true love for him! No one compares to him at all! Not even close!

Viggo stops with his hand on the doorknob and looks back at Amari over his shoulder. "It Garrett lived and it was me that got killed. Would you have loved Allah, then, too?"

"Yes." Amari hesitates. "Because he was more than a mentor to me and I was in denial of my feelings for him to quite some time."

"And who would you have chosen at your coronation?"

Tears form in Amari's eyes as she thinks about, looking down.

"That's what I thought," Viggo growls. He opens the door to leave.

"You," Amari puts in as she looks at him, stopping him from walking out. She shakes her head as she comes to a realization. As much as she loved Garrett and would have loved to have him by her side, she wouldn't be able to stand to lose him as her commander. She's still trying to get used to Adam as her new commander! And he's gone more than Garrett was!

Viggo looks back at Amari. "But I would've been dead."

"Viggo, let's be honest. No magic works on you."

"A titan spiritwalker is what killed Garrett." Viggo turns around and faces Amari. "That would've been my death as well. We both know it."

"And we also both know that you put up a hell of a fight. You've outsmarted a titan spiritwalker plenty of times before. To the point it looked like it committed suicide."

"This time it would've been different," Viggo says lowly. "I wouldn't make it out alive with a second one and you know it," he growls with a snarl, curling back his lip.

It kills Amari to see him like this, but she lifts her chin and keeps eye contact with the love of her life. The man that she will choose over and over, again. "And I would've brought you back like you did me. With Sunni's help, of course. She knows you were meant to be husband and god. And once Garrett passed away from old age or sickness, I would've chosen you anyway."

"Then why." Viggo snaps, slamming the door behind him as he stalks towards her. "Are you in love with Allah?" He truly looks heartbroken and Amari wants to fix that more than anything.

She gets on her tiptoes and feathers her lips on his, holding the back of his neck. She lets her brown eyes settle on his. "Because he let me in the end," he whispers. She shakes her head. "And I wanna forget that I ever loved him. I had a choice. Yes. At my coronation. And I chose you. For more than one reason. I'll *always* choose you. Remember that."

Viggo's eyes race side to side, searching Amari's for a reason not to give up. "Then why? Why me?"

Amari lets her fingers run through Viggo's short hair that's he's grown out a little and she scratches the back of his head reassuringly. "Because I didn't just make a promise to Garrett. I made a promise to myself." She searches his eyes for a way in, lovingly. "That I would only choose what's best for me. And Hallam. I'm not gonna lie. I kept the best for Hallam in mind as well. But I thought about it on my way to you. Where Washington is in Homba. About what would be best for me. And even though Garrett is the one I loved first. You'll always be my first choice, Viggo," Amari says softly.

He searches her eyes wildly and tears form in his for the first time in the time she's known him. She firmly grips the back of his neck reassuringly.

"I'll always. Want. You. *Need.* You. And yearn. For. You." Amari shakes her head and lets her eyes flicker from Viggo's eyes, to his lips, and back up to his eyes, again. "I'm madly, irrevocably, and truly in love with you. Just think of Allah as a manstress that I intend to give up. Very soon."

Viggo takes a deep breath before crashing lips on Amari's in a brief, strong kiss. His arms wrap around her torso and she finds her feet off the ground as he holds onto her tightly. She buries her face in his chest and holds onto him in a hug, her arms wrapped around his torso. Her hands on his shoulders.

"I love you," Amari says softly as she presses her lips into the front of Viggo's shoulder. "Forever and always. Until the end of time. I will always follow you no matter where you go." Quoting her vows, she remembers them word for word.

Viggo quotes them with her, adding that low husky tone to her soft loving one. He sighs and his hands fall down her back as he relaxes.

"No more sex with others, Mare," Viggo says roughly after a moment of silence. "Please. It hurts."

"It'll be hard to give Ada up, but I'll do my best," Amari says softly, adding the but before she can get a growl of warning from her beloved husband.

"Thank you," he says lowly and roughly, his chin on her shoulder.

"We need a new plan," she adds softly.

"One that we can both agree on."

"There's always Manny. He can take Hapoor's place once the traitor is killed."

"The men of that whole pack were raped by Mavis. While they deserve the best, Manny deserves better."

Amari nods before she sets her chin against the front of Viggo's shoulder, looking over it. "Well, we need someone else to take over it. And it's not like Allah's child can take over it once it's born."

"Wait… Allah's having a…"

Amari nods, against. "He fertilized one of Ada's eggs in me. I gave it back to her, but she's not very happy that I did."

"Amari," Viggo starts in a matter-of-fact tone.

"What?"

"Ada. She has alpha blood in her veins thanks to Hapoor. The Asgard Light Moon pack is practically hers when he goes. Kill or demote him and it automatically goes to her."

"But she was trained to be a luna. Not an alpha."

"Same diff."

Amari shakes her head. "No, it's not. Lunas take different responsibilities. They look after the finances, bookings, and the pack while the alphas smooth things over with rivalries, watch the borders, and stop wars from breaking out."

"Good thing I know how to do those things," Ada says at the door. "Thanks to Manny."

Amari looks at her over her husband's shoulder to see Ada leaning into the doorway with her arms folded across her chest. "Do you wanna take your father's spot in the Asgard Light Moon pack," Amari asks slowly.

Ada's blue-green eyes sparkle mischievously as a smile plays at her lips. "That's a better plan than before."

"Just think of it this way. You're about to have an heir in nine months."

Ada smiles evilly. "Thank you, Allah." She seduces.

Viggo growls warningly and Ada throws her hands up as her eyes meet with his, Viggo turning around to face her.

"Sorry, your Eminence. It won't happen, again. I promise."

"Good." Viggo stands in front of Amari protectively and she can tell he wants her all to himself. "Let's talk strategy."

Ada nods. "I know someone that Hapoor fell in love with years ago. When they were just kids. She'll be of good use to us." She shrugs. "It would also be nice for her kind and mine to have an alliance."

"You better give me her name before I decide not to promote you as the new alpha," Viggo warns.

Ada smiles. "You better call Ambroz. Cause you're going in the ocean."

Amari's heart sinks to the floor at the news. Fuck. She hast to go to the one place she has an intense fear of. Great…

15

Allah looks up from his desk as a few knocks sound from the door and it opens, revealing Amari and Ramein with Viggo holding his and Amari's son behind her.

Where's Emma? Is she with Lillian in Homba, again? Allah wasn't planning on any visitors today, but he's grateful to see Ramein. As much as he's in love with Amari, he knows he'll never have her. She made her choice. And all he can do is respect it.

Amari and Viggo walk into his office with their two youngest children and Allah walks around his desk, his eyes on Amari. She looks like she just got the talk from Viggo, staying close to him her nose red and her facial expression dull. Allah knows Amari has allergies and it can explain her nose being red since her eyes are shining with love every time she looks at her husband.

But her facial expression shows she had *the* conversation with him. That means Allah and Amari are done for good. His heart breaks at the thought of letting his best friend go. But it seems she's sticking with her choice.

Ramein runs over to Allah and he bends down to pick her up. He takes her in his arms and rubs his nose on her cheek, finding comfort in his future luna already. She provides it well.

"Are you being good for your parents," Allah asks Ramein in a low tone.

"When am I ever bad," Ramein replies, throwing her little arms around Allah's neck.

He chuckles. "When you're having a bad day."

Ramein shakes her head. "I've been good."

Amari talks softly to Viggo and Allah focuses on their conversation, heightening his hearing. But before he can hear what they're saying Ramein cuts in, sounding louder and making him wince at the pain that hits his ears.

"Mom wants me to play with your sister's grandkids."

Allah lets his hearing go back to normal and gives his attention to the little person.

"Are they here?"

"No. But my Beta and Delta have grandkids that are your age and they're going to be here in just a little bit."

Ramein nods. "Okay." She looks at her parents. "Can I stay in here and play with Allah," she asks them in her sweet, innocent voice.

Amari looks at her lovingly. "No. We gotta talk business. I'm sorry, sweetie."

"But there's no one else for me to play with!"

"I just saw Marcus with his grandkids. Have an omega take you to them, please." Amari looks at Allah. "Can you please mind link with him and Tali to come up, please? We need to have an important conversation that involves them and the rest of your lycans."

Allah nods as he puts Ramein down. *Marcus. Tali.* He starts in a mind link. *Amari and Viggo need to speak with us. My guess is it's about Hapoor and the war he's trying to cause.*

On our way, Marcus responds.

Allah closes the mind link with his Beta and Delta and Ramein walks out of the office, taking the hand of Allah's new omega he took in after the war with Kera was over. She's a lycan that no one knew about, her lineage in question. She smells like Allah's mother and has the battle tactics of a warrior. But she asked to be an omega and no more.

Allah wonders if maybe she's the illegitimate child of Allah's mother and the manservant she slept with before his father came along.

"Allah," Amari says, bringing him out of his trance and back to the present.

He looks at her.

"Are you okay?" She sounds sincere.

"Yeah." He walks over to the couch opposite of the one Amari and Viggo are sitting on with their son sitting in front of them on the floor. Allah sits down and looks at them. "Is there a new development with Hapoor?"

Amari looks up at Viggo and their brown eyes meet. They look at Allah. "We made some discoveries. And made a new plan."

"What about the other…?"

Viggo growls in response and Allah looks at him. Oh, he had the talk with her.

"Plan," Allah backs off. "Sorry," he says lowly as he gets a death glare from the god of Hallam.

Marcus and Tali walk into his office and close the door behind them. Marcus joins Alah on the other end of the couch and Tali sits in the chair on their right.

"What's going on," Tali asks, her black slim business dress hugging her slim body and hips.

Amari looks at her. "May got raped last night. By Hapoor."

Growls echo in the room and it takes a moment for everyone to calm down. Nervous that Hapoor saw right through the plan, Allah sets his jaw and leans forward.

"That's impossible," Tali puts in with a growl. "The plan was fool proof."

Amari shakes her head. "I'm afraid not," she says lowly. "I had a feeling it wouldn't go as planned."

"So, what do you suggest we do? We can't just have you sleep with Hapoor, now! He'll know it won't be your child!"

Amari nods. "He and everybody else would suspect the worst. What with Ada pregnant with Allah's child and May taking the morning after pill."

Allah winces. He didn't share that piece of information with his Beta and Delta.

"Woah, woah, woah, wait," Marcus puts in. He leans forward, his eyes on Amari. "Ada's pregnant?"

Amari nods.

"How's that possible? She won't let a man near her!"

"Well, when a woman is born with the rare gene," Amari starts, trailing off.

Allah feels his Beta's eyes on him. "You slept with Amari, again?"

"Well," Allah starts, trying to defend himself.

"That's not important," Amari snaps, cutting in before the conversation can veer the opposite direction. "With Ada pregnant, May on the morning pill, and a few of their eggs are inside my ovaries Hallam is going to know the child isn't actually mine."

Marcus looks at Amari. "I hate to ask this… But is May…"

"She'll be fine. I know you worry about her, Marcus. She's your sister."

"I wish she'd come home."

"She felt as though I needed a couple lycans in my estate. And it's been great."

"I didn't even know she was bi until it was too late."

"It happens."

"So, what's the plan?" Tali cuts in. "I mean… We can't honestly wait for Hapoor to attack with his new alliance with the rogues."

"It's not a new alliance." Amari looks at Tali.

"What do you mean?"

"Hapoor found Heaven's Light."

Allah, Marcus, Tali, and Viggo all growl at the news. This isn't good. When did that happen!

"The night he raped me. On our way women Vixen sent scouts to follow us and hold us back so he could catch up. Luckily, Madi came and killed one. One she let go after discovering the rogue was pregnant and she just broke the leg on another."

"She kills way too much," Tali snaps. "Why did you make her goddess of Hell's Fire?"

"Because that's what the god and goddess of Hell's Fire do." Amari snaps. "Think about it. My grandfather didn't want Madi to be the goddess of Hallam He wanted her to the goddess of Hell's Fire, so he gave her dreams where she kills. Keep the population at bay."

"She killed all the lieuts!"

"She had no idea what she was doing at the time. But, please, let me tell you what I know."

"Yes," Allah puts in. He leans back in the couch. "Tali, Marcus. Let Amari finish. I have a feeling she's getting somewhere."

"Sorry," Tali whispers. She soothes out her dress then leans back in her chair. "Please, Goddess Amari. Continue."

"So, outside of Heaven's Light Hapoor told me he's always helped the rogues. Some of his pack have families with them and are just afraid to let them in since they're rejects from other packs."

"So, he has a soft side," Marcus puts in. "Big deal. The issue is he has them working for him."

Amari nods. "That's where Ada comes in."

"Ada… What does she got to do with this?"

"She's Hapoor's daughter."

Marcus slowly leans forward, cautious at the news. "That's impossible," he says lowly. "He had to be twelve to have her!"

Amari nods, again. "Mavis raped him at that age and got pregnant with Ada."

"More like she raped him when he was eleven."

Amari shakes her head. "Whatever." She dismisses the comment with a wave of her hand. "But the point is, Ada can get the Asgard Light Moon pack back under control. She's the rightful heir to it thanks to him. Mavis raped and killed his sons and recently his luna Zara just passed away from ovarian cancer. Doctors removed a lump when she had breast cancer a few years ago."

"Oh, my gods," Tali breathes softly.

"They didn't anticipate for there to be a second lump. Mavis found it but didn't say anything. That second lump was near Zara's ovaries."

"When did she," Marcus starts, feeling guilty for not staying in the loop with the pack that his sister was supposed to marry into after she met Hapoor at a high council meeting.

Allah marked May so she couldn't leave. Marcus asked him to find a way to keep her from going to a brutal pack that likes to rape their women, not wanting her to fall to that fate.

"Just yesterday. It was a short reunion between Hapoor and Zara. So, he's grief stricken. When he discovered that May was me last night… He turned it around and raped your poor sister." Amari says with empathy, getting a growl from Marcus. She knows first-hand how brutal Hapoor and his pack are. She fought with him many times over it and then he raped her here in Allah's kingdom just a few weeks ago.

She's lucky he didn't get her pregnant. "Ada has alpha blood thanks to him. And she's his first-born. Allah can demote him, but he's not going to go without a fight." Amari looks at Viggo, who gives her a nod. "So, we decided to Ada and May fight their way into the pack and change it. All the men that are raping their women… Will either be killed, put in Hell's Fire prison, or cast out as rogues.

They get to choose their destiny. Of course, they're all going to put up a fight. So, we need all the help we can get."

Marcus nods.

"Count me in," Tali puts in, leaning forward. "My wolf is itching to teach that pack a lesson."

"Same," Marcus puts in. "And we have warriors here that have a personal agenda on that pack. Their sisters or wives were once victims. Heck, we can even have a couple of omegas we've caught training with Lillian to better their battle skills because they were victims of the pack."

Amari nods. "The Silver Lake pack took in a few of those women. I'm sure they'd be willing to help as well."

Marcus smiles. "They'll be surrounded," he sneers with pride.

"You can count on me, Mare," Allah says softly, leaning forward. Gray eyes meet brown eyes. "I'll be there to fight right by your side."

Amari nods and Viggo gives Allah a warning glare. He leans forward.

"We want to think of every possible outcome," he puts in lowly. "We don't want any room for error. You attack and it doesn't go as planned the first time, revert to the next tactic right away. Don't try the same thing over and over. They'll pick up on what you're trying to do and they'll come up with another plan."

Marcus nods as Allah looks down at the floor. He peeks through his lashes at Amari as he asks her the question through his eyes. Something's up with Viggo.

Amari gives Allah a small nod. Great… Viggo's been acting this whole entire time! Of course, he feels the pain! What was Allah thinking?!

"Let's figure out what we wanna do," Tali puts in. "And when."

∞

Amari walks into the bedroom after a successful day. It felt good to do business alongside Viggo. She needs to include him more.

He's really a good asset in the meetings. He was very professional with Allah and kept it that way. He didn't let his personal problems with the lycan king get in the way. Even though Viggo has respect for him, Amari knows he would like to kill the man for touching her. That's what turns her on the most.

Viggo knows when to be professional and when it's okay to go after someone. He's perfect and Amari doesn't deserve him. She knows she's about to lose Ada as her mistress. Allah, Marcus, and Tali all agree she should be the alpha of the Asgard Light Moon pack. She's got what it takes and has May to be her luna.

Right where May should be.

Amari walks over to the closet as she gets rid of her black ankle boots, a slit on either side of them to show off her ankles. She puts them in their cubby then takes her pearl earrings out, puts them in a little case that was once for soap, and replaces them with little diamond earrings.

Viggo follows her in and takes his tribal belt off. He never leaves without it. The buckle has the earth dragon and fire dragon circling around the buckle, chasing each other's tail. Their four sets of claws are tucked into them to show peace towards each other, while they circle around the emerald gemstone that's in the middle.

The stone shines brightly. But the moment it's hung up the light dies down.

"That was successful," Viggo says lowly, untucking his shirt from his pants.

"Yes," Amari says lowly, watching her beloved husband as he starts taking his clothes off. "It was."

He takes his shirt off and the three scars that start at the top of his neck from the side trail down it and to the front of his chest, stopping just above his rib cage. His well-toned body compliments his role as the god of Hallam. His twelve-pack abs are nicely toned and show how he stays in shape.

Whenever he's not wrestling sea creatures or dragons, he's doing sit-ups and push-ups to keep him so in shape. Amari gets lost in watching her husband's biceps bulge with just the simple act of hanging his shirt up that she doesn't hear his question. She'll never get tired of looking at him.

Viggo walks over to Amari and brushes her bangs back, tucking them behind her ear and letting his fingertips feather against her temple.

"Hey," he whispers. "You with me?"

Amari shakes her head, pulling herself out of her lustful trance. "Yeah," she says softly. "Sorry." She looks up at him and he wipes the corner of her mouth. "Were you saying something?"

"Yeah." He cups her chin and their brown eyes lock. "You did good." His thumb traces over her bottom lip. "You know what you're doing. I couldn't be prouder."

Amari lifts her chin out of her husband's hold. "I have you to thank. I've never been the greatest at battle tactics and you're started to rub off on me."

Viggo lets his hand trail across Amari's shoulder and then down her arm. "Klauss has been there to help as well."

"He's so busy with his kingdom he hardly has time for me anymore."

"But he still reaches out." Viggo pulls something out of the back pocket of his jeans and he hands a cream-colored envelope to Amari. "This just came for you. It's Klauss."

Amari takes the mailer from Viggo and looks at it, Klauss's handwriting on the front.

"I already opened it because I was curious in what he had to say. It's a coming-of-age invitation."

Amari pulls out the card in the envelop and looks at it. Her best friend's eldest is turning seventeen and being crowned as the princess of the takals. Wow! Time sure has flown! Amari remembers when Arendil was just little and she was just old enough to choose her creature!

They met in one of her dreams and Amari helped her choose wisely with what she loves most. Arendil now rides a beautiful white Pegasus with gray around its muzzle and hooves. Amari looks at the beautifully done invitation.

Arendil looks so much liker her mother, her blond hair and blue eyes shining bright in the sunlight as she looks back at the camera in her leaf green v-neck dress with lace, her green crown of leaves and blush roses on her head. The train on her dress is laid out and her Pegasus is in the background with its wings spread out. The rose bushes with blush roses make the setting absolutely beautiful.

Amari looks up at Viggo. "I have to go," she whispers.

"We both do," Viggo says lowly. He sets his hands on Amari's hips, keeping eye contact with her. "It's not only our duty. But he's your best friend and Nikolas would hate me if I didn't go."

"Well, he's your cousin. So…"

Viggo kisses Amari's forehead then rests his there. "I love you, Mare," he says lowly and softly.

She lifts her head and gently presses her lips into his in a soft kiss. "I love you more," she says softly.

Viggo slips his tongue into Amari's mouth and their tongues spar against each other. It doesn't take long before he unzips her dress and slips it off her shoulders. She undoes his pants then pushes them down with his boxers.

Viggo picks Amari up by her thighs, getting in between them as he pulls her into him. They kiss. She holds onto him with her calves as she uses her core to keep herself upright and un-clasps her bra from behind. He turns the light in the closet off as he backs out.

Amari lets her bra fall down to the floor and lets her hands roam around Viggo's naked ass as he walks over to their bed. She shifts the air and turns off the light. Their tongues sparring, he lays her down on the bed on her side, staying on top of her.

He doesn't pull away, slipping two of his fingers inside of her with her panties just set to the side. She gasps. Oh, he's just getting started. Amari knows what's next and he rubs her clitoris with his thumb while he fucks her opening with his two fingers. She moans into his mouth, pleasured enough already.

But he doesn't stop.

Amari's hand holds the back of Viggo's neck as he lips land on her mate mark. If he's going to upgrade it, again, she's got to do the same thing to him. She won't let him get away without it. He sucks on it, getting a gasp from her at the tingling sensation of change. There he goes. Pleasuring her more than necessary once, again.

Viggo puts his free hand next to Amari's head and she pants, seeing white and rolling her eyes to the back of her head. She feels as though she's on cloud nine and she doesn't want to come down. She wants to stay on her cloud while her god makes love to her all night.

It isn't until it's the middle of the night that Viggo finally lets up on her mate mark and spreads her thighs open, slipping her panties off of her. He enters himself inside of her and her core tightens around him to pull him in deeper. He groans and takes his time with his thrusts, stroking her insides and taking her to her climax.

Amari throws her head back, pressing her naked breasts into Viggo's pecks. His arms wrap around her as he thrusts her hips into him with every thrust of his hips. She gasps, panting as he slips inside of her deeper and hits her spot. She rolls on top of him and rides him, bringing herself down on him in thrusts. She lets him hold onto her hips and watch her.

Her breasts bounce. She takes one of them into her hand and massages it, letting herself go. Viggo thrusts into her as she comes down on him and they get into a rhythm, meeting each other in the middle with every thrust. He hits her spot continuously, making her have an intense orgasm. She feels like she's still on her cloud.

Amari groans with her head thrown back and Viggo sits up, pressing his chest into her breasts. He thrusts into her so hard all she can see is the back of her head. He groans into her neck, his mouth on her mark. He spills his seed inside of her.

Amari lets her lips land on Viggo's mark and she upgrades it. It takes a couple of hours, but they wind up falling asleep not long after. They both sleep like a baby.

<h1 style="text-align:center">16</h1>

Amari stands on the deck of the ship and stares out at the ocean. Nervous, she's not sure how well this is going to go for her.

She has galeophobia and thalassophobia. The fear of sharks and the fear of the ocean. She has no problem with lakes. But since her experience with a humpback whale that tossed her around and protected her from a shark, Amari has never been the same with oceans. They terrify her to the core.

She shudders. She prefers to stick with lakes and rivers. An orca comes up for air near the ship, making Amri jump and take a step back. Viggo grabs her from behind and gives her a reassuring hug. She pants in pure terror, not wanting to get in the ocean. She can't do this… It's too much!

"Viggo," she breathes. She shakes her head. "I can't do this."

He kisses her cheek. "I can go," he says lowly, reassuring her with softness and a firm hug. "It's okay."

Amari shakes her head, again. "No. She… doesn't like you."

"She tried to eat me. What do you expect?"

Amari shudders a sigh. "Mermaids… They prefer…"

"Women and mermen. I know. But I got someone to protect me." A shift in the water is heard and droplets are heard hitting the surface of the ocean. A few hit the deck of the ship.

Amari gets nervous, not wanting to look up. Dear, lord… This is rough.

Amari shakes her head to try and clear it. It's okay! They'd never hurt you, Mare! You used to have one! Until… Amari shudders, ready to shut down. Her tafala. He was the sweetest thing. But she couldn't protect him when two wild tafalas attacked him. He was protecting her, keeping her safe from them. But when Ambroz came along it was too late.

Amari's tafala was gone. Dead and at the bottom of the ocean. She gave him a proper farewell and his siblings did the ritual they do for a passed loved one. Amari slit her arm open and let her blood seep into his skin to break the bond. She misses him… She wishes she had him by her side right now.

But when did Viggo become a rider?

Purrs come from the tafala behind Amari and it soothes her, making her close her eyes and remember Wicks.

"Brother," Viggo starts. "She's nervous. Scared." He goes quiet and Amari knows his tafala is speaking to him.

Tafalas can't just mind link with anyone. They can only do it with their rider. With that in mind, Amari dares to turn around to find out who chose her husband. She looks up at the biggest tafala of the oceans and seas. The king. The alpha.

With his eel-like head that's a little more box shaped, Ambroz brings a little comfort to Amari. He looks at her and their brown eyes meet. He lowers his head and presses his muzzle gently into her abdomen. Amari's arms instantaneously wrap around his head. Viggo chuckles after a moment.

"He missed you, too," Viggo says lowly.

Amari pulls away and looks at him, comforted have Ambroz on their side. "Would he be okay if I rode him with you?"

Ambroz nods his head and lets his body glide over the ship, looking back at Viggo. He dips his head then gets on his companion's back. He offers his hand to his wife.

"He'll offer you some air."

Amari nods and takes his hand. He pulls her up onto Ambroz in front of him, wrapping his arms around her protectively. Ambroz dives into the water, gliding easily over the ship, and Amari moves her body with him as the water envelopes her.

She holds her breath for a minute before the air hits her lungs. She's able to adapt to breathing underwater thanks to Ambroz's gift. She leans forward as he dives down towards the village of the mermaids, Viggo leaning forward with her, pressing his chest into her back.

Comfort sweeps over her, being trapped against her husband with the tafala king underneath her. The ocean is dark and lifeless at first. But when they get deeper, anemones scan over the ocean floor. A turtle hovers over one, getting attacked by two little clownfish. They protect their home from the intruder, but the turtle doesn't give up as it searches for food.

A plesiosaurus swims above Amari and Viggo. She watches in awe. It still lives here! That's *amazing!* Here, Nessie, Nessie! Ambroz swims underneath a stone archway and a few mermaids come up to him, running their palms over his skin. Mer-people love the companionship of a tafala, specifically the king. He blesses them with just a touch.

A mermaid moans from behind Amari and Viggo, who look back at her to see her enjoying Ambroz a little too much. She caresses her hands over his tail while she's underneath him. He thrusts his tail into her, getting a moan of pleasure from her and filling her up with his semen.

Mermaids technically don't have fated mates and they'll mate with tafalas and their own kind. But sometimes their fathers will promise them to a merman to be their spouse and mate. A different mermaid takes the moaning one's place as she accepts Ambroz's gift. The new one receives the same one, moaning and squealing with his massive release inside of her.

Amari shakes her head and looks ahead, dismissing the horny mermaids. Mating season… Mermaids get way too horny in the fall, the season being the time when they're most fertile and ready to have a child.

Viggo gives Amari a reassuring squeeze as Ambroz dives down into a hole where there's a village of mermaids and mermen, swimming around and greeting

Ambroz. The mer-people are shocked see Amari and Viggo. But they don't stop the tafala king as he swims over to the home of a mermaid that's in love with a life form on earth.

She can help Amari and Viggo with their plan. They want to include her. Besides… She has a personal agenda against Hapoor himself and she would love a chance to get back at him.

A third mermaid is heard mating with Ambroz, squealing and moaning. Amari quickly gets off of his back, Viggo following. Her air supply gets cut off the moment she's not in contact with Ambroz anymore and she holds her breath. Amari and Viggo swim over to the door of the home, her vision blurry again. He opens it for her.

Amari steps inside as she holds her breath. Because of Ambroz she was able to see and hear things clearly, not just breathe under water. Now, it's all back to blurry and muffled, a mermaid getting off on Ambroz and begging him for more.

The moment Viggo closes the door behind him the water is out of the house and their feet meet the floor. Amari takes a deep breath of the ocean air and the smell of fish hits her nose, mermaids still going at it with the tafala and heard clear as day. Amari looks back at Viggo.

"Why do mermaids get off on tafalas so much," she asks lowly. "I don't get it."

"They have bigger penises," Viggo says lowly. He joins Amari at her side.

"We prefer to mate with them, actually," Athena, the mermaid Amari and Viggo came to see, speaks up.

She walks out of her bedroom. "And you just interrupted my mating with your entrance."

Amari looks Athena over with a brow raised. "You, uh… mate a lot, do ya?" She teases in a seductive tone.

Athena gives her a stern look. "He's very specific with who he mates with, actually," she states matter-of-factly.

Amari looks at the man that walks out of the bedroom while zipping up his pants and realization hits her. Lord Poseidon! Of course! The king of all mer-people and mate of Athena and Sirena! Amari knew she was pushing it when she made Sirena the queen of the sirens and gave Matt a second chance. But Sirena deserved to be happy. She didn't seem thrilled to come to back to the ocean.

Poseidon grunts and his arousal is obvious.

"I am," Amari starts. "So, sorry, King Poseidon." Her brown eyes meet his glaring deep green eyes. "My… Please, accept my most sincere apologies."

"You took Sirena from me," Poseidon says lowly. "Now, I'm here with Athena twenty-four, seven."

Amari cautiously tucks her wet hair behind her ear. "She wasn't happy. Sirena."

"I know." A mermaid is heard over him, screaming in pure bliss. "But she's not like any of the mer-people. I wanted her to be happy, so I didn't touch her in that way." Poseidon seems to be irritated.

"Matt."

"She missed him like no other." Another mermaid is heard calling out Ambroz's name and

Poseidon snaps. "Get your hands off King Ambroz! All mer-people! Stop mating with king!" His voice booms out for all of his kind to hear and everything goes quiet.

Poseidon looks at Amari after an awkward quiet moment. "Mating season. Mermaids are so horny at this time of year they'll mate with anything."

"Sounds like someone else I know," Amari says, getting a snort from Viggo.

They both know who she's talking about. A lycan in the Odinfah lycan pack always has his sights on a beautiful creature to nail. He's so horny he can never think straight! But at least he tries. And he protects all life no matter the cost. He's a good man. You just to have to find a way around his always naughty mind.

"Well, hopefully they'll stop for the time being," Poseidon says lowly. He lifts chin, looking at Viggo as he prefers to talk to him. Of course. Mermen prefer to talk business with other men, making the women feel bad. "What can we do for you, your majesty? Is there something going on?"

"I'm afraid so," Viggo puts in, putting his hand on the small of Amari's back. "A war between the Asgard Lycan pack and the Asgard Light Moon pack is about to break out. We were hoping to talk to Athena. We need her to do something for us."

"Absolutely not!" Poseidon doesn't hesitate.

"H-hole on," Athena speaks up, all too interested in the conversation. Her green gaze lands on Amari with an all too knowing look. "Hapoor is causing trouble, again?"

"As always," Amari replies.

"Athena, I am not letting you," Poseidon starts. Athena cuts him off with a gentle hand on his elbow.

"You know this would benefit the both of us," she says lowly.

"It would benefit you!" He snaps. "I am not letting him impregnate you! It's out of the question!"

"Think of it," Athena soothes, her tongue flicking over her lips.

Amari shares a look with Viggo.

"Your daughters were killed. By Kera. If I agree to let him get me with child and you and I marry, we'll have a place in the lycan world, again."

"I gave up on that," Poseidon growls.

"Poseidon, please," Athena begs as he walks away from her. She watches him start for the bedroom.

"No!" King Poseidon snaps, making up his mind and looking at his mate. "It's just you and I, now! Freda and I are done! And so are you and Hapoor! Forget it!"

"Poseidon!" Athena takes a few steps towards her mate and king, but he stops her with a lift of his hand.

He slams the bedroom door behind him and leaves her alone with Amari and Viggo. Amari starts for her, but she gets stopped by Athen holding the one moment finger up.

"Just give us a moment," Athena says lowly.

Amari lets her hand down and gives Athena a brief nod. Athena walks over to the bedroom door and gives it a few soft knocks.

"Poseidon, baby. I'm coming in." She walks in and closes the door behind her.

"You are not taking part in this," he yells, his voice booming.

"It'll be good for us, Poseidon!"

"Good for you! You've been wanting Hapoor's child since you were nine!"

"She needs the help! Sei! Think of the alliance!"

"I am not!" The kitchen wall next to the bedroom shakes as Poseidon hits it and makes Amari flinch. This isn't going well. "Letting you do this!"

"Oh, so it was okay for you to have children with the love of your life, but I can't have any with mine?!"

Silence. And it's way too quiet. Something slams into the house and a bang on the door follows. A mermaid's squeal of pleasure is muffled by the door.

Sounds like Ambroz is getting it on with mermaids! Tafalas can scent when a mermaid is in heat. The two creatures may be different in species, but they somehow have some of the same ancestors that make it possible for them to reproduce.

Amari and Viggo press their lips together in a smirk as they listen to the mermaid at the door continue to have the time of her life with the tafala that's eager for crossbred heirs. This is how sirens are usually born. And it never happened until now.

∞

Poseidon gives Athena a broken glare, staring at her in disbelief. He can't believe she just said that! He's always been in love with her! And Sirena when she came along! Freda was just a childhood crush and fling!

Poseidon once tried to make the move on Sirena, but she wasn't interested, still needing time to get used to this new role. That's when he met Freda for the second time. Allah's lycan omega that had a thing for mermen.

Poseidon fell in love with her during his time at Allah's kingdom and wound up having two love children with her. Twins. And he misses Amy and Lexi more than anything. Poseidon should never have left without them.

He hears King Ambroz on the top of the house and mating with every mermaid that he can get his fins on. Having him here makes it impossible for any merman to mate with his wife! Having the opportunity to mate with a king is an honor and no mer-person will pass that up!

Poseidon sets his jaw in a light clench, staring at the woman that he has been in love with since the moment he set his green eyes on her. In the middle of the courthouse of his father's kingdom when they were just six years old.

"I'm in love with you," Poseidon breathes softly, his broken glare on Athena. "No one else."

Athena growls and walks passed him, pushing him aside with the back of her hand. "What am I? Number three? Or wait… Five. That's right." She starts packing her bag.

His boner forgotten Poseidon stands in the middle of the bedroom as he lets his mate pack up. She's got a point. And he hates it. He *never* let that rapist werewolf near her. He didn't want her to get hurt by the man. Hapoor may have lycan glood in his veins more than werewolf blood. But he's still a mutt that Poseidon can't stand. And he has *every* right to hate the man!

"But either way, I'm going," Athena orders. "I want that baby." Her arousal is so strong it's hitting Poseidon all over him, begging for him to take her here and now. "And it'll be good for us. The alliance is needed."

"I prefer you didn't," Poseidon puts in.

"Oh, like you have a choice!" Athena snaps. "Sei! This is our goddess and god that need my help for once. I've *never* been called to a battle. This is my chance to do the right thing!"

"Goddess Amari may have the last order, but you're my mate." Poseidon orders as he turns to face his beloved mate his father chose out for him. "We don't have fated mates, but if we did you and I would be matched. *Fated mates.*" He shakes his head. "I don't wanna lose you, Thena."

"I will get my baby." Athena starts in a threat. She grabs her slick dagger that Poseidon made for her with the spikes from a dead sea urchin he found while out hunting. "And I'm going to end him." She walks over to him as she puts her dagger in her bag. "He broke my heart and killed my sister. Literally."

"You're not going."

"Then why aren't you stopping me?" She starts past him and grabs her brush from the nightstand.

"Because I love you." Poseidon turns to look at her and she stops dead in her tracks. "Athena, I may have loved Freda and Sirena, but they came after I met you.

We were six years old and in the courthouse of my father's kingdom."

"May he rest in peace."

Poseidon shakes his head. "We locked eyes…and I fell in love, Tin. With you. And it's *always*. Been you."

Athena keeps her back to him.

"I just didn't say anything because I wanted it to happen naturally. And then my father promised you to me. But on his death bed…"

"He promised you Sirena as well. He wanted you to marry her. Make an alliance with her and her future sirens."

"Yeah," Poseidon says softly. "But I've been wanting you," he continues softly as he starts for his beloved mate. He stands right behind her and her scent drives him crazy, making him caress her arm and put his nose in her hair. "And I want you pregnant with one of my hairs. Not his."

Athena shakes her head. "You have five so far," she says lowly. "Just give me this one. Please. I can get to Hapoor with no suspicion. No necklace. No spell. Nothing."

Poseidon's heart breaks and for the first time in all of his years, tears form in his eyes. He's not one to cry and his father isn't the only reason, teaching him to be tough and be able to take on everything. But he is his own man, hardly ever showing his soft side to anyone.

Athena only gets it when they're in bed together!

Poseidon kisses her head of blond hair and brown hair, his heart shattering at the thought of Athena being right. He's going to have to give up this one child for a werewolf that he doesn't like! A rapist! And a murderer! Poseidon doesn't like this, knowing he has to agree to the plan one way or another.

"And I still love him," Athena says softly. She turns around and looks up at him, her breasts brushing against his chest. She's just a few inches shorter than him. They're both still the tallest of the mer-people. "Please. I need this closure."

Poseidon's deep green eyes search Athena's sea green ones, trying to find another reason for her to stay. But he can't think of one. Finally, he gives in. He holds the back of her neck and kisses her for the first time, their lips clashing together. Usually, mer-people don't kiss. They don't ever show any signs of affection! They're not ones to fall in love so easily. They mate for life and devote their lives to each other, but they never confess their love to each other or anyone else. Mer-people are a stubborn, independent species that don't rely on anyone.

Athena opens up and Poseidon slips his tongue into her mouth. Their tongues clash and spar, Athena dropping her bag. Her arms wrap around Poseidon's neck. He picks her up by her thighs as a mermaid is heard screaming out in pleasure outside, getting a growl from him. He needs to be done quick.

Mer-people may mate for life, but if the king of tafalas is here all mermaids take the shot to mate with him and have his first crossbreeds. It becomes an alliance between the two species when it happens.

Poseidon takes Athena over to the bed and lays her down, getting on top of her and tearing her pants and panties to shreds. He pulls out his pulsating member and guides it into her, not wanting to wait any longer to relieve himself. He makes it quick, thrusting into her and not spending a moment to prolong their orgasms.

Their breaths mingle together as he continues to thrust into her, feeling her tightness all around him and pulling him in with every thrust. Athena makes a small sound into Poseidon's mouth and clings onto him as his cullions jump. He spills his seed inside of her with no hesitation. She has a small orgasm and he joins her. But it doesn't last long when she realizes what he did.

"Fuck, Sei," Athena whispers. "It's supposed to be Hapoor's."

"Then go to the bathroom," Poseidon says lowly into her lips. He thrusts into her one more time then goes limp. That's the fastest they've ever done it!

Poseidon pulls out of Athena and leaves her on the bed as he arranges himself. He turns his back to her and she goes to the bathroom in the back to relieve herself. He pushes his limp member to the side of his boxers then zips up his pants, settling them on his hips. He looks at Athena's black bag on the floor and picks it up as Ambroz gets busy with another mermaid, making her come with a scream.

Looking inside, he finds that she's taking her teddy lingerie. Oh, no she doesn't! She can seduce Hapoor in a different way! Poseidon quickly takes Athena's lingerie out of her bag and replaces it with his shirt that he's wearing, wanting her to have his scent with her at all times. He wants to claim his mate in front of the world and let her know that she's only his. That's better.

Satisfied, Poseidon throws the bag onto the foot of the bed and stuffs Athena's lingerie underneath the mattress. That's the last place she'll look! After a few minutes, Athena comes out and notices his lack of shirt.

"Where are they," she asks, knowing what he did. Nothing gets past her!

"Hm," Poseidon asks, acting clueless.

Athena raises her left brow and he copies her.

"Oh, I threw them out into the sea. You won't be seeing them anytime soon."

She sighs in disgust and grabs her bag. "I'll ask Amari for a teddy then."

"Absolutely not," Poseidon orders slowly. He easily slides his hands into his front pockets. "You can seduce your childhood lover a different way."

"We never did it," Athena says lowly.

"You might as well have."

Athena looks at Poseidon in disbelief, her jaw agape. "I'll see you in a few days."

"No." He walks over to his mate and casually slides the ring in his pocket onto her wedding finger as he interlaces his fingers with hers, his eyes on hers. "You'll be back tonight."

Athena's lips land on Poseidon's in a loving and passionate kiss. "I'll be back after the war is over," she says into his mouth. She pulls away from him.

His eyes closed all he feels is her presence as she starts for the bedroom door. When he hears it open, he opens his eyes and watches the love of his life leave.

"Ready to go," Goddess Amari asks.

"Yeah," Athena replies. "I convinced him."

"You always have a way with men."

Athena giggles. "Viggo can attest to that."

Viggo moans in disgust. "Don't remind me."

Poseidon listens as the front door opens and the house is instantly filled with the ocean. His legs change into a tail when the water hits him, but he stays in one spot with ease. The moment the door closes all the water is chased out. And Poseidon is left alone, standing on two feet. He quickly walks over to the front door and opens it, wanting to see his mate and future queen off.

His legs turning back into his orange and blue tail, he leans into the doorway as he watches Athena swim off with Ambroz, Viggo and Amari on his back. Athena looks back at her mate and their green eyes meet. He dips his head to her, his heart breaking at the knowledge that he's got to let her fulfill a promise that Goddess Amari just asked her to make without having to actually say the words.

Athena and Poseidon knew she was going to ask the moment she stepped foot in this house. Athena's blue and purple tail fades into the void ocean and Poseidon is left with a shuddering breath as he tries to hold back the tears. He wants her to come back and forget about all of this. But he knows Amari didn't come because she wanted to. If anything, she tries to avoid the ocean as much as possible ever since her incident with the humpback whale back in Homba. Poseidon only knows about it because one of his mermen slipped through a portal by accident and saw the whole thing. He knows Amari would only come here in a desperate time of need.

She'd never come into the deep sea willingly.

17

Ragnar paces as Allah can't stop thinking about her. Amari… Where is she? Is she okay? Did something happen yesterday? Or maybe earlier today? Why isn't she here yet? Does Allah need to send a scout for her?

Ragnar growls at Allah for all the questions about Amari, but he can't help himself. He worries about her! He knows she can hold her own, but sometimes he just can't stop. Allah is still trying to get over her for Ragnar! She promised them Ramein, their *real* second chance mate, as their alliance. But that's going to be at least fifteen years from now!

Allah notices his team watching him and Ragnar as his wolf paces. A few whines and pants come from a couple of them. Ragnar stops to glare at the mating couple. Now?! Of all times and places! They just had to choose now! Why did Allah even agree to let her come on his team?! She's in heat in wolf form! Allah should've just ordered her to stay home!

Randy's wolf makes eye contact with his king as he pants, pretty content with himself with a smile on his face. He stops in mid-hump as realization hits him in the face. Randy gets off of his wife instantly. They're probably impatient for all of this to go down just as much as Allah is. And it doesn't help when the females are in wolf form at this time of year and not already pregnant!

The males go crazy over their scent! The very few females that don't have mates are fought over by males wanting to court them. And after further investigation Allah found out that was the case with his omegas Amy and Lexi. His pack kept that a secret from him since they knew Amy was once his favorite.

Ragnar shakes his head and gets back to pacing. At their stations for the attack, Allah, Marcus, and Tali are covering the borders on the west, north, and east. The Silver Lake pack are on their south border with the Asgard Light Moon pack and they're on high alert. They sent their best warriors to keep an eye on it at all times.

Ragnar shakes his head, again, as he starts to get more impatient, ready to tear some flesh and teach this pack of rapists a lesson. They should *never* have taken Mavis in! A twig snaps and makes Ragnar stop to sniff the air. That's when it hits him and he starts growling at the scent of pine sap and sandalwood. Zane. The son of a bitch has come to walk right into Ragnar's paws, meeting his death after raping countless women in just the past year.

"I'm sorry, Zane," an all too familiar female voice says. What is she doing here?! She's not part of the plan! "But I fear as though my father isn't well enough to lead the pack anymore. And as his rightful heir, I'm challenging him."

"And we accept your challenge," Zane speaks up, his husky voice filled with a challenging tone. "But we also must decline at the moment. Hapoor is busy with some plans of renovations right now.

"That is not acceptable." Ada gets in front of Zane as they come into view and her lips are on his. That's not right… Ada wouldn't kiss Allah! Why would she kiss Zane?!

Unless… Is this some sort of hoax? Maybe Amari's signal?

"You must accept the challenge now or I will take it by force."

A growl escapes Zane's chest. "Nice try. May. But we both know Ada won't kiss a man."

"You got the wrong woman," Ada says lowly.

Ragnar stalks towards Ada and Zane as he takes the signal, baring his teeth in a low and soft snarl with his golden eyes on Zane. He's ready to attack. Ready for Amari's word. Ada, or say Amari, turns away from Zane and thrusts the necklace off of her, turning back into herself with the beach blond hair turning golden-brown.

"Have fun in Hell's Fire," Amari says lowly. "He's all yours, boys." She stalks into the forest, towards the south border.

Zane's eyes meet Ragnar's. The wolf snarls at him as he stands over the man, towering over him at a few feet. Fear radiates through Zane and he's only able to get five seconds ahead before Ragnar takes one bound and snatches Zane in his jaws. He clamps down for a firm hold before shaking the man like a ragdoll. Ragnar clamps down harder to break his spine in half. He drops the dead body and looks back at his team.

They give him a brief nod before they start
stalking through the grass, splitting up to cover more
ground. Six men are seen leaving the pack house, laughing
full heartedly. Allah recognizes one of them as the man
that raped and killed a twelve-year-old human girl. He's
alive?! Allah thought he was hung for his crimes! Well,
he's about to be unalived, now!

Ragnar stalks around the men before finally
picking off the murderer, bounding in quietly and taking
him without a sound. In the grass, he pulls the man's
intestines before he can scream. It's about to get uglier
than this.

Allah would never have thought of this plan! This
is more of a masterpiece for werecats! They're
masterminds at pulling the Beta and Delta away from the
alpha and the rest of the pack, killing them before they
can mind link anyone about the danger that's surrounding
them.

The alpha of the opposing pack is reserved for
the alpha of the werecat clan as it's usually a war between
the alphas of the werecat clan and werewolf pack.
Werewolves always lose because of this battle tactic. Well,
it's about time for them to be outsmarted by their own
lycan king!

The remaining five men quickly get picked off
with no detection by the others and Ragnar takes another,
ripping the man's head off his shoulders. Howls are heard
at the south border, letting Allah know a few men
ventured that way and are now giving a warning.

Fuck…

Hapoor walks over to his Delta after failing to mind link with Zane. Where is he? Why isn't he answering?

Hapoor tries to reach out, again, but this time the mind link is gone. There's no connection. Fuck. Something's going on. A few howls are heard from the south border, making Hapoor frantic.

They're getting attacked?! Who ordered the hit?! If it's the Silver Lake pack finally having enough, Hapoor is here to finish the job! He's wiping out Alpha Kane once and for all!

"Astrid, did you get the reports from the patrols," Hapoor asks, getting down to business before joining the fight.

"Yes," she replies. "And there's nothing to report."

"Then why can't I get a hold of my Beta?" He turns to his side table and looks at the paperwork on it. "And why are the reports right here? They should be on my desk!"

"You were busy with that little omega earlier we didn't want to interrupt."

"I wasn't fucking her if that's what you're trying to imply." He gets impatient as he looks over the reports. "Where's my Beta?" He orders. Where's Zane? Was he killed? Hapoor growls at the thought.

"We don't know what you're thinking anymore, Alpha. You've gone completely rogue and you fucking act like one," Astrid says in disgust, her nose wrinkled up in Hapoor's peripheral vision.

She looks cute when she does that.

"She and I were merely having a conversation about May. Her cousin. I was asking her what May's next plan of attack would be, because, clearly, she's the one that's got the hit on me. Not my daughter. And she's working with the Silver Lake pack." Hapoor slams his hands on the side table and looks at Astrid, their twin blue eyes meeting in matching glares. "Where's Zane?!"

Astrid motions at the file in her hand with a glance at them. Her eyes land on his. "I don't know. He went offline an hour ago when I tried to reach him about Ada being here and wanting to talk to you. I was trying to talk with him, but he just snapped at me and then cut me off."

Hapoor growls then turns around, stalking towards his office.

"I wouldn't go in there if I were you."

"Why?"

"Because you'll walk into your sister doing it with her mate and husband. Do you really wanna see that?"

Hapoor stops where he is and he growls. Anywhere but there! He told his baby sister she could do it anywhere, but there! That's his personal space! Hapoor turns back around and walks over to his Delta, taking the contract that's in her hand.

"What is this," he asks as he looks at it, looking for keywords.

"Ada's challenge to you," Astrid puts in. "She and I were talking earlier and she mentioned that she changed her mind about the pack. She wants to take it from you."

Hapoor growls, again, but at the contract. Not Astrid's words. She's lying! This contract is from Amari! She's taking the pack from Hapoor and handing it to Ada!

"There's no challenge, Astrid."

"What are you talking about? I went over that contract with Ada earlier." Astrid stays professional as she converses with her cousin.

"Amari's taking the pack from me!"

"There must be some kind of mistake." Astrid takes the contract from Hapoor and goes through it. "I swear we talked about a challenge."

"There's no challenge, Astrid," Hapoor snarls.

Astrid looks up at him in horror. "Alpha Hapoor?"

He shoves the contract into her chest, hoping to throw her off. "You think I'm stupid, don't you?"

"I... I don't." Astrid shakes her head, looking flustered while she holds the contract to her chest. Her eyes stay locked on Hapoor as she plays dumb. "Understand."

"Oh, you understand *clearly*." Hapoor snaps, inching closer to the only cousin he ever liked and got along with.

It seems it's about to bite him in the ass this time and there's nothing he can do about it. Astrid shakes her head in disbelief.

"Hapoor, I would never-"

His hand dashes out and wraps around her neck, his claws digging into her skin as he chokes her. "You went to Amari. You've been wanting the alpha position since you were *ten*. Astrid. And when you couldn't get it, you worked on becoming my Delta because *that's.*" He shakes her violently. "The blood line you were born into! And now that it's not enough you wanna get rid of me!" It was all starting to make sense, now.

Astrid barely gets a breath out. "That's..."

Hapoor tightens his grip on her throat and he gets in her face threateningly. "Don't. Fucking. Say. It." He snarls.

"Absurd," Astrid whispers before her air supply is completely cut off, gaining a growl from her cousin.

"Let her go, Hapoor," a familiar female voice says behind him. "She had nothing to do with this."

Hapoor's eyes trail back to his left with a glare as if he can see her. "Give me one good reason why I should," he snarls. "Amari."

May wouldn't be stupid to try, again, would she?

"It's 'your majesty' to you. And she's innocent. Let. Her. Go." Oh, it's Amari alright!

Hapoor gets a better plan. Feeling betrayed, he snaps his Delta's neck in half, looking into her lifeless eyes. His cousin... Gone. Dead at his hands. And he feels nothing. Hapoor lets her go and her body falls to the floor with a thump. He turns around to look at Amari and that's when it hits. The sweet smell of her arousal and a pull he can't quite explain.

It also doesn't help that she's in a light blue chemise with light blue fishnets and white lace panties barely showing through. Oh, she plans to seduce him into signing the contract!

He has to admit she's doing a pretty damn good job at making his mind go places that he shouldn't. With

Amari as his goddess, he should respect her. But when she's dressed in lingerie his wolf is going nuts over her body and the smell of her arousal. Something's off, but Hapoor shakes his head. He walks over to the woman in front of him, forgetting about the war that's just right outside his door, only hearing her heartbeat.

It lulls him closer to her and he wants to have a real taste of her. He wants to know how she *truly* loves her man in bed.

"You." Hapoor starts seductively. "Are. Fire." He thrusts Amari into him, her breasts pressing into the top of his rib cage.

She looks at him as if she's turned on by his roughness, her brown eyes landing on his lips. She's acting differently. But there's no necklace around her delicate neck to indicate she's someone else. A growl comes out of his chest as he gets reassured this really is her and she wants to seduce him into a contract.

Well, that's not going to happen. All she's going to get is his pups.

"But you're not getting me to sign anything," he says roughly.

"That's too bad," she says lowly. "Because well." She unbuckles his belt and undoes his pants. "The only way you'll get pup from me is if you sign it."

"A counterstrike." Hapoor is impressed with his goddess, making him admire her. "I'm not surprised. But I only want pups that will take my place." He shakes his head. "My daughter is a bastard child, so she doesn't get it."

Amari thrusts Hapoor's hips into her and he gets turned on by her roughness, growling and looking at her lips for a release. "You sure you wanna give this up," she asks lowly. "What you really want?" She lets her lips feather his.

Hapoor shakes his head. "I will rape you again and again if I have to," he says roughly, his blue eyes looking into her brown eyes as they light up with silver rings. As much as he enjoys the screams of a successful rape, he wants to make love to this woman instead.

Feel every single inch of her skin and make her come. Loudly. Uncontrollably. She's the goddess of his world and she's absolutely stunning, the most beautiful thing in this world.

"Mmm," Amari moans seductively. She gets on her tiptoes and puts her lips to Hapoor's neck, where his mate mark disappeared after Zara's passing. "Too bad you won't get the chance," she whispers. She gets a growl from him.

He thrusts her into the wall. Wedging his thigh in between her thighs, he slides her up it. "You're not going anywhere," he threatens. He groans with the feel of her against him. She's so intoxicating! "And I get to do whatever I want with you."

Amari pants, her breath tickling Hapoor's lips. "Make it fast," she seduces in a whisper. "Cause I got places to be."

Hapoor hikes Amari's chemise up to her hips, wanting to obey her order for once. His pulsing member strains against his boxers and Amari quickly pulls it out, stroking it with her hand in a smooth rhythm. She gets

Hapoor going before he can even enter her. He groans at her scent and arousal, tearing her lace panties to expose her down there.

With a swift move, she helps him guide him into her. He takes her in fully, thrusting into her and feeling her out.

"Who am I," Hapoor growls into Amari's golden-brown hair.

"Daddy," she manages out through her pants of pleasure. Her head rolls forward. "Fuck. Daddy!"

He growls at the nickname she has given him, but it's not the one he's looking for. He thrusts into her hard. "I'm your what? Amari." He thrusts into her harder and the pictures on the wall shake.

She chokes on an orgasm. "You're my…" She throws her head back, exposing her neck.

Hapoor thrusts into Amari hard and stills himself deep inside of her. "Say it," he growls threatening.

"Alpha," she says after a moment of hesitation. "You're my alpha."

He growls at the victory. "That's my girl." He thrusts into her and she wraps her arms around his shoulders.

They come together as he quickens the pace and she screams her release, his name on her lips, as he spills his seed inside of her. But he's not done with her just yet. He's taking her up to the bedroom.

∞

Athena opens up for Hapoor as he takes her, towering over her and holding onto the headboard for just a little bit of control. Disguised as Amari, Athena is able to fool the man she fell head over heels for when they were just pre-teens.

This is just what she wanted. Closure. And a child with the man she's so in love with. Yes, he killed her sister. Yes, she wants revenge. But with this child she'll be able to take over his pack with it and have an alliance with the Asgard Lycan pack that Poseidon so needs. That's the revenge that Athena wants. She wants her mate and future husband to be happy. And she will get it.

Hapoor continues to thrust deeply into Athena, having no idea that it's actually her. He thinks he's having sex with Amari. And when a mermaid is the mastermind of manipulation, she can turn into someone else. Someone that another loves. Hapoor must feel something for Amari if he can be gentle with Athena in bed! He grunts and pants, railing into her.

She sees stars and her eyes roll to the back of her head. She can hear the war going on outside, but Hapoor is paying no attention to it. He just continues to thrust into her, deep in her spell. He lays down on top of her and she wraps her arms around his torso, her hands on his shoulder blades.

She lifts her head and pants in his ear, her legs intertwined with his. She pulls his hips into hers, clenching her thighs into him. Hapoor growls and wraps his arms around Athena, stilling that she's Amari. His touch... His skin... His lips...

Athena enters Hapoor's mind with ease without him knowing, wanting to know the reason for his soft caress. She doesn't have to dig very deep to find what she's looking for. Hapoor is gentle with Amari when he wants to be, but its her disobedience and attitude towards him that makes him want to discipline her. But if he could have his way completely... Hapoor would be the man to love Amari.

This news makes Athena growl, making him growl with her as he shudders his release inside of her. This should be good. Enough. Athena now has enough of his semen to be able to get pregnant.

She rolls on top of him and sinks her teeth into his neck, where there was once a mate mark. He thrusts his hips into her and makes her rock. But all of a sudden, he stops, stilling himself inside of her. Athena sits up as she straddles him and she rides him, his hands going to her hips. He watches her with lust, but she can tell someone is talking to him through the mind link.

Zane is dead! And Astrid was on Amari's side! Who else could be talking to Hapoor?

He thrusts into Athena as she comes down on him and she throws her back in delight, showing off her luscious breasts and neck. Hapoor rolls on top of Athena and rails her into the bed, not letting up on his thrusts or his grip. He's getting more aggressive, showing that he knows something is going on. He brings Athena's hips into his and his fingers dig into her, making her wince in pain.

"You fucking liar," Hapoor growls, sounding betrayed. Is he talking to Athena? "She's right here underneath me, you fool." He thrusts into Athena harder and makes her come, having an orgasm and feeling like she's on cloud nine.

Her fingernails dig into his back and she lets her hand trail down it. Athena sneaks her dagger into her hand as Hapoor finishes up, keeping her in her orgasm. But she's able to think clearly. Athena rolls on top of Hapoor as he thrusts into her and orgasms. She raises her dagger above her head, ready to strike.

Athena instantly transitions back into herself and Hapoor looks up at her after a moment of recoiling. Fear strikes him as realization shows on his face.

"Athena!" His eyes go to her dagger. "Wait. No!" His hands come up to protect his face.

I want him, a male voice says in Athena's mind somehow. *Bring him to me. Please.*

Athena throws her dagger down and it meets Hapoor's pillow, landing right next to his head. He looks at her in fear and disbelief.

"Now, I'll have your baby," she growls, her green eyes glaring into his blue eyes. She shakes her head. "Just like we always wanted."

Athena gets off of Hapoor and she gets dressed in normal clothes as she walks out of his bedroom. She's done with him. She got what she came for. Amari and Allah can have the final decision on what to do with him.

"Athena," Hapoor calls out, drawing out his first love's name. "Wait!"

She ignores him and makes it down the stairs with her bag in hand and normal clothes on. She listens to him as he tries to defend himself.

"I made a mistake. You know I love you."

Athena makes it to the bottom of the stairs and she starts down the hallway.

"I met my fated mate and I was all over the place. I wasn't thinking. I'm sorry."

"Sorry doesn't get my life back," Athena growls. She opens the door, but Hapoor slams it shut, leaning into it.

"Hey!" His blue eyes pierce her green eyes. "Give us a moment. Please."

Athena glares at Hapoor. "Your goddess is killing off your pack of rapists and you'd rather talk to me?"

He winces. But he shrugs it off. "What do you expect? Fucking shit happens." He doesn't sound very happy at the moment. Good.

"Sign the contract and be done for." Athena picks the file off the floor and shoves it into Hapoor's chest. "I don't want you."

Hapoor slams the door closed as Athena opens it. "You're not going anywhere," he threatens. "We're talking this out."

"We're done. You're done. You raped Amari and May and your own daughter wants nothing to do with you! That says a lot about how much you've changed!" Athena shakes her head. "I want nothing to do with it! With *you*!"

Hapoor winces. "Athena, please." He cozies up to her and kisses her forehead.

She flinches and pulls her head away from the touch that she once enjoyed from this man. "I hope you go to Hell's Fire for this," she growls.

She opens the door and leaves him behind.

18

Amari punches one of Hapoor's men in the nose then elbows him in the temple.

Most of them are dead, but there's a handful that are tied up. Amari drags the man in the grass then throws him with his buddies. Allah ties his hands behind his back then frisks him for weapons, getting a growl from him.

Allah pulls out a couple knives and tosses them aside, making eye contact with the man. Marcus's wolf growls at one of the tied-up men when he eyes one of the knives. Amari kicks it into the grass before the man can grab it. It hasn't been easy. But they've taken care of most of the criminals.

Luckily, all the women in the Asgard Light Mon pack are innocent. They prefer not to get in trouble with their lycan king or goddesses. Werewolves and lycans believe in the Moon Goddess and the Hallam Goddess and God. They know Amari and Viggo can do something with the criminals if they're caught. That's why there's not much crime here.

The criminals get tortured in Hell's Fire before being considered forgiven and start that trek for the trials. Voices are heard and Amari recognizes them immediately. Marcus's wolf stops growling and perks his ears up, looking towards the arguing couple. Amari starts for them but stays hidden in the tall grass, not wanting to get caught. She wants to savor this hailing victory.

"Athena," Hapoor snaps. "Don't you dare walk from me," he threatens with a growl.

Amari peers through the grass and watches as he takes Athena's wrist.

"Not, again."

Athena whirls around to face the man she once loved and slaps him in the face. Amari hears a few of the lycans behind her snicker quietly. This pretty entertaining. Two old lovers have come together one last time, but only because Athena agreed to it. She wanted her revenge after all.

"You don't get to order me around," Athena orders. "I'm not your luna and I never was!" She snaps.

Hapoor looks at her with broken disbelief. "I can change that. You know that. All I've got to do is announce it to my men-"

"You honestly think I'm gonna believe you after everything you put me through?" Athena cuts him off, pissed at him for thinking it's as simple as that. "You killed my sister!"

"It was an accident!"

"You call this?!" Athena holds her shirt up to reveal a scar where she was stabbed. "An accident?!"

Amari doesn't know the story, but she does know it's part of the reason why Athena wanted revenge.

"Tina."

"No!" Athena snaps in a booming voice. "It wasn't an accident! You wanted her dead! When you

found out she tricked you. You stabbed her through me!"
That makes Amari wince.

"Athena, I… I'm so sorry."

Athena shakes her head, glaring at Hapoor. "You used to be loving. And caring. You took care of everyone including! The rogues that were rejected by their packs! Now, look at you! You're raping women and letting your own men get away with rape and murder! You're mistreating others as if they're just some… *Pawn* in your game!"

"Athena, I changed after you left. What do you expect?"

"For you to change for the good!" Athena growls angrily.

Amari hears the grass moving swiftly behind her and she looks back to see Allah in wolf form, stalking towards Athen and Hapoor.

"Allah," Amari whispers. "No!" She tries to grab him as Athena continues to snap at Hapoor.

"Not for the inconsiderate!"

"Allah," Amari snaps in a whisper as he slips through her fingers. "Stop!"

"When I found out that all you wanted was Goddess Amari, I couldn't help myself! I *had* to trick you into believing I was her so I could get pregnant with *your* baby! That's all I ever wanted!"

Hapoor looks at Athena with broken blue eyes, panting in disbelief with his lips parted. He truly looks heartbroken. Amari almost feels bad for him. He must truly love Athena.

"I wanted us! As a family! And you wouldn't give me that ten years ago!"

"May got in the way. I'm so sorry. I should've…" Hapoor shakes his head, not noticing the lycan that shifted, towering over Athena in a protective stance.

Amari watches him in lycan form, awestruck and falling in love with him all over, again. But she knows she shouldn't. She's devoted her life to Viggo and her kids. She needs to get out of here before anything can happen. Before she throws herself at Allah and changes their alliance. He deserves to be happy even if it means giving up Ramein to him. Amari noticed the way Allah treats her daughter and she knows it's for the best.

"I should've rejected her in the first place," Hapoor says lowly.

"We're done," Athena growls. "Hapoor. I got what I came for. Now, you can rot in Hell's Fire." She turns towards the grass and stops at the sight of Asgard, Allah's lycan.

Asgard opens his mouth in a snarl and his saliva drips from it as Hapoor grabs Athena to protect her.

"She's the reason," Amari speaks up as she pushes through and reveals herself, deciding to intervene at this point. Realization runs through her mind as she thinks about what's going on.

Hapoor looks at her in disbelief as she stands next to Asgard.

"Athena's the reason for you mistreating women. You betrayed *her*." Amari points at him. "Not the other way around. Remember that."

"Amari, what are you doing here?" Hapoor continues to protect the woman that he once loved, keeping her behind him as he stares at Amari.

"Taking over." Amari puts her hands in her front jean pockets, grateful she got them made just for her. "You're no longer alpha of the Asgard Light Moon pack. I made a mistake. I should never have asked Allah to give the title back to you. You don't deserve it."

"Call him off or I'm calling my men," Hapoor threatens with a growl.

Amari bursts out laughing. "Good luck with that. Cause." She wipes a tear away at the corner of her eye then looks at Hapoor. "Most of them are dead. You only have a handful left that we have tied up back there." She motions back at Hapoor's men with her head, her eyes on him. "It's your move."

Hapoor looks between Amari and Asgard in fear.

"Sign the contract." Amari threatens.

Hapoor shakes his head at her, showing his stubbornness. "No."

"Then the rest of your men die."

Hapoor growls at her with a glare as he gets aggressive.

"Sign it."

"Forget it," Hapoor snarls, flashing his canines.

Asgard walks forward and grabs him by the neck, choking him as he lifts the werewolf off the ground. "I, Allah Ammon King, declare Hapoor Blackfoot as a rogue. I strip him of his title and make him nothing. Any who cross him and his followers may kill them without questioning."

Hapoor struggles as he fights for control. He shifts into wolf form to try and gain it, but Asgard keeps him from shifting completely, keeping his tight grip on Hapoor's neck. The pathetic looking man hangs limply from Asgar'ds hold, deciding to stay in human form. A whine escapes his throat.

"Make your move," Asgard growls challengingly.

Amari can see why Allah shifted into him. Asgard has all the power he needs to make a wolf crumble at his feet. Bigger, scarier, and meaner. He can make an order and a wolf will yelp in agreement, rushing to do what he was told.

Hapoor struggles against the lycan as he tightens his hold.

"Kill 'im," Amari orders lowly. "He deserves it."

Asgard snaps Hapoor's neck in half and his lifeless body dangles in the lycan's hand. Asgard drops him to the ground and turns to Amari. He starts to shrink as he shifts to Allah.

"No," Amari starts, taking a step towards him. She wants to see Asgard for just a little longer. "Stop. Don't shift."

Asgard grows back to his size, wanting to obey his goddess. "Amari?" His voice deep and husky, he awakens her down there.

She looks over at Athena and their eyes lock. "We need to start cleaning up." She looks up at the lycan king. "And it'll be easier if you stayed in this form. Also, you need to persuade the rest of their fates. They won't suffer here if they choose death."

"But they'll suffer in Hell's Fire."

"Only if Madi chooses to." Amari lifts her chin, keeping eye contact with the lycan that she must give space. She can't see him for quite a while. She loves her husband too much and wants to stay with him more than anything. She *has* to work it out with him.

Asgard starts for the remaining living rapists. Amari has a hard time watching him walk away, but she has to.

"Allah," she speaks up.

He stops his back to her.

"Ramein will be the only one coming to see you for now on. I will be too busy with my role as goddess. I'm so sorry." She can't lie to him. She's been putting off some important things that come with her role just so she could see Allah. It's time for her to step up.

"Our alliance stays the same, though. I'll just see you when I see you."

Asgard nods before he walks back into the grass. The tied-up men are heard crying out as they writhe in pain with the decision that they choose, suffering from being killed slowly.

∞

Amari walks out of the castle and through the courtyard.

Someone new is here and it's about time. He needs to rest. He may have a wild side that makes him attack the innocent. But he did that when he was the Eye of Hallam. Since it was no longer needed, he never grew out of it as he aged. It kept him feeling young.

Amari stands a few feet away from the gates and they open as he finally steps through, looking battered and beaten. Oh, the poor thing! He relied on flying to his cavern that he probably fell most of the way down with his wing that never healed right! Amari's heart reaches out to the poor dragon.

As he walks inside Amari takes a few steps back. He walks over to her and the gates close behind him. Amari holds her hand out to him and rests his nose into it, looking young, again.

"Hey," Amari says softly, facing the first creature she ever dreamt about. In her dream, she was the last hope to get gold and jewels that were protected by this dragon. She only calls it a nightmare, because she fell to her death. "Welcome home."

"I've been waiting for this day," Jarom says lowly.

"I know. It's been so long. I should've come to visit you. I'm so sorry."

"It's okay. I'm here, now."

Amari dips her head. "Raja let me know just moments ago she downed you when you went after Klauss. I can only imagine all the feet you fell to get here."

"I fell to my death trying to get here. Sadly, I cannot return to Hallam to take you anywhere, now."

"That's okay," Amari says softly. "I got others."

Jarom dips his head in a nod. A dragon calls for him in the distance, welcoming him home.

"You got a cavern waiting for you. You know where to go."

Jarom lifts his head and looks towards the mountains in the distance. His permanent home with a loved one there already.

"Feel free to come visit anytime."

"Thank you." Jarom hugs Amari with his head before taking off.

∞

Allah gets out of the shower and grabs his towel. He dries his face, pressing it into his towel as his thoughts start racing, again.

The pack that killed his wife… Defeated. The men that were behind her murder… Dead at Allah's hands. He found every single one of them and tortured them with the very few that were tied up. As much as he feels relief, Allah also feels regret.

He should've proclaimed the Asgard Light Moon pack as non-existent. Never to be formed, again. Hearing the pack name still haunts him. Thinking about it makes him shudder. After finding out what really happened…

Allah can't get it out of his head. All day every day. He's haunted by the images that play in his dreams. The blood. Selena… Her weak cry for help… Allah's Beta before Marcus…

She sent the Asgard Light Moon pack to defend Selena. Alpha Blackfoot, Hapoor's father, came back with her blood all over him. Allah shouldn't have fallen for his lies. He sighs and sags, closing his eyes and leaning into the faucet. Rage fills his heart as he can it all, now.

Selena… Killed by her own brother when he found out she would take the pack after hiss passing instead of his own son. Allah swipes his hand and shoves everything off of the countertop, turning and looking up at the ceiling.

He named the pack Asgard Light Moon for a reason! And finding out that his wife was killed for it to stay in Hapoor's family is dark… And cold… A few knocks sound on Allah's bedroom door and he wraps his towel around his waist. He clears his throat as he tries to mind link with person that's there, but he can't get into their mind, their presence being blocked.

Knowing it's someone that's not in his pack, Allah walks over to the door to open it. But Amari walks in before he can. Their eyes meet and he knows she's here for a reason. The alliance and nothing more.

"You know you can have your daughter come here," Allah puts in as he walks over to his dresser.

"Emma's too young at the moment," Amari puts in as Allah opens his underwear drawer. "And Ramein is sick. She has the flu."

"My apologies, Mare. Truly."

"It's fine. She'll be okay." Amari's fingers run over Allah's scars made by Ragnar six year ago. They never healed properly due to infection.

"I did all that I could do. She just fell asleep with her dad."

Allah nods his head as he drops his towel. He puts his boxers on, trusting his best friend. "Tell her King Allah wants her to get better soon so we can play."

"I will." Amari takes a moment before continuing. "I want Asa to teach Ramein your guys' history," she says softly. "Every single bit of it. It's important to me."

Allah nods. "Okay," he says softly. He turns around to look at her.

Her scent envelopes all around him and he can't stop himself from breathing it in, letting it hit his scent glands and calm his nerves.

"You really shouldn't be here," Allah says in a low warning tone.

"Ramein is sick," Amari says lowly. "Someone had to come so everyone knows we still have an alliance."

Allah nods, again, this time in understanding. "Your husband could've come."

"He's watching our daughter. And I know you don't like him. He's not a fan of you either. It was best that I come."

Allah looks at Amari's lips, wanting to kiss her. But he knows he can't. For once, he's able to resist, knowing the outcome if he did. His heart breaks as he turns around and grabs his towel from the floor, throwing it in the dirty hamper a moment later. He ignores the pang in his heart.

"Amari, it's a few days after Hapoor's killing and I still got a lot of things to do. And make up. So, can you please make this short?"

"I thought you'd want to talk business."

"It's nine o' clock in the morning, Mare." Allah snaps softly. "I have paperwork to take care of since Ada's taking over the Asgard Light Moon pack. I have to do business with my ex-wife." Worked up with Amari's choice on the pack, Allah wants to take care of it sooner than later so he doesn't have to deal with it for very long.

He's using as a cover up to Amari for his anger towards the late pack that killed his beloved wife.

"I know how that must be frustrating," Amari says softly as Allah feels her eyes on him.

He gets a pair of jeans out of his dresser and gets them on. "You think?"

"You wanna get it done sooner than later."

"Like no other."

Amari hugs Allah from behind, settling her head in between his shoulder blades and throwing him off with her softness. "I understand." She kisses one of his scars gently and he shudders at the sparks that she ignites inside of him.

Her touch… No matter what she does… She will *always* have him wrapped around her finger. And she will always be his world. His everything. Oh, how is he going to get over her?

Allah leans into his dresser with his hands on the smooth top, regretting everything that he did to Amari six years ago. He should've fought for her! With persistence!

"What are you going?" He teases, knowing he can't pass this opportunity up. If there's *any* way to change Amari's mind and make her choose him, this is it.

"Saying goodbye. What do you think I'm doing?"

"Trying to get in my bed." Allah flirts teasingly.

Amari snorts. "I got a husband that can pleasure me just fine." She teases. "I don't need you in that way. I just want you."

Allah turns around to face his best friend, his heart aching and breaking for her. He so wishes she wasn't doing this to him. He can't stand another goodbye.

"Yet here are you," he says in a low and teasing tone as he holds her chin with crooked finger underneath it and his thumb on the nub.

Amari lifts it as she keeps her brown eyes on his gray eyes. "And here I go," she teases in a low seductive tone.

Allah kisses Amari's high cheekbone, letting his lips feather against her skin. He puts his lips to her ear as he wraps his arm around her middle.

"Don't go too far," he says lowly.

Amari snorts. "Oh, I wouldn't dream of it."

19

Hapoor screams in pain as he gets burned with a stoker, Madison on the other end of it.

It's possible she doesn't know he made it easy for Amari with her attack. Sure, he had no idea when she was going to do it. And yes. He'd prefer if he was still alive. But there's something more sinister at play and Hapoor isn't going to give up any information when Madison comes asking. But hey. He's got a new woman to rape. And he's going to have fun with her.

Hapoor looks up at Madison as he growls in pain, his body shaking at the intensity of the burning. He holds her brown gaze and she finally lets up after a moment.

"That's for raping my cousin," Madison puts in.

Hapoor laughs. "Call it what you want. But she *enjoyed* it. Every. Single. Moment."

Madison moves quickly. His head is thrown to the side with his right cheek stingy. "I better not find out you're working with Kera. Or you'll be moved." She threatens.

Madison walks away, putting the stoker back in the burner where it belongs. Hapoor gets thrust up on his feet by two men that work for her. They escort him out of the torture chamber and down a long corridor. In an estate that was built to accommodate a witch and a werewolf, Hapoor is now somewhere he enjoys.

Sure, he misses his pack. And all of his men are here. But if Hapoor behaves, he'll be able to get room service and roam wherever he wants. That includes Madison's castle. And when that day comes, Hapoor will have *all* sorts of power.

He stands in front of a set of double doors after going up a flight of stairs and the men take his shackles off of his hands and feet. He rubs his wrists after they're relieved from the handcuffs and he turns towards the two men, getting down to business.

"How do you like your jobs," Hapoor asks casually.

The tall brunette twists his mouth in consideration as he thinks about his answer. "Eh."

"We enjoy it," the dirty blond says, just a few inches shorter than his friend. "I mean… We may have died in Hallam, but we still get to cross between there and Hell's Fire since we behave."

"What do you mean?" Hapoor turns to face the man, curious as to what he's talking about.

"We came here on a technicality," the brunette speaks up, his blue eyes almost green in this lighting. "We robbed a bank."

Hapoor laughs. "And you came here because of that?"

"Not all of us stay here forever," the blond says.

Hapoor looks at him.

"If we behave, we get jobs. If we continue to behave, we're able to go between Hallam and Hell's Fire.

It we're *forgiven* for our actions on Hallam. Not everyone gets the pleasure, though."

The brunette shrugs. "Well, also it's not just the people you hurt that forgive you. You also have to be forgiven by Amari and Madison. And *then*."

"Once your forgiven of all your sins and you pass the test Madi gives you with flying colors… You're able to take the trek from here to Heaven's Light and Amari will give you another test."

"If you pass that one with flying colors then you're now in Heaven's Light and your wolf becomes your companion, able to come and go as he pleases from Heaven's Light to Hallam."

Hapoor drops his jaw in disbelief. "How long did it take you two to get to where you are, now?" He points at the men.

"Pfft." The brunette smacks his lips together, pulling his head back. "Only two months for us to be honest. We didn't do something as sinister as *you* did."

"How long would it take for me?" Hapoor points at himself, his finger on his chest.

The two men look at each other then at Hapoor. "You…" The blond bounces his head from side to side in consideration. "Probably at least three to five years to get to our point. Then at least another twelve years before you're able to take the tests."

Hapoor nods. "Thank you. I'll do my best."

The two men laugh. "Good luck. We hear Kera is a *real* bitch."

"More like a whore." The brunette puts the back of his hand on the blonde's chest, looking at him. Their eyes meet. "She'll sleep with you if you let her." The blond bursts out laughing, doubling over with his hands in his pockets.

"I'm so glad I don't like witches," he says through the tears. He wipes them away as he looks at Hapoor. He clears his throat. "Just… When she hears you're a cat she treats you very well. When she hears that you're a wolf…" The man shakes his head. "She treats you like the dog you are. So, be careful."

Hapoor nods, again. "Thank you. I appreciate the advice. But have any werecats really come to Hell's Fire?"

"On technicalities like ours. But they're never here for very long. With their honesty they're forgiven super-fast."

"Last on we had was literally just here for five minutes," the brunette says.

"Yeah, that's a new record. But it was a mistake anyway."

"They thought she murdered someone when she broke into a house. Turns out the guy was already dead and she broke in after hearing the fight. Though she could save him in time."

Hapoor pulls his head back in disgust. "I hate cats."

"They're way too honest in my opinion." The blond looks at the brunette then back at Hapoor. "Let us know if you need anything. Kera is quite crafty and she never has a roommate for very long."

Hapoor nods for what seemed the tenth time. "Thank you." He opens the door to the living room and his blue eyes meet Kera's brown eyes, who is standing next to the min-bar. He smirks at her. Oh, he already knows what she's here for!

Kera puts her finger to her lips and waits a few moments before speaking up. "You have what I want."

Hapoor nods, again. "Ada."

"Oh, yes indeed."

**Immortal Dreams Trilogy continues
and ends with Traitor of Dreams!**

Immortal Dreams Trilogy:
Different Shades of Dreams
Mother of Dreams
Traitor of Dreams

**Find out what influenced Amelia in the prequel
Amelia's Flaws!**

**Want to know what happens after the events of
Mother of Dreams?**
Ada's Rule

**Find out the aftermath of Traitor of Dreams in
Malech's Wrath!**

Want to read about another world? Check out the new
series!

Don't Forget Me Series:
Dreamy Nights
My Dreams or Yours
Alechi's Mate
Raising Ashley
Abraxas' Fate